The Genesis Project

Greg Van Arsdale

The Advent

Chapter 1

Bullets buzzed by the man's head, the crack of automatic rifles all but drowned by a flash of light and ground-shaking boom of thunder. Running in an all out sprint across a barren stone slab, he ducked beneath the swarm of lead. The sudden move threw him off balance and he sprawled forward on the rain splattered slope.

One hand landed against the rocky terrain. He pushed hard and then was up, lunging to the right. He immediately stumbled again on a craggy ridge and rolled left.

A staccato beat of lead ripped the ridge.

A slug tore through his jacket, burning his shoulder. He dodged right and dove headfirst over the first of two boulders. Fiery tracer rounds streaked the night. The deadly barrage smashed into the massive rocks front and rear. Chunks of gravel, gouged from the larger stone behind him, fell on his head and shoulders. He gulped huge drafts of air into starved lungs and listened to the sounds of the war ravaged night.

The stranger cringed beneath the ugly smack of lead on stone. Dozens of ricochets whined into the darkness. A cannonade of thunder rumbled overhead.

Then a pause in the assault.

He chanced a quick look around as lightning seared the midnight sky. The jagged bolt struck a distant rock, detonating it in a shocking display of sight and sound. It was over in an instant. A brief moment of brilliant light, but enough for what he wanted to see.

He was on the edge of a circular clearing of solid rock about one hundred yards wide. A dense forest of giant oak and pine surrounded the barren slab. Sheets of rain obscured details, but on the far side, a group of men were just entering the clearing. They spread in a platoon-wide battle line. Some of them slipped on the slick rock. Most jammed fresh magazine clips into their weapons.

And then the light was gone. Darkness once again enveloped the earth. And with it, the assault resumed.

The man slammed his back behind the safety of the first rock. *Who are those guys?* he wondered. *Why do they want to kill me?*

Another brief flash and he scanned the scene in front of him. The forest resumed just ten yards from where he crouched. Hundreds of bullets zipped through the rain, smacking stone bare inches from his head. Others swished by, striking the same trees marked for his escape. Ten yards of open terrain. Ten

4

yards of solid rock slab without so much as a pebble for cover. He shook his head, wiping rain and from his eyes. Ten yards of pure luck.

Another flash.

He took another plaintive sweep of the land, searching desperately for any other way out. There was no other choice. He rose to a sprinter's crouch, waiting for the lull when they reloaded.

He peered a cautious eye around the now heavily gouged boulder. The soldiers were close enough to see their faces now, clothed in military camouflage uniforms. An officer behind them cursed the men forward with wild gestures of what appeared to be a silver sword.

A final barrage of lead finally chewed through his protecting rock. He ducked lower. His eyes darted left and right. He didn't have much time.

The rate of fire dropped.

Instantly, he bolted into the open, pumping his legs as hard and fast he could. Ten yards, not more than five steps, but that night it seemed like a mile. Time passed in agonizing slow motion. Boots splashed through rivulets of mud streaming across the strata.

Five yards. Still alive.

The rifle assault remained focused on the two boulders. *They must be firing blind.* Two more pounding steps. Seven yards. A distant flash of light.

That's when all hell broke loose.

They saw him. Fifty rifles fired as one in his direction. The man ducked low. He cringed as a lightning bolt seared overhead, striking a nearby Pine tree. The trunk exploded like a cannon shell, the sap instantly vaporized into a thousand fiery fragments. The blast knocked him on his back, his clothes in flames. He rolled in the muddy water, dowsing his smoldering jacket. Bullets kicked rock chips in his face, but now he looked up with newfound fear. The giant tree, its middle gone, was falling toward him.

Frantically, he rolled left then scrambled on hands and knees, barely managing to dodge the thickest branches. And then he was up, pushing needles aside, using the fallen foliage for cover. A few crouching steps and he disappeared in the forest gloom.

He instantly turned right. The ground, hidden by drenched shadow, was covered with thick undergrowth and snaking ground vines, making footing difficult and treacherous. He constantly tripped and fell. He turned left about twenty yards in and hit an exposed root, sprawling headfirst into a thicket. Long thorns sliced his face. Blood, diluted by sweat and rain, washed into his eyes.

He tugged against the snaring barbs. His breath continued in ragged gasps. His body begged for rest. But there was no time. He had to keep moving.

Finally, he ripped free of the thorns to stand behind a large oak. He took a tentative peek around the bole. A burst of gun fire shredded the tree bark. Splintered shards stung his face and outstretched hands. Instinctively, he ducked right, then jumped a hedgerow and disappeared into the shadows.

"Here!" someone shouted. "He went in over here!"

Three sharp blasts of a shrill whistle carried against the wind.

"Left flank, move up. Box him in. Box him in!"

More tracer rounds converged on where the man had been. He hooked an arm around a sapling and turned hard right, barely escaping the assault. He drove his legs ever harder, dodging left then right.

In the darkness, he never saw the steep incline. Arms and legs flailed in an ungainly tumble. Forty bone-bruising feet later, he rolled onto a granite surface, panting for breath. Dazed but not seriously hurt, he looked around. He might as well been blindfolded.

Gale force winds and slanting rain once again pelted him with unimpeded force. He struggled to his feet, pushing against the wind while shielding his eyes against the stinging rain. A heavenly dagger struck the Earth. What he saw in that brief flash made his heart sink.

He stood on another flat slab of rock. But this one was larger, so much so he could not see the other side. There were no boulders, nowhere to hide—but also no snaring vines to impede his way. With quickened speed, might reach the forest on other side before the soldiers found the clearing. There had to be trees there. If not . . . it was better not to think about that. He was gone before the lightening bolt faded into a trail of evaporating fireballs, sprinting blind through the night without caution.

Time and again he looked over his shoulder, wondering if the soldiers had yet found this clearing. Then he would snap his head forward, squinting for the first sign of cover.

Nothing.

He kept moving, leaning low against the torrential conditions. *Were they there already?* He glanced back. If caught in the clearing, he was a dead man. Panic mounted to terror. He raced into the heavy wind, a force that sapped his waning strength. Every step longer, more laborious than the last until he was practically falling with effort.

That was when he came to the end of the world.

There were no trees at the clearing's end. There was nothing there at all. Had it not been for a fortuitous blast of light and thunder, the man never would have seen the cliff edge just fifteen feet ahead. It glistened in the shuddering streaks of ebbing light. Beyond this was the empty black of nothingness.

He threw himself backward, hitting the ground in terrified desperation. He kicked and clawing at the merciless, flooded rock. It was too late. He was moving too fast, the ground slick with mud. Nothing to grab onto, no stopping his slide.

He rolled over on his stomach and gouged the stone with both hands. The hard stratum scraped skin and nails from his fingers. Both feet scrambled against the earth in vain attempt. Terror turned to horror when his feet slipped clear of the ledge.

He reached for a small bulge. The slippery rock escaped his grasp.

The sharp shelf ripped up his shins.

Water poured off the cliff in sheets to disappear in the blackness below.

One hand chanced upon a small crack, but the brittle shale broke away. He reached again but came up short as the weight of his legs now pulled him ever faster into the abyss. All hope seemed gone. He dragged his fingernails against the stone, but it was no use. His legs now clear, he began to fall.

And then he stopped.

Pain stabbed his stomach. He looked down to see his belt buckle lodged against the edge. The lower half of his body hung free, legs dangling in the empty night. His weight pushed the steel buckle deep into his sternum, but he barely noticed the pain. He was just glad to be alive.

Careful to make no sudden moves, raw hands groped the cliff top. He found a crease in the rock and jammed bleeding fingers into the split. He then lay still, wind and rain pounding his back.

An excited shout from the far off trees penetrated the howling maelstrom. "Sir! Scuff marks. He went down this way."

The shrill whistle signaled the others. The leader shouted, "Everyone, lower level. There's no way out. We've got him now!"

Teeth gritted with strain, the stranger tried to pull himself up, but quickly collapsed.

At least fifty men scrambled down the slope leading to the clearing.

Desperately, the man swung one leg up for the ledge but came up short.

Flashlights snapped on, swaying left and right.

On his second attempt, the man managed to hook a knee over the edge. Slowly, carefully, he inched his way up and rolled onto solid earth. He collapsed on his back, shaking with fear, gasping for air.

A rapid succession of lightning bolts crashed

around him, obliterating all they touched in a ball of flame and electrified shockwaves. They illuminated the scene below.

The craggy ledge marked the beginning of a near vertical drop. Two hundred feet down, an ocean raged frothing white. Massive waves crashed against equally huge boulders that littered the shore, their own thunderous roar almost lost to the storm's screeching howl.

A thin ledge, perhaps thirty feet wide, skirted the mountain halfway between cliff top and ocean. Cluttered with thick brush, it extended left and right as far as he could see.

The man beat the rock with a bloody fist, realizing he had been driven here like a hunted animal. He was trapped. To go down that cliff wall was suicide. Maybe an expert climber could make it in good weather, but not on a night like this.

The row of men with their sweeping flashlights crept closer.

The man glanced left and right along the cliff's edge. The entire side of the mountain was one giant vertical wall. There were no trees anywhere, absolutely barren landscape of exposed rock on either side. He looked back and all thoughts of escaping along the ledge were instantly gone.

High intensity beams swept the rock. The men had spread into wide line, cutting off escape the way he came. They were no more than fifty yards away now. His only chance was down. He turned to probe the cliff with one foot.

A single shot came from the line of soldiers.

The bullet hit hard, propelling the man off the

cliff and into the murky night. At first there was silence, but then the hurricane slammed his body against the cliff wall. A scrub pine grew from a rocky crag and he grabbed it with both arms, but he was already moving too fast. The gnarled trunk snapped at its base. The stump snagged his coat and spun him into a head over heels roll, dislodging rocks as he fell.

Countless times the wind slammed him against the jagged wall. Each impact gouged another bit of flesh. He crashed against a rocky outcrop, his left leg crushed beneath him. His agonized scream, choked with fear, never cleared his throat. He rebounded into the darkness and fell with the silent rain.

His only sense was of the advancing ocean roar. So dark was the night that he did not see the massive boulder until a thunder bolt struck the flat stone just before impact. He landed with a vicious thud.

The collision crushed the air from his lungs in a whoosh of torment. For a lingering moment he laid still, his body wrapped across the boulder like a rag doll. Try as he might, he couldn't move. The impact had knocked the wind from him. His starving lungs craved the life-giving oxygen that simply would not come.

He had just managed to roll over and suck in the smallest sip of air when the boulder shuddered beneath him. He tensed in absolute stillness. The lightning blast must have dislodged the giant slab from its delicate perch. Slowly at first, the massive stone yawed forward. The man leaned back against the increasing pitch, wild eyes staring at the deadly dark below. For one transitory moment, the giant rock stopped, producing a brief illusion of hope that seemed terribly unfair. And then the base broke loose and everything fell away beneath him. Somewhere down the incline, his head smacked the stone wall . . .

~~~

A thunderclap reverberated overhead, sending tingling currents through the soaked ground, jolting him awake. He opened his eyes with a flutter, blinking hard, but there was nothing to see. The night was now pitch black. Oddly, there was no wind or rain, but he could still hear it. Confused, John felt the darkness with bleeding hands.

He was lying on his back in thick, gooey mud. He smiled, letting the slime ooze through his fingers. By sheer luck he had landed on the middle plateau. Of this he was certain. Only the ocean lay below. The thick goo had softened the impact and saved his life. He was lucky to be alive—but luck doesn't last forever.

His entire body ached from countless cuts and bruises. His head throbbed, pounding with every heartbeat. The bullet wound burned his left side and his leg felt broken. He tried to sit up but immediately struck his head against rock and slumped back into the mud. He reached out. A flat rock surface extended as far as he could reach in either direction, the ceiling no more than six inches above him.

His first impression was that the dislodged boulder had followed him down the mountainside and landed on top of him. As improbable as it seemed, this had to be the case. He leaned farther left and right to confirm his suspicion. Rock walls on both sides. By chance, he had landed in a stone crevice at the base of the cliff. The V-shaped split held the massive stone aloft.

That's when horror struck him. It took a moment for his pain-numbed mind to realize it, but when it did a cold chill shuddered down his spine. *He was buried alive!*

His thoughts ran wild. How many stones lay atop this one? Hundreds of them. Maybe tons of rock cascaded down the cliff in an avalanche of stone, and he was at the bottom of them all. How was he going to get out? How was he going to breathe?

The thought of suffocating in that claustrophobic tomb brought a new sense of fear. He pushed against the rock in futile effort.

A wet gust of wind touched his head. He looked up to see a small opening, no more than six inches wide. Outside, lightning licked the landscape. Small consolation, but at least he wouldn't suffocate.

The flickering bolt strobed the night. Water droplets pouring off the rock above seemed to falter in mid-fall, glittering in beautiful sparkling contrast against the black caldron beyond. Broad leaves, whipped by the wicked wind, thrashed against the opening.

The man reached up to clear mud from the portal then stopped. Faint noises filtered across the narrow strip of land. He strained a wary eye to see the darting searchlights advancing from his left. Soon, uniformed soldiers were everywhere. Men driven to desperation ripped through thick shrubs that infested the land.

With just the occasional lightning flash, he

could not see much, just malevolent shadows. Brilliant beams probed under bushes, beneath fallen trees, anywhere that offered shelter to a man.

Behind them, that same commander drove them on, cursing his men with an endless stream of obscenities. The stranger couldn't see his face, but the commander wore a rain slicker over a military uniform and high-topped black boots, the only one so equipped. He also noticed it wasn't a sword he carried. It was some sort of silver scepter or cane which he used to beat the men to greater speed.

"Find him!" His shout carried rage. "Find him now. I swear to God I'll kill the man who lets him escape. Everyone, form a line. Shoulder to shoulder. Shoulder to shoulder. I want this man dead. Tear up every bush if you have to, but find him!"

In rapid succession, the commander turned and beckoned two men. "Johnson. Murphy. Come here."

A rustling of brush. Running footsteps. A man shouted, "Sir!"

"Go scour the base of the cliff. He may have missed this ledge entirely. See if you can find his body on the rocks below."

Heels clicked to attention. The men turned to leave but their leader stopped them. "Wait. Come back here."

"Yes sir?"

"Who fired the first shot? I gave orders to hold fire until my command. Whoever it was gave away our position too early. He warned our suspect to run before we were close enough for a sure kill."

A moment's hesitation before one said, "Phillips, sir."

"Yes sir. Phillips," the other echoed.

The commander's voice was cold. "Bring him to me."

Footsteps drifted to the distance. In a moment, three men returned, breathing heavily.

"You wanted to see me, sir?" Phillips said, his voice quivering.

The flack crack of a pistol shot merged with the thunderous crash of light that shook the ground. John looked up to see the soldier fall, his dead eyes staring directly at his. Rain diluted the blood oozing from a hole in his forehead that streamed across a blank face. And then the flash was gone, the face an empty silhouette.

"Johnson," the commander's tone was indifferent, "when you're finished inspecting the shoreline, dump this piece of trash over the side."

Johnson hesitated. Finally, he stammered, "Y-yes sir."

The dead man slid from view.

John looked on in amazement. *What kind of commander would shoot his own men?* he wondered. *Who was he?* Despite hearing his voice and seeing Phillip's face, he still had no clue who these men were or why they were so bent on killing him. He spent a long time searching his mind but could not come up with one single thing.

His mind was blank. John's head throbbed with the effort of thinking. That's when he realized something that pushed all other thoughts aside. Not only did he not remember why they were after him, he had no recollection of his past at all. At first, he thought it was amnesia from being knocked out. But he ruled that out when he recalled events before the fall . . .

He had been standing in a forested area on top of the rocky mountain. It was dark, the gathering storm not yet the howling maelstrom it was now. Water had trickled through the leaves and onto his upturned face.

He heard it first, the rush of distant rain coming at him through the darkness like a train, but coming fast. Trees began to thrash and sway, moaning beneath the torrential force.

He had been on the edge of the clearing. The sudden wall of wind knocked him to the ground. At that moment something whisked overhead, striking a tree where his head had been. With wondering eyes he looked back, barely able to make out men running through the forest. Dozens of bright tracer rounds then pierced the night. The forest absorbed most of the onslaught. That's when he started running, dodging bullets . . .

The commander moved out of sight. The man pressed forward, straining to see more, but the small portal blocked the effort. All he could do was listen.

Men shouted, uprooting bushes. Logs tossed aside rolled through the heavy brush, every bit of earth the subject of brutal inspection. A soldier threw remnants of a plant over his shoulder. The shrub landed in front of the stranger, blocking his view. He pushed it aside. It was a stupid move, for no sooner had he cleared the hole than a flashlight shined directly in his eyes!

The man buried his face into the mud. He didn't move, afraid to even breathe. All he could do was pray that no one had seen him.

Boots stopped in front of the hole.

The man's heart pounded. He cringed, waiting for that hot blast of rifle fire that would end his life.

Nothing happened.

As quick as it came, the light turned away. There were no shouts, no cry of alarm. No one fired a shot. He looked up, and what he saw brought a sigh of relief.

In front of him were those dreaded pair of black, high-topped boots—but these weren't ordinary boots. They belonged to their leader, someone the soldiers obviously feared a great deal. Although the man had been exposed, no one looked his way. As he watched, the soldier holding the flashlight seemed to look for an excuse to be somewhere else, his eyes averted, looking anywhere but at his commander. The man smiled at the irony. The very presence of the one looking for him saved his life.

A call came from the ocean cliff. "General Logan? Sir, I've found something!"

Every man trudged toward the cliff. All flashlights focused on one man who raised a ragged jacket for everyone to see. With all those high-energy beams trained on him, he virtually glowed against the black backdrop of surging storm and sea.

The rain, though steady, had lessened to a steady drum. The gusting wind tore some words across the landscape more than others. But he heard the soldier say, "This is definitely his coat. It was snagged on the ledge. He must have gone over the cliff, sir. And from the upper shelf, that's a two hundred-foot drop straight down. Nothing but rocks and surf down there, the kind that tears a body to shreds. If he's down there, there's nothing left but pieces by now."

He turned to shine his light over the edge. Others followed suit. "We tried scanning the shoreline, but the rain makes it impossible to see much from up here. But it's certain he's dead. No one could have survived that fall. Even if his body wasn't mangled on the rocks, the rip tide would have washed him out to sea."

"If he is down there," General Logan's voice was even, penetrating, "I want his body found. I'll believe he's dead when I see his corpse with my own eyes."

An officer spoke from behind. "But sir, there's no way to get there. We didn't bring climbing gear. And with all due respect, in a freak storm like this, it would be suicide to try. Can't we wait till morning and this storm blows over? I mean, if the guy's dead, he ain't going nowhere. We stand a better chance of finding the body in daylight."

A sharp crack reported the backhand slap across the officer's face. "Shut up! Lieutenant Carpenter, as of right now this storm is the least of your worries. I don't care how you do it but you will get down there. You will find his body and you will bring it to me. And you will do it tonight, not tomorrow."

The General pressed close to Carpenter's drained face. "Do I make myself clear?"

The menace in his voice made the lethal threat very clear. The stricken soldier held his bleeding lip, his eyes wide and staring. But the expression on his face was not of respect or even fear. It was . . . terror.

The lieutenant stood transfixed in the baleful glow of lights, trembling, uncertain what to do. Tension filled the uneasy silence until a few men gently tugged Carpenter from the General's paralyzing glare and hurried him away.

They walked quickly past the stranger's hiding place. The lieutenant's voice quivered as he shouted orders on his radio to bring climbing gear. The stranger looked at those left behind. They huddled off to one side looking miserable, seeming to huddle against the storm as much as from Logan.

A few flashlights remained on the General. He stepped to the cliff's edge, seemingly oblivious to swirling wind and the perils a hundred feet below. He looked out over the sea as if contemplating its blackness. He tapped his leg with the silver cane. The ebbing storm rumbled overhead, its faint flashes a meek reminder of its once awesome power.

Suddenly, Logan cocked his head to one side and looked up as if listening to the wind's dying moan. The men stared at him. Logan remained transfixed like a stone statue for some time, coattails fluttering in the wind.

At last he turned to face his troops. When he did, he noticed Phillip's body lying at his feet. With a contemptuous sneer, he kicked the body over the side. Logan leaned over the ledge, watching it impact the rocks below. Satisfied, he whirled and marched toward the cowering group of soldiers.

"He's not dead," Logan said. "He got away."

The soldiers instantly began to back away. "But how . . . ?" one began, only to be stopped short by

Logan's menacing scowl. The man shrunk into the cowering crowd.

Logan stepped forward. Every man looked at him, uncertain faces full of fear. With a wave of his shimmering silver cane, Logan split the squad into two groups. Indicating those on his right, he ordered, "I want you men to search the forest from here to the city. Beat every brush. Shoot anything that moves. Don't use the trucks. The noise will warn him of your presence. Search the houses, too. Break down the doors if you have to. If anyone resists, tell them I sent you."

He turned to a burly brute of a man. "Sergeant Fishetti, your shot definitely hit him. God only knows how he made it down that cliff alive. Between his wound and that fall, the man we're looking for is in dire need of medical attention. I want you to take the rest of the squad and stake out all the hospitals and clinics in town."

He glanced to his right, raising his cane in a vicious swipe at the lingering soldiers. "What are you men waiting for? You have your orders. Get moving!"

The men scurried off into the night, their footsteps fading in rhythm with the rain. Fishetti's group hurried into formation and then marched away, but Logan held Fishetti back. As they strolled by, Logan spoke in hushed tones. Fishetti nodded.

At last, the stranger was alone and breathed a sigh of relief. He laid his head on an outstretched arm. His body ached. The bullet wound burned like fire. The throbbing pressure inside his head increased with every heartbeat. The night, thick as it was, grew darker. All sounds faded into the distance. And then everything went black.

Chapter 2

Jack Logan barged through the front door of his State Police Special Force Station. It looked like most police stations. Desks and cubicles lined in rows, one of which led to the captain's office. The sun was still rising when he marched through the building wielding his silver cane like a baseball bat, smashing everything in reach. Uniformed officers scrambled from his path as he made his way to the back office of Raul Petra, the Precinct Captain.

"Petra!" he screamed. "Petra, where are you?"

Gone was the military uniform of the previous night, replaced by a custom tailored suit and thousand-dollar shoes. His black hair neatly combed straight back. His coal black eyes flashed fury.

He scanned the room, glaring at all who dared to stare at him. "You are all useless. All you had to do was kill one man. One man! Fifty against one and you couldn't even do that!"

He swung the cane with both hands on a desk nameplate. The woman shrieked, turning her back against the flying shards. Not satisfied, Logan crushed her family picture, repeatedly pounding the desk with the heavy knob of the cane.

Nothing was sacred, no one safe from his wrath as he littered his path with destruction. Tall, lean, and well muscled, he swung the metal scepter in a powerful arc to send the remains of a ceramic coffee cup high into the air.

A full-length mirror adorned a central post. Logan stopped, turning left and right to admire his image. He leaned forward to smooth a lock of hair back into perfect place. After straightening the lines on his suit, he nodded satisfaction and abruptly smashed the glass with three vicious swipes before resuming his march to the captain's office.

"Isn't that the Governor?" a young man whispered to an older man.

The veteran cop nodded. "Yep, that's him. And he's in one of his moods. Let's just say it's best to stay out of his way when he's like this, which is often and unpredictable—so stay on your toes."

Logan spun toward them. "What did you say?"

The older man glanced up, his eyes wide. "Nothing, sir. Private Parker here just didn't know who you are."

Logan glared at them a moment then turned away and called again, "Captain Petra!"

Raul Petra appeared in his office door the same time Logan tried to barge through. Raul was a big man, standing three inches taller than his boss and outweighing him by more than fifty pounds. Gray hair adorned his temples, contrasting with a mass of black, curly hair. His wide shoulders exemplified a natural strength enhanced by hours in the weight room. He was an imposing figure, a brute of a man three years past fifty who looked anything but old.

Forced to a sudden stop, Logan glared at Petra

who then stepped to one side, crossing massive forearms across a Herculean chest. Logan pushed into the office. Pivoting on one heel, he slammed the door. The violent shockwave threatened to send dozens of pictures and award plaques crashing to the floor.

"What is wrong with your organization, Petra?" Logan shouted. "When I asked for fifty men, I expected trained veterans.

"It was a simple assignment: Kill one man. I led them to the spot. All they had to do was shoot him. I couldn't have gift wrapped him any better. And yet they still let him get away. What kind of department are you running here?"

"A good one, sir." Petra's response was even, steadfast. "My men are well trained and in excellent condition. You must admit there were extenuating circumstances last night that contributed to the escape of your suspect. As good as my men are they have no control over the weather."

He held up a calloused hand to stop Logan's interruption. "However, as you directed we are continuing to search all houses and the surrounding forest area. Lieutenant Carpenter is still on the beach with ten men searching the shore one mile in either direction of the plateau. I've got five men in scuba gear in the water and two helicopters scouring land and sea. Fishetti is raiding all medical centers and emergency clinics. However, as of his last report, nothing's come up. But don't worry, sir, we'll find him."

Logan's lips curled in a beastly snarl. "You better. It's your job on the line!"

He slapped the silver cane on the conference

table. The impact cracked like a gunshot. "I do not tolerate incompetence, Petra. I put you in charge of my Special Force Unit because of your record. I want men who know how to kill, men who can follow orders. If you can't handle this job you better tell me now because I'll get somebody in here who can!"

He pressed close to Petra. "Do you understand me, Captain?"

Logan retained the threatening pose a moment. He glared at the bigger man, but Petra never blinked, returning Logan's malevolent glare without a word. Both arms remained crossed as the impotent threat died against his war decorated walls.

An involuntary muscle twitched Logan's cheek. He turned his back to Petra's silent confrontation and regally strolled to the map covering the far wall, both hands clasped behind his back. As he passed the table, he retrieved his cane with an exaggerated flare.

The map detailed the city and every hill, creek, and valley within a ten-mile radius of the city. Logan indicated an area labeled Rock Hill, an aptly named outcropping of granite nestled tight against the ocean five miles north of town. It was on its upper plateau where he and his men had waited in ambush the night before.

Stepping closer, Logan stabbed the location with the sharp point of his cane, deliberately ripping a jagged hole. Petra's lips compressed into a tight white line as his prized map tore.

"This is where we found him," Logan said. "On top of Rock Hill. Fishetti shot him, but he was too close to the cliff edge and fell off. My instincts tell me he can't be far from this spot. With a chest wound and most certain injuries from his fall, the man has got to be one hurting unit."

Petra interjected, his tone bitter. "You say Fishetti shot him? In that case, this guy's dead for sure. I never heard of Nick missing a shot—and I mean ever. He's the best man with a rifle I've ever seen. He's also an expert with guns, knives, martial arts. You name it, he's the best at it. The man's a certified killing machine.

"He was a sniper during the war. One shot, one kill. That was their motto and he lived up to that standard every time. During the war, he did over a hundred jobs for me behind enemy lines. He was in and out without ever being seen, a ghost, a shadow in the night. You don't know he's there until you're dead. In every mission, he neutralized every target with just one shot each. Counting the war and his service here, he has the record for most consecutive one-shot kills. It's something he takes great pride in."

"Well, he can take his one-shot pride and kiss it good-bye. Fishetti hit him, but I assure you the man I'm looking for is still alive. Don't ask me how I know, I just do. And that means we have serious problems."

Logan's cane tore a line in Petra's map from the mountain to the city. Petra's hands knotted into fists.

"You say your men searched everything from Rock Hill to here," Logan said. "But in that storm, there's no way they could have done a good job. I want them to do it again. I want two-man teams sweeping the entire area. I don't care if they have to bulldoze every tree and bush. Just find him.

"I also want you to concentrate on the house to house search here in the city. Start from the north end. With the shape he's in, he would have gone to the first house he saw. Then work your way south."

Petra threw his arms wide. "But Governor, I don't have the men to do all that!"

"Then activate the National Guard. Call the city police. They can help."

"The National Guard?" Petra took an agitated step forward. "You mind telling me how you can possibly justify calling them into this?"

"Well," Logan waved him off, "make up something. Tell them he's a serial killer. No! Even better. Tell them he's a terrorist. That will push their hot button."

"Not until you tell me what's going on." Petra's eyes narrowed. "Last night, I didn't ask questions when you commandeered my men because you're my boss. Now we're talking something entirely different. Outsiders make me nervous. We've got a hundred pounds of heroine in our deal going down tonight and I don't like the idea of having a lot of other guns around.

"Who is this guy that warrants jeopardizing our whole operation? What makes him so important? Just this once, why don't you drop your little Napoleon act and level with me?"

Logan marched straight toward Petra, his eyes wild. He raised the silver cane in muted rage, but again Petra returned Logan's angry glare with his own and even took a retaliatory step forward.

The move stopped Logan midway across the spatial office. He hesitated, lowered the cane, and then looked away, pretending something was in his eye. He coughed lightly and signaled Petra closer, lowering his voice to a conspiratorial tone.

"He can destroy us, Raul," he said. "He knows about our drug operation. He knows how and when we get shipments, how we launder the money through state accounts, everything."

Petra throttled a hoarse shout. "Why didn't you tell me?"

"I didn't want to alarm you unnecessarily. As you said, we've got a big deal going down tonight. I didn't want our buyers getting wind of this and back out. My plan was to kill him before anyone knew he existed. But we're past that now. We have no choice but to call in every gun we can get our hands on. The longer he lives, the more risk we run of going to jail for a very long time. All he needs is a computer that can access state systems. Once he goes public, we're finished."

"But I don't understand." Petra shook his head. "We covered our tracks. We've been through investigations before and come out clean. No one has ever connected us to anything. We're bullet proof."

Logan shook his head. "Not this time. This man has proof. If we don't find him, we're going down."

Petra threw back his head, rolling his eyes. "Oh, my God!"

He turned away, cursing under his breadth. He stopped. His head came up as he spun around to march straight at Logan, an accusing finger stabbing the air. "How could he possibly know all this? Only you and I know the accounts—and I didn't tell anyone!"

Logan took a step back. "Well neither did I! All

I can tell you is what my source told me. But I admit the reception was bad. I didn't get all he said."

"All who said? Who is this informant of yours? How do we know we can trust him?"

"I'd trust him with my life."

"Who is he, Jack? Your snitch. Tell me who he is."

"I can't tell you." When Petra took another step forward, Logan hurriedly added, "Not because I don't want to. I'd tell you if I could. Fact is I've never seen him. He initiates the contact and tells me things. He's never been wrong. Everything he's ever told me has been dead on. It was he who said the man we're looking for would be on top of Rock Hill at midnight. And he was there, right spot, right time."

Petra squinted, his head cocked slightly to one side, but his glare never left his target. He shook his head with a deep frown.

"Look." Logan forced a smile. "We can't waste time blaming each other. We're in this together, remember? Let's stay focused on the real issue and that's killing this man before he hurts us. If I were you, I'd start trying to figure out a way to do that before it's too late—for both of us."

"Well can you at least tell me his name, what he looks like?"

Logan shook his head. "That's part of the problem. Like I said, reception was bad. I think it was Newton or Norman. Something like that. I don't know for sure."

"Well, then give me a description. You were there. You saw him. Describe him to me." He picked up the phone. "I'll get Fred in here to do a character sketch—"

"Don't bother." Logan shook his head. "I only saw him from a distance. Plus, it was pitch black and raining. All I can tell you is he's medium height, medium build, and I think black hair."

Petra hurled the phone against the wall. The shattered debris clattered across the tile floor. "Oh, this just keeps getting better and better! There's a guy out there who can bring down our entire organization. No one knows what he looks like, and no one knows who or where he is. Just how am I supposed to put out an APB on a faceless ghost with no name?"

"I know it's not much, but it's all we've got!" Logan shot back. "Look, it can't be that hard. Stop whining about what we don't know and look at what we do. The man is a stranger. Right now, no one but us knows he's here. That means he's alone. And don't forget he's critically wounded. A man shot, beaten, and bleeding to death has got to stand out in any crowd."

Silence hung a pregnant moment. Petra's eyes shifted left and right, his brow knitted in studious frown. "You say he needs a computer," he said.

Logan nodded.

"What kind of computer?"

"A big one." And then Logan's eyes brightened. "And where is biggest, most powerful computer around?"

"The University!"

"Yes. And because it is a State facility, it can access State systems."

Logan straightened and said with a

commanding tone, "Station men at all the University's computer terminals. If anyone even remotely suspicious tries going near one, I want him brought to me. I'll know if it's the man I'm looking for the minute I see his face. No one kills him till I see him. Got that? I want to see him die with my own eyes."

He turned to the wall map, dismissing the captain with a regal flip of the hand. "Now go. You have your assignment. The sooner this man's in a body bag the better for both of us."

Petra nodded and opened the door.

"Raul?"

Petra turned his head.

"Better play it safe. Run a check on all companies in the area that have a computer. I want anything bigger than a PC put under surveillance."

A curt nod and Petra left the room shouting rapid-fire orders at everyone he saw.

Logan watched him go, malevolent eyes glaring. "What an idiot! I can make you believe anything, anytime. If you only knew the truth of why I need this man dead, then you'd be scared of me. Once this man is dead I will put a stop to your insolence. Who knows? Maybe you will find out the truth, but by then it will be too late—and I will be invincible!"

He turned with a contemptuous sniff to study the map once more. He crossed his arms, one hand rubbing his chin as he concentrated on the area surrounding Rock Hill.

Chapter 3

The stranger woke at dawn. The rain from the night before now rose in a ghostly vapor that hung in the still morning air. Sunlight streaked through the trees, creating shifting shafts of bright gold that danced in the mist.

He tried to sit up but the knifing pain in his side stopped the effort. That's when he heard the distant chop of helicopters. He peered from his rock tomb to see two Army aircraft roar overhead and into the distance, out to sea. As they faded into the distance, he watched and listened in anxious anticipation.

A nearby bird called a friendly morning and others answered in kind. The ocean surf, still agitated from its own midnight turmoil, churned the rocky shoreline below. The world, spent of its anger, seemed calm.

Satisfied he was alone on the ridge, he started to dig his way out. The cramped confines made the task of clearing the mud with just one hand hard work. He could barely move his left arm. The mud was soft, but it still took an hour before the opening was large enough to squeeze through.

Pressing both palms into the slime, he inched forward on his back. His head emerged first and he squinted against the sun's glare. Sweat rolled down his forehead and stung his eyes. The heat reflecting off the mountainside sapped his waning strength, forcing him to stop many times to rest. His shoulders were the hardest to fit through, but by turning and twisting he managed to make it. Hips and legs followed easily.

Then he was born from the Earth.

Soaked with blood and sweat, he sat against the cliff wall, breathing hard. He looked at his left side and understood the reason for the weakness and throbbing headache. The bullet entered below his rib cage and passed clean through, exiting his lower back. Judging by its angle, no vital organs were damaged, but he had lost a great deal of blood. It must have stopped bleeding during the night for his shirt was stained a dry dark red. His digging efforts had reopened the wound. Blood now seeped from the jagged hole and dripped steadily onto the sodden earth.

He looked down to see his left hand in the sticky ooze. He jerked it back, staring in slow realization at the crimson stain dripping down his fingers. If he didn't get help soon, he was going to die.

His head drooped. He leaned back against the cliff wall, letting the welcome relief of unconsciousness engulf him. No sooner had he closed his eyes than a voice inside his head shouted, *Get up. Get up. Get moving*!

The man forced himself unsteadily to his feet, but he rose too fast. The landscape whirled and lurched at a feverish rate. Overcome by nausea, he bent forward retching violently. When the vomiting stopped, he waited for his vision to clear before rising—more slowly this time.

By now, the sun was hot over the horizon. Rolling blue waves glistened in the gathering heat. The narrow shelf opened to his left. Forest trees swayed gently in the morning breeze. He would be safe from the choppers beneath the trees should they return. Pushing off the wall, he staggered toward them. Somehow, he knew his destination lay in this direction.

Walking was an arduous task. His left leg worked but swollen twice its normal size. Each step brought shooting pain from heel to hip. Hundreds of cuts and bruises covered his body, all of them stabbing him with each step he took. Every cluttered bush or fallen tree became an obstacle to be conquered—and there were many obstacles. It all made for dreadfully slow progress.

By the time he reached the end of the plateau, sweat drenched his tattered clothes. The plateau gave way to a rocky slope. He leaned against a small pine to catch his breath and survey the countryside below. The terrain was flat. The dense forest spread to the west in an unbroken green carpet that disappeared into a horizon of purple haze.

To his right was the rocky seaboard. The forest ran almost to the cliff's edge, which was still over fifty feet high here. Only at the edge did the trees thin out, leaving a few sparse sentries to take the brunt of the wind's daily attack. These outer trees were thinner then their brethren. Barren, wind-tortured branches bent landward in permanent deformation.

A creek gurgled through scattered stones at the base of the rocky slope. The water flowed from his left, dancing sprightly among the moss-covered rocks before streaming over the cliff. Buffeted by the ocean breeze, the flow dissipated into a fine mist that never reached the sea. Sunlight reflected off the spray to form a beautiful rainbow.

At the sight of water, the man broke into a stumbling run. He slid down the broken shale and fell beside a small pool created by the larger rocks. The cool water felt good on his parched throat and he drank his fill. He rolled into the stream, letting the gentle current caress his wounds. Thick, green leaves rustled overhead, shading him from the harsh sun.

Distant shouts shattered his respite. *Soldiers!* Frantic, he struggled out of the stream. He had to keep moving but was simply too weak to go on. His only hope was to hide.

He crawled to a nearby tree and collapsed at its base. He shifted to a sitting position, the thick trunk shielding him from any landward view. The dense stand of trees blocked the sky. To be certain, he covered himself with some branches torn off by the storm. Then he cast a worried look in all directions. It wasn't much, but it was the best he could do.

At last, he leaned against the giant pine. He jumped at the faint sound of a whistle. Nervously, he pulled the brush higher around head and settled down to wait.

Chapter 4

The man woke with a start. How long had he been asleep? Glancing at the sun, he guessed a few hours. He listened. No sound of the whistle. No helicopters. Satisfied they were gone, he crawled back to the mountain stream and bathed his wounds. He took his time, allowing the clear water to float the grime away.

Suddenly, his mind erupted in a series of brilliant flashes of white light. He shook his head to clear his vision, but the quickening bursts continued. Suddenly, rapid pictures erupted in his mind. A gunshot. A woman lay dying in his arms. Blood was on his hands. And then the pictures faded to black as a haunting voice echoed with laughter.

Who was she? he wondered. Had he killed someone? Was this why the men were after him?

Then slowly, haltingly, a woman in a white sundress came into view. She was young, her soft brown eyes deep and inviting. Long, auburn hair captured the rising sun, surrounding her slender face with a gentle radiant glow. She looked like an angel.

She laughed, beckoning him to follow her. When he didn't rise, she approached with an enchanting smile, her hand reaching for his.

The man could not refuse her. He struggled to

his feet, using a tree for support. He reached for her hand, but when he did the image faded from view. He blinked a few times, staring at the empty space where she had been, and slumped back against the tree. The woman seemed so real. He was wide awake. It could not have been a dream.

He knelt to drink more water and then staggered to his feet. The stream's invigorating chill fueled his determination to renew his journey north. Somehow, he knew he would find friends there.

However, the water's rejuvenation did not last long. An hour of trudging through thicket with the rising sun had already sapped him, causing him to rest more and more frequently. As time dragged on, he thought many times of giving up the struggle. It would have been so easy to just lie down and die.

Time and again he forced the morbid thought from his mind. He would not give up. Every time he fell, he found a way to force himself back to his feet. Something inside would not let him stop.

He came upon a trail and followed it. This made walking easier, but he still fell on a regular basis. And each time he collapsed, it was harder to rise. His leg ached miserably. Though the bleeding from the bullet wound had slowed, it still seeped down his shirt. Every step drained a little more of his life onto the dusty trail.

Soon, the path turned inland and he collapsed against the bole of a giant oak. He tried to get up but couldn't find the strength. He struggled to rise only to fall back again. He hung his head, his breath coming in ragged gasps. He couldn't hold on much longer.

That was when he saw the house.

Two A-frame sections flanked a central span, the structure forming a square U-shape. The center part of the house was half the height of the two side structures and contained a porch made of red brick. Four bleached white columns produced a southern antebellum look. An iron handrail lined the seven steps on the right side of the porch that led to double wide doors.

The trees around the house were cleared a hundred yards in all directions, allowing for an unobstructed view of the magnificent ocean cliffs. In their place, a carpet of lush, green grass made for a beautiful meadow. Only a few trees remained close to the house, performing a servitude of shade, which they did well.

Four chimneys adorned the rooftop, one for the front and rear of each A-frame. Smoke came from the rear stack on the left.

Someone was home.

The man managed to stand one last time, stepped off the dirt path and onto a walkway of gray river stone leading to the porch steps. Flowering plants and bushes formed a colorful apron along the entire front. They were neatly groomed, their bright hues lending an intrinsic beauty to the home. Honeybees, doing what they do best, made their busy sounds as they buzzed among them.

Grabbing the iron handrail, he dragged himself up the porch steps and pounded on the door. He leaned against it, grateful to have finally reached his goal. Being at that house gave him a sense of security that he could not explain but desperately needed.

He rapped again, harder this time. He held tight

onto the doorpost. His knees trembled with the simple effort of standing. A full minute passed and still no one came to his call.

Dark shadows began to crowd his pain-wracked mind. On the verge of passing out, he again reached for the door but could barely lift his arm.

He tried to swallow against the nausea but his mouth was too dry. The pressure inside his head continued to slowly pound out the light of day. With each passing second, the world grew ever darker.

It was then, at the point of utter collapse, that locks and latches turned on the inside. The door jerked open in an agitated rush.

Confronting him was a man in his early sixties. Long snow-white hair extended past his collar, the thick mane matched by an equally majestic white beard.

He was sixty pounds overweight, but what struck the stranger most were his eyes of sky blue, still sharp and clear. At present, their rage transfixed him. A half-bent pipe clenched in strong teeth vented his fiery temper. In his hands was a shotgun.

Though his eyes glared hostility, there were also deep laugh lines etched at their side. This man was no stranger to hardship, but he also knew compassion. The stranger saw all this at a glance.

The old man blocked the open door, shotgun ready for action, but then his eyes went wide at the sight in front of him. The pipe fell from his gaping mouth to clack across the white ceramic tile at his feet.

The stranger rolled off the doorjamb and said, "Doctor Lazlow. I need your help."

With that, everything let go and he fell into Lazlow's arms. The doctor dropped the shotgun and caught the man before he hit the floor. He shouted something over his shoulder into the house, but the stranger could not hear what he said, only muffled, slow moving sounds. He mumbled in his delirium and Lazlow's face snapped toward him with a look of utter astonishment. And then everything drifted to black again.

Chapter 5

The glow of a cigarette illuminated Sergeant Nick Fishetti's face. He sucked hard, breathing the acrid smoke deep into his lungs. Fishetti was a big, muscular man, the product of years of combat training. His pockmarked face and square jaw were covered with three days growth. Standing six-foot-three with a thick, barrel chest, he looked every bit the seasoned war veteran that he was.

Fishetti was a member of Logan's Special Force Unit, only tonight his job was not to fight crime, but to protect it. Behind him, concealed in an alley of deep shadow, a major drug deal was going down. There were some big names in that alley, dangerous people, and a lot of money. The money is what necessitated his presence there.

He leaned against a brick wall and snuffed out the spent cigarette, his tenth one that hour. He looked at his watch under the illumination of an overhead streetlight. It was late, almost two o'clock in the morning, and he was cold. Groaning a heavy sigh, he dug into his coat pocket and pulled out yet another smoke.

"What's up, Fishetti?" A voice called from the darkness.

Fishetti rolled his eyes toward the approaching sentry, keeping his hands cupped around the flickering flame of the match head. He drew deep on the smoke and whipped the match to extinction before sending it spinning into the night.

"I'll tell you something, Miller." Smoke clouded his face. "This has got to be the most boring detail I've ever pulled. How long have we been standing here? An hour? And for what? There ain't nobody going to try anything, least of all with these guys. I should be in bed like everyone else."

"I'd like to be home, too."

Fishetti smiled. "Who said anything about home?"

Corporal Tony Miller laughed. He was a lean, likeable kid with light hair and a quick smile. A police patrolman for three years, he joined Logan's unit just two weeks prior. Captain Petra assigned Fishetti to be his mentor, a job of which Nick was not particularly fond. Fishetti preferred to work alone.

Tony motioned for a cigarette. "At least you got a post that's out of the wind," he said. "I've been standing around the corner where it's blowing cold right through me. I should have put on thermals. After that front moved through the other day, the night air really got nippy."

Fishetti shook out the smoke for him and looked at his watch. He peered down the alley one more time.

Tony shivered, lit the cigarette, and pulled his collar up around his ears. "How much longer is this thing going to take?"

Fishetti shrugged. "Who knows? By all rights, it

should be over by now. But with Logan so tight lately, he's not taking any chances."

"Yeah, he's been acting kind of strange." Miller blew a thin stream of fog-laced smoke. "What's up with him? I heard he came in smashing up things yesterday and read Petra the riot act."

"Don't know for sure." Fishetti shrugged and glanced over his shoulder. "All I know is that we're gonna be wasting all day tomorrow looking for a dead man." He checked his watch with pressed lips. "We're supposed to muster at Bishop's Field at 0700. That gives us only five hours."

Tony said, "It don't matter if he's dead or alive. Logan canceled everything until we find him, and I mean everything. This is the last shipment."

"Yeah, he's worried, all right. No doubt about that." Nick nodded. "But if you ask me, we're wasting our time. The guy is fish food."

"How can you be so sure? Lieutenant Carpenter had men searching the cliff base all day and came up empty. If he was on the plateau, we'd have found him that night. If he's in the water, the divers would have found something, don't you think? How can you so sure he's dead?"

"Because I'm the one who shot him, that's why!" Fishetti stepped in Miller's face. "You saw the jacket. It was a clean shot. All we have to do is wait a few days and watch the shore. His body will wash up sooner or later—what's left of it, at least."

"But I still don't know how you can be sure. What makes you the expert?"

Fishetti grabbed Miller by the jacket and pulled

him in close. "Look, boy, I won best sniper ten years running. I did five tours back to back. Are you listening? Back to back. I'm the best of the best. I can't tell you how many people I killed, most of them behind enemy lines. One shot, one kill. Check it out if you want. I got a perfect record. Every mission, never missed a shot."

Fishetti released him.

"What do you mean, never missed a shot?" Tony said, straightening his jacket.

"What, are you stupid or just hard of hearing? I mean I never miss. One bullet, target down. How simple do I have to make it? Over a hundred missions. It's a world record as far I know. Probably never be broken, least of all by a no-account drifter."

"Well, whatever." Miller shrugged. "You and I are assigned the north forest. Petra's brought in the National Guard so at least we don't have to do the city door-to-door search."

Fishetti's head snapped up. "The National Guard?"

Tony nodded. "Turns out he's not a drifter. Petra said this guy is a terrorist. He's already killed five people. Anyhow, Captain got a tip he's camped in the woods somewhere and he wants us to get him before he kills again."

Fishetti flipped the glowing butt into the street. "Oh, that's just great! Not only am I not going to get any sleep, I got to spend all day trekking through the woods looking for a dead man."

He stepped back to the corner, peering yet again down the alley. Handshakes were being made. Briefcases full of money snapped closed. Suit cases of heroin shut. The guards standing behind their players looked tense, the two sides eying each other with mutual mistrust.

Fishetti signaled Miller and they both checked their weapons. Safety switches snapped off. If anything was going to happen, it would be now.

Fishetti's voice softened, but the bitterness was unmistakable. His eyes were on the men down the alley but said to Miller, "I don't know how Logan knows so much, but he's usually right. If he says the man's in the woods, then he might be. But I'll tell you this. If he is alive, I guarantee he won't be for long."

He pulled his gun and pointed the Beretta at Miller's face. The move was casual but the threat clear. "You keep this between you and me, you got that? If he is alive, I'm going to find him myself and dispose of the body where no one will ever find it. If anyone asks, I killed him that first night. There ain't no way I'm gonna let some drifter—terrorist or not— blemish my perfect record."

Chapter 6

When the stranger awoke, a small table lamp on his right dimly lit the darkened room and bathed the simple surroundings in a soft, warm glow. A glass of water sat beside the lamp and he scooped it up, draining it empty in three long gulps. He slammed the glass down, wishing for more.

He pulled the covers aside to sit on the edge of the bed and examine his condition. His swollen left leg moved stiffly, but it functioned. The bullet wound, wrapped with clean, sterile bandages, no longer hurt. Broad strips of surgical tape held the packing in place. Scabs and bruises of various degrees covered the rest of his body. No part had gone unscathed. But overall, he felt surprisingly good.

His hands, severely lacerated from clawing the rock, each missed the nail on three fingers. A tightly taped sling held his left arm across his stomach to immobilize his damaged shoulder. However, no bones seemed to be broken.

The man's clothes were gone. No big loss as they were bloody shreds anyway. He now wore blue, long-legged pajamas. The matching shirt lay draped across the footboard and he picked it up. He put his right arm through and draped the left over his shoulder, letting it hang open at the front. Grabbing the canopy post, he pulled himself erect and stood there a moment, gaining his balance.

A faint glow filtered through the half-open door and he decided to find out where he was, starting with the hall outside. He took a faltering step, checking the weight on his damaged knee. Satisfied with the results, he let go of the bedpost and limped against the nearby dresser while he peered through the opening, anxious to see what lay beyond.

His room was at the end of a long hallway. Several low-watt night lights lined the left hand wall, providing pools of illumination revealing many doors—all of them closed in stony silence.

Dozens of pictures of all shapes and sizes filled the empty spaces on left wall, scattered in random distribution along the entire length. On the right, a handrail opened onto the front foyer. At the far end, a soft light flowed up a set of stairs.

Someone was still awake.

He ventured forward, eager to find out more.

The wooden floor creaked beneath his weight. He moved to one side where the boards were less worn and tip-toed down the hall. Approaching the first pool of light, he paused to examine the photographs.

Some were simple snapshots chronicling the events of an old man's life. Others were professional portraits of children, a boy and a girl at various stages of growth. The boy's pictures were newer, their color brighter, more bold. Though both children's photos were taken at roughly the same age, he guessed by the clothing style they were separated in time by twenty years.

There were baby pictures of all kinds, photographs of kids at play and vacation, but they all seemed remote. Just colored paper filled with unfamiliar faces. None sparked memories or emotion. None, that is, except for one.

The picture showed Doctor Lazlow standing on the deck of a fishing trawler, proudly displaying his worthy deep sea catch. He was much younger then, his thick mane mostly black and he was much slimmer.

At first the man thought it might be someone else, but those piercing blue eyes and smoking pipe clenched in strong white teeth marked him for who he was. He stood triumphantly with one leg atop the prized Sailfish.

The girl, perhaps 18 or 19-years-old, danced beside Lazlow, her lithe form caught in mid-jump, clapping with glee. She had the thick hair of the family, but hers was more red, like auburn leaves. Her developing figure was tantalizingly concealed beneath a bikini top and hip-hugger shorts.

Something in this big fish story seemed familiar. The man leaned in close, squinting through the dim hallway light. As he stared, strange sounds seemed to emanate from the picture itself. As if by magic, the hall disappeared and he was drawn into the scene before him.

He heard the girl squeal when Lazlow heaved the mammoth fish flopping onto the deck. The sea breeze carried the rank odor while Doc bellowed with pride. He flexed his muscles in a mock display of brute strength. The girl giggled and jumped for joy. And then the scene stopped, the memory melting into the darkness and the man found himself back in the darkened hallway, staring at the portrait once more.

He moved on to the next picture. It was newer, showing Lazlow much older. He played ball in the yard with the little boy. The now fully grown woman stood off to one side, her arms folded in front of her.

The stranger leaned in for a closer look and his eyes went wide. It was the same woman he had seen in his vision. He found this both fascinating and confusing. She was more beautiful than ever, but her eyes held an emptiness that hadn't been there before.

The last picture before the stairway showed Doctor Lazlow, the woman, and the boy standing in front of a rocky mountainside. Half way down the cliff, a huge boulder hung impossibly balanced on an escarpment of rock. The stranger was amazed that something so large could protrude that far into space and still not topple into the sea below. It loomed over the lower plateau, defying gravity to bring it down. In the corner of the snapshot, someone had scrawled *The Three Amigos at Hanging Rock*. The man peered at the picture through the dull light. He knew that rock.

Slowly, he descended the carpeted steps. Half-way down, the stairs turned back on itself one hundred and eighty degrees. A bay window adorned this turnaround landing that also overlooked the front foyer. To his left, the front door. He recognized the white tile from when he arrived. At the bottom, a short hallway led to his right, the kitchen the first door in front of him.

Beside him, on his right, another door stood ajar. The light beckoned him onward. The man peeked inside only to find a similar set of stairs descending to the basement area, this one completely encased in wood.

These stairs also doubled back, ending in a large game room. A bright rectangle of light from an open door on his right illuminated a cluttered mess of furniture and household trinkets: A bear-claw card table, a pool table, a variety of exercise equipment, two televisions, a long couch, and a bar—though he could see no sign of alcohol. Children's toys littered the floor.

He approached the open door, moving silently. At least he did until he stepped on a baseball bat concealed in the shadows. His right leg flipped behind him, sending the bat clattering across the hard Spanish tile. He lunged forward in an ungainly effort to catch himself against the doorframe with his one good arm. In sheepish embarrassment, he stepped into the room.

The large study contained two doors on opposite corners. Books lined the walls on either side of the door in which he stood, mainly reference novels relating to psychology, psychiatry, and other technical matters. Posed pictures, plaques, and diplomas decorated the far wall. Heavy red velvet curtains covered the windows, now closed against the dark world.

The door in the far corner also contained a window, indicating this wasn't a basement at all. The house was built into the hill, not just on top of it. This other door opened onto a backyard of lower elevation than the front.

A large wooden desk spanned the corner to his right and faced the center of the room. Its neatly arranged piles of paper suggested it belonged to someone both meticulous and busy.

The old man sat in a recliner along the far wall. A porcelain lamp of a Sailfish arching out of a foaming sea illuminated the huge, leather bound book in his lap. The stranger watched him scribble notes with one hand while the other maintained a point of reference in the mammoth manual.

A long, overstuffed couch sat a few feet out from the bookcase wall on the left and ran parallel to it. A posh rug covered the area enclosed by the desk, couch, and recliner, completing a comfortable and relaxing study environment.

The old man glanced up from his reading and looked at him over gold, half-rimmed glasses. His wary expression was nevertheless inviting, his unwavering eyes locked on the stranger in front of him. Doc didn't say a word, which the stranger took as a reserved welcome.

The man took a few, short steps and noticed a small mirror setting on the left shelf—and what he saw wasn't pretty. The hunchback of Notre Dame had nothing on him. Mental images of mothers pulling screaming children off the street as he walked by forced a painful smile to chapped lips.

His face, smashed by stone after stone during the fall, was puffed, discolored, and swollen. An ugly, red gash ripped across his forehead, ending somewhere above his right ear. A large knot at his hairline possessed every disgusting color imaginable and leaked clear fluid into the scab of a missing eyebrow. Both eyes were black, as well as yellow and green.

He gave Doc credit for not grabbing the

shotgun, which he noticed was nearby, propped in the corner by the back door. All Doc said was, "You should be in bed."

"Oh, don't worry about me. I feel better than I look." And he meant it, too. The hundreds of cuts and bruises were but a dull reminder of their former self and his strength vastly improved. "How long was I out?" He dabbed the leaking clear fluid with a tissue.

"Almost three days." Doc puffed his pipe while tamping the bowl with a tobacco-stained finger. "And I will tell you, not a more disturbing sight have I seen for quite some time. You were in a bad way, young man, but you were lucky. Had you come a few minutes later, I would have been fishing with my grandson and you most likely would have bled to death on my front porch. That would have been a very messy prospect indeed." The last with a smile to erase all affront.

"I'm sorry, Doctor, but I didn't mean to frighten you. I don't even know how I found your house."

Doc grunted a jovial smile and heaved the heavy book aside. "Oh, that's quite all right, my boy. You broke the tedium of this place. Being so far from town, we seldom get visitors. And those we do get are the type I don't want around." He nodded at the shotgun by way of explanation.

He pushed his massive frame to his feet, extending a pudgy hand. "I'm curious. You know me, but I'm sorry I don't remember you. What is your name? Who are you?"

The man grasped his hand to complete the greeting ritual, but stopped in mid-breath. His mouth opened to reply, then stopped. He could think of nothing to say. They stood holding hands a few embarrassing seconds before the man released his grip to rub the back of his neck.

He looked at his feet. "I, uh, I don't know. I can't remember anything beyond last night."

Doc stroked his thick white beard, studying him with a raised brow and appraising eye. At last he said, "That's understandable, my boy. With the severity of your injuries, amnesia should be expected. Given time, however, your memory should come back."

He retreated to the recliner and motioned John to the couch. "Sit down, sit down. Let's have a little chat. Maybe I can help jump start your mind."

The man sat on the plush couch. Large pillows enveloped him, pulling him deep into their softness.

Doc picked up his pipe, knocked out the old tobacco, opened his pouch, and began packing a fresh load. "Tell me what you can remember," he said.

"Not much, I'm afraid. The first thing I recall is walking through the woods on top of a mountain. The next thing I know, a bunch of men started shooting at me."

"Do you know why they were chasing you?" Doc lit a match. His tone was professional and soothing, as if he had done this sort of thing a thousand times before.

"No. There was a terrible storm. I remember running through heavy rain. They cornered me against a cliff. That's when one of them shot me and I fell off. Yes, I hit my head several times during the fall. But if it was amnesia, why can I remember all that and not know who I am?"

Doc glared at the man with a skeptical sneer,

the lit match momentarily forgotten. "Are you telling me you fell from the top of Rock Hill? Son, I find that rather hard to believe. No one could survive that."

"Well, believe me, I had plenty of rocks to break my fall," he said with equally heavy sarcasm.

Doc regarded him a moment before lighting his pipe and blowing the spent match to extinction with a smoky cloud.

"Besides," the man continued, "I didn't fall the entire way. I landed in a deep wash of mud on the middle plateau. That alone saved my life. I then hid beneath a pile of boulders while the men searched for me. I must have blacked out because the next thing I knew it was daylight and all I could think of was to head this way. I seemed to know I would find this house. And when you answered the door, I suddenly knew your name. Why, I don't know, but I did."

Lazlow puffed his pipe and looked at the man with a pose of studious concentration. It gave him a detached, scholarly look which the stranger was sure took years to perfect. Lazlow's eyes scanned the other man's body actions and facial expressions for hidden clues, an impossible task considering the face was a swollen mask.

"Have we met before, Doctor Lazlow?"

"Call me Doc. Everyone else does." Then he shook his head. "I don't seem to recall you, though. But then, my memory is not what it used to be—and neither is your face. But that's quite all right, my boy. It will come to me.

"Seems to me you were likely the victim of one of the gangs that's been terrorizing these parts. Strange they ventured so far from town, but not unheard of, not unheard of. That's the reason I keep this shotgun handy. Never go anywhere without it these days. Just in case. There's a bunch of them, gangs I mean, and they're all a murderous lot."

"It was no gang."

"How do you know that?"

"Unless these gangs you mentioned are armed with machine guns, it was no mere gang. They were something else."

Doc looked at the stranger in a hard but brief pause then said, "Anyhow, it wasn't my decision to keep you here. It was Mary's idea. She's the one who insisted we take care of you instead of calling 911. She has this sixth sense of such things. She was convinced that whoever shot you would check the hospitals to finish the job. Probably right, too. Probably right. I had my reasons, too, you know, but more on that later.

"I've never seen her so adamant. She's been, shall we say, a bit reserved for quite some time. No matter what I said, she was absolutely determined to take care for you herself." He smiled. "She also made me swear not to tell anyone. She was afraid if word got out, whoever it was after you would come here. It's like she knew you were in trouble and she had to protect you.

"Like I said, Mary hasn't been herself for quite some time. But for some reason, your survival gave her a renewed sense of purpose. She came alive again for the first time in years. I found her attitude and energy so uplifting I had no choice but to go along."

"Who's Mary?"

"Geez! You must have been dead to the world.

Mary is my daughter. She's the one who's been buzzing around you like bees on honey ever since you got here. She got you through the fever, nursing you non-stop night and day.

"She seemed obsessed with you, absolutely determined to keep you alive. And as I understand it, things were touch-and-go there for a while. But I'm glad she did what she did. This experience has been good for her. She's not shown that much attention to anyone, much less a man, since her husband died."

"I'm sorry to hear that. I saw what must be her picture in the upstairs hallway. She's a pretty woman."

"She is a beautiful person," Doc corrected, pointing with the tip of his pipe. "Pretty is only skin deep. Beauty goes to the bone. She's one of the most caring and smartest people you'll ever meet. Even when she was a kid, she acted ten years older than what she was. And curious!" He slapped his knee and laughed. "Every new bug she came across had to be examined. She would ask me question after question until I ran out of answers. And then she'd come into my office, pull out the encyclopedia or go on the internet and study the critter until she knew everything there was to know about it."

He paused, smiling, his head slightly bent, his eyes glinting.

"That's very unusual." The man gave the obliged nod. "You must be proud."

"Pride doesn't say the half of it. She's never satisfied, that one. Even today, always wants to know more. David, my grandson, is just like her."

"Looks like a fine kid," the man said, recalling the photographs.

"He is. He's never disrespectful and always minds his manners. Why, he didn't even cry when he was born, just kind of yawned and laid there, looking at us. He's air-headed like any nine-year-old, but a good boy nonetheless. He doesn't remember his father, of course. David was just a few months old when the man died."

"His father? I don't recall seeing any picture of a man on the wall other than you."

Doc shook his head. "Given the situation how he died, I decided not to reinforce that particular event in our lives, so I hid his pictures. I didn't want to be continually reminded or have to explain, well, you know . . ." one finger idly traced the pattern of his worn book.

He looked up. "I guess you might say I'm now his father now. We go fishing and do a lot of things together."

"What happened to his real father?"

Doc hesitated, taking a deep breath before answering. And when he did, he was blunt, his voice bitter, his expression transformed to an ugly scowl.

"He was hung."

"Why? What did he do?"

"He didn't do anything!" Doc shouted, his blue eyes blazing. He ripped the pipe from his clenched teeth and aimed the tip at John. "And I don't see that's any of your business."

The man bowed his head, averting his eyes.

Inexplicably, Doc added, "Someone set him up, that's what it was. They accused him of rape and murdering a little girl. They even bribed a couple of drunks to say they saw him do it. But it was a lie. It was all a lie. Paul would never do anything that hideous." He shook his head. "That lynch mob didn't even bother with a trial. They came to this very house, dragged him outside, and hung him from a tree in our front yard!"

He returned the pipe to his mouth, puffing hard and fast, and stared into the dark corner in silence for a long moment. Somewhere in the game room, a clock chimed eleven o'clock. The sound startled the old man from his reverie. World-weary eyes flitted about the room, his voice so faint John could barely hear, "Mary thinks Jack was behind it all, but I can't believe that. You can't convince me a fine, enterprising man like that could do such a vile thing."

"Who's Jack?"

"Jack Logan is our Governor." His tone was loud and authoritative, but his eyes nervously scanned the floor. "Duly elected government officials just don't do that sort of thing.

"Besides, Jack is my patron, my friend. He personally funds my research. If not for him, I'd have nothing. Why would he want to kill Paul? Why would he kill my son-in-law?"

"Logan, you said?" The man asked, alarmed. "Jack Logan is your Governor?"

"Yes, why? Do you know him?"

The stranger shrugged but said nothing. It was obvious Doc liked this Logan and, not knowing what situation he had fallen into, he decided to keep his thoughts to himself.

For some reason, Doc went on praising Logan. Maybe it was to prove Jack was a good man. Or maybe it was to recite the rhetoric once more—and maybe this time he would believe his own story. Whatever his reason, the man thought he could learn something by listening to answers of unasked questions. He reclined on the couch, idly listening to Doc's glowing description of his idol.

After an hour of Doc's drone, the man's head drooped. He snapped upright with a jerk, blinking away the bleariness.

"Oh, listen to me rambling on," Doc said. "Why don't you go on back to bed? Rest is still your best medicine. Tomorrow, if you're up to it, we'll try using a device I've just invented that may help you regain your memory."

"What sort of device?"

"Oh, just something I've been dabbling with. It's supposed to resonate with the alpha rhythms in a person's brain and induce a calming effect. I think if we can get your mind adjusted to a neutral state, you won't block your past anymore."

Doc spoke with practiced professional poise. "That's what you're doing, you know, blocking. I'm hoping my invention can coax repressed memories to the surface. You'll be my first patient. So what do you say? Shall we give it a go?"

"If you think it can help." John shrugged. "I'm willing to try. I'm haunted by this feeling there's something terribly important I should be doing. So yes, I'm game. At this point, I'm willing to try anything."

"It's agreed then." He slapped the armchair with a happy hand. "Tomorrow we will awaken your mind and see what secrets it holds. In the meantime, if you agree to be my test subject, I'll offer you refuge from those trying to kill you. Agreed?"

The man nodded. "Fine with me. And thank you."

Refuge

Chapter 7

The next morning brought a soft breeze that caressed the sheer curtains of John's open bedroom window. Sunlight flowed inside with the wind, transforming the billowing white lace into a glowing, dancing wraith. Outside, rustling trees whispered a soft song as the ocean tide beat its steady rhythm. Nature was in harmony.

The door clicked softly. The stranger watched it swing open and the ruddy face of a small boy peer through the opening gap. It was David. His big, round eyes absorbed everything as he spied into the mysterious world of a stranger. He craned his head to look behind the door.

"Hello," the man said.

David's head snapped around with a gasp, eyes wide, and then he hurried away. Running footsteps retreated down the hall. The man smiled at the curiosity of a child.

The aroma of breakfast wafted through the open door. His churning stomach reminded him it had been four days since he had eaten solid food and urged him to follow the delicious odor. He quickly buttoned the pajama top as best he could and descended the stairway.

The kitchen was large, with all manner of pots and pans hanging over a center cooking island. Beyond the kitchen was the vaulted ceiling of a living area furnished with a wraparound couch, a large flat-screen TV, and stereo. No walls separated the two rooms. The couch extended across the middle, marking the boundary.

On the right, a windowed door led to a circular driveway. The solid window wall on the left side of the kitchen revealed the other side of the U-shaped house. In the middle, a rose garden was in full bloom. A breakfast alcove protruded into the inner garden, providing an unfettered view of the dew-dampened roses.

Doctor Lazlow sat at the round table inside the nook drinking coffee and reading the newspaper. David was beside him, playing with his pancakes.

"Good morning," the man said.

"Ah, good morning, my boy!" Doc dropped his paper. "Come in! Come in! Have a seat. I trust you slept well the rest of the night?" He spoke in rapid-fire fashion. "Would you care for something to eat?" But he was already on his feet, not waiting for an answer. "We have pancakes, eggs, and bacon." He heaped piles of each onto a plate. "Coffee's in the pot. Fork's in the top drawer." He nodded his head to indicate the directions.

The man poured himself a cup of coffee and sat down at the table, gazing at the panoramic view of the inner courtyard garden and the red brick path winding through blossoming shrubs. Sitting in that serene atmosphere, surrounded by Nature, he was comfortable, at peace with the world. It felt like home.

"What's the matter?" Doc said. He set the plate in front of him with a heavy hand.

The man looked up, his mind snapping back to the present. "I could swear I've been here before."

Doc didn't reply, choosing to sit in idle contemplation. The man looked at the boy. "You must be David."

He nodded.

"How old are you?"

"Nine and a half," he said, blushing with a quiet voice.

"Wow!" the man acted surprised. "You're big for nine and a half."

The childish compliment brought an embarrassed smile, but little else. *Some master conversationalist I am*, he thought. He ate in uncomfortable silence before remembering the bat he tripped over the night before.

"Hey, David, do you like baseball?"

"Yes, sir. It's okay. I like to hit, but I can't catch very good. I like football, too. But I think soccer's the best. It's fun."

"And he's getting pretty good at it, too," his grandfather said. He then terminated the conversation. "Are you finished, son?"

"Yes, sir," the boy said with the exaggerated nod of a playful heart.

"Go brush your teeth and then you may go outside."

The stranger watched in amused silence as the

boy carefully carried his dishes to the sink. A tiny bit of tongue peeped out the corner of his mouth, his eyes glued to the plate and fork. He set the plate and the half-empty glass of milk down with a loud clatter and then bolted from the kitchen and up the stairs, doing his best to take them two at a time.

"He's a good kid," the man noted when David made the stairway turn.

"He is at that." Doc nodded. "His heart's pure gold and I love him to death. He's not grown beyond his years like his mother was at his age. I suppose girls grow up faster. But then, boys don't mature till they're what, fifty?"

"I don't know," the man laughed. "I'll let you know when I get there."

They set their plates in the sink and Doc rinsed them off before putting them in the dishwasher. Above the sink, a window facing the circular driveway gave a breathtaking view of the ocean. To the left, down a rather steep slope, a wall of dense trees surrounded a large back yard.

"By the way," the man said, "where is Mary? I'd like to thank her."

"Oh, she's an early morning person." He pointed out the window. "She likes to walk along the cliff at sunrise whenever she can. She said something about having some errands to do and that she would be back this afternoon."

The last of the dishes done, he looked at the stranger up and down with an appraising eye. "You need some clothes. We had to throw yours out, torn up as they were. But I think we can make do. Come on, follow me."

They left the kitchen and turned left down the hall. He stopped short of the door leading to the garage and pulled on a thin rope hanging from a ceiling trap door. As the door swung down, a ladder unfolded.

He motioned his guest to stay where he was and scurried into the attic more nimbly than one would think possible for a man his bulk and age. After a moment of silence, there came a number of shuddering thumps followed by boxes sliding about. Finally, Doc appeared at the opening with a few of them.

He called in a mock bombardier's voice, "Look out below!"

He dropped a three-foot square box at the man's feet. The stranger had just bent over to pick it up when another box hit him on the back of the head.

Doc clicked off the attic light and scrambled down the ladder. He turned to see John rubbing his neck, looking up at the attic.

"What's the matter now?"

"Huh?" the man looked at him, unaware he had been staring into space. "Oh, nothing. Just that creepy feeling again that all this has happened before." He gestured to the boxes. "Paul's clothes?"

"Yep." Doc mopped his brow. "How did you know that?"

The man shrugged. "Wild guess."

"They did belonged to David's father. Don't know why we didn't throw them out. Out of sight, out of mind, right? Anyway, looks like it's a good thing we didn't. They're a might musty, but I think they'll fit you fine. You look to be the same size he was." He slid open a set of folding lattice doors behind him to reveal the laundry room and wasted no time dumping the boxes indiscriminately into the washing machine.

"Mary always fusses at the way I do clothes," he said with an air of defiance. "But she's not here now and, personally, I don't think it matters what gets washed with what." He closed the lid and started the cycle. "Why don't you let me show you the house while these are running? As long as you're my guest, you should know your way around."

A few steps toward the center of the house brought them to the front foyer. Save for the double-wide front doors on their immediate left, there were no other doors there, only high archways leading to two other rooms. Doc's heels echoed on the white tiled floor as they passed crossed into an immaculate music room on the far side of the foyer. To their right, between the kitchen and the music room, a long, stone table filled the formal dining room

The music room was immaculately outfitted in various shades of white. The deep pile carpet, the leather couch, even the molded columns supporting the intricately carved mantle over the white brick fire place were all complimenting hues of ivory. An overstuffed leather couch occupied the middle of the room, facing the fireplace. The only exceptions to the pallid scene were a large oil painting and a beautifully polished, solid black grand piano. Most notable was the entire inner wall of the house was made of solid glass, allowing an unobstructed view of the inner garden from any room.

Doc talked as if giving a museum tour rather than his home. His boring drone lasted for hours. The old man wasn't satisfied with simply pointing out the artifacts he collected over the years. For some reason he felt compelled to recount all sorts of personal stories about each room and the objects they contained, especially the ones concerning David and Mary.

The stranger smiled at those stories, like the time a baseball crashed through the dining room window while the governor sat at the table. He could almost hear the commotion, security guards scrambling into defense position with guns raised around the governor, although he was sure Doc didn't laugh then as he did now.

Doc also told of happier times when he would crawl on his hands and knees on the plush white carpet with young David riding his back like a horse while Mary played the piano. As the man listened, he could almost touch the memories he painted—almost, but not quite. For whenever he reached for them in his mind, the images vanished, leaving him with nothing but the echo of empty words.

Finally, mercifully, David interrupted and asked for something to drink. The clothes were dry. Doc excused himself and the man retreated to his room to sort through the pile of shirts and pants.

He was glad for the respite. The loaned memories only served to fuel the desire to discover his identity. The more Doc talked, the more he felt the foreboding presence of impending doom and the nagging certainty that he should be doing something to stop it.

He entered the kitchen to find Doc and David sitting at the table. John said, "So, Doc. When are we going to try that invention of yours? I'm dying to know who I am. Not being able to remember anything is driving me nuts."

Doc nodded, stroking his snow-white beard. "You mean the Alpha device? We can do it now if you're up for it."

"Doc, at this point, I'd try anything to find out who I am. If your gizmo thing can help me know who I am, then I'm all for it. As far as I'm concerned, the sooner the better."

David excused himself and said he was going outside to play and Doc took a moment to review the essential safety instructions of staying in the yard. Judging by the look on the boy's face, he had heard the same speech many times over. He nodded and danced in anticipation until the lecture was over and then bolted through the side door. He hit the ground running full out.

"That's good." Doc watched him kick a soccer ball with a smile. "He can keep himself occupied for hours. Mary should be home in a little while anyway. It will give us the time we need to be alone."

With that, he walked briskly out of the kitchen. The stranger hesitated, casting one last look at David. He felt sorry for him, the boy forced to invent yet another solitary make believe game. No friends to play with. And then he hurried after Doc, who was already halfway down the stairs.

"What's this thing going to do?" the man said, feeling apprehensive.

Doc paused at the switchback landing. "It won't hurt, I assure you. The entire process is completely passive. The machine will surround your brain with a rather unique energy field. But not to worry, not to worry. It's not strong enough to endanger your brain's natural electrical circuits so there's no danger whatsoever of convulsion or neural damage."

He proceeded into the game room, talking over his shoulder. "I must tell you that the device and the energy field it creates are classified top secret, so I must ask that you please not tell anyone. I'll inject you with a sedative to help you relax. That's it. You should remember everything after that."

They walked into his study and Doc motioned him to the couch. He took his assigned place and watched Doc tilt a blue book in the center of the bookcase. A subtle click and then he swung the entire middle section inward on hidden hinges. A room filled with electronic test instruments and workbenches lay beyond the wall of books. Flashing computer panels lined the back, making for a quaint little workshop.

"A secret lab?" the man's eyebrows rose.

Doc shrugged with a demure nod and walked inside. In the middle of the room, on top of a two-foot high metal cart, sat a mysterious black box. The cart had caster wheels with two doors on the bottom.

He rolled the unit in front of his guest. He plugged it in and switched it on, initiating a slight electronic whirring noise of a cooling fan inside. He instructed the man to lie down on the couch and then opened the cabinet doors to produce two expandable bands. The smaller of the two went around his right arm. The largest encircled his chest. Both sensors connected to the front of the black box by coiled cables.

He then went back to the cabinet and carefully

extracted a strange looking helmet which he placed on the man's head. It had a dozen transducers, tiny discs connected by a tangle of wires that collected at the back of the helmet and led into Doc's computer. The final step was to open his shirt and tape six probes to his bare chest, one over the heart.

"This is a just a precaution in the event a problem does occur," Doc said with an official tone. "This is the first time this unit has been used. By monitoring your blood pressure, breathing, and heart rate, I can determine your state of distress. If anything *does* happen, I will terminate the session immediately."

He moved a chair in front of the unit and sat down at the control console. While Doc made last minute adjustments, the stranger busied himself studying the computer and the sensors attached to him. It didn't take long to recognize the contraption was a lie detector, an elaborate and complicated one, but a lie detector nonetheless.

The man glanced at the unsuspecting doctor with a twinge of resentment but did not say anything. After all, by his own account, he was a wanted man. If he were Doc, he would have done the same thing. How else could Doc be certain he was telling the truth?

The man shrugged. It didn't matter. If this so-called alpha device could unlock his mind, then Doc could do any lie detection he wanted. He had nothing to hide, or so he thought. He reclined on the couch, allowing the soft cushions to embrace him.

At last, Doc finished his preparations and approached him with a syringe in hand. He injected a clear substance into his arm and turned off the lights, all the while reminding him not to resist the drug. In a few minutes, the man grew drowsy and his head drooped.

Doc immediately flipped a switch on the machine. A series of lights came on, illuminating his face. He spoke to him in a low, monotonous tone, something about focusing on the light above his head.

The stranger had been wrong about that device being lie detector.

Doc energized the circuits in the helmet. For the first few minutes, he constantly adjusted the dials. He chuckled at something and scribbled a note on the paper strip chart rolling out of the side. His pudgy middle jiggled with mirth. He flipped a final switch.

That was when the room lost focus.

Doc squinted at the monitors above the black box and grew suddenly serious. He turned another knob and the room instantly began spinning like a cyclonic time warp. The man blinked hard, trying his best to hold on, but the room continued to fade away.

Doc flipped another switch and radiating star bursts blurred the man's vision. He felt himself propelled through a black mist, the room violently exploding from view.

And then in one brilliant flash everything stopped and he found himself alone in total darkness. There was no sound, not even a breath of air. He felt like a wraith floating in the emptiness of deep space.

Doctor Lazlow's voice echoed through the darkness, instructing him to relax. He turned at the sound but could no longer see him. He looked around, fearing the foreboding isolation. And as he did, a small light materialized in the distance, zooming toward him at great speed.

The light brightened into a vision of a room similar to Doc's study but slightly different. The man found himself standing in a room that had the same leather sofa fronting a book-filled wall. But across from this was a recliner chair of matching white leather. Between them was a glass-topped coffee table.

A middle-aged man reclined on the sofa. The stranger couldn't see his face. He sat hunched over, researching a book clutched on his lap. He had thick hair black but streaks of gray spoiled his massive beard.

As the scene focused, the man on the sofa looked up from his reading and the stranger saw those clear, sky-blue eyes. It was Doctor Lazlow when he was a younger man, just like the picture he saw upstairs. Rings of sweet fragrance encircled Doc's head as he absently puffed his ever-present pipe. He peered through the lingering cloud, eying someone in the recliner with a concentrated stare.

The vision moved as a disembodied spirit to see who was sitting in the chair. And when it did, it stopped dead still. The man in the chair was none other than *himself*! Like Lazlow, he was also younger, maybe his late teens. He squirmed with barely bridled excitement, his legs constantly dancing with nervous energy.

In the vision, Lazlow smiled and said, "Calm down, John. And stop fidgeting! You're going to wear a hole in that seat cushion. Just sit back. That's it. Take a deep breath and tell me what's on your mind."

Doc set the heavy book aside and leaned back,

crossing his arms on top his pudgy middle. One hand held the pipe to pursed lips.

John! The stranger said to himself. *My name is John.*

He saw himself obediently scoot back in the chair. However, no sooner had his head touched the cushion than he bounced forward again, sliding to the edge of the seat. "Listen," the boy said. "Do you remember the optical device I've been working on?"

"That thing supposed to make blind people see? Sure, I remember it. As I recall, it flopped. Why are you so excited about a failure?"

"Because I didn't fail. Well, yes, I did, but I didn't. What I mean is, because of that, I finally realized feeding electrical impulses to dead brain tissue is a waste of time. Sure, we can stimulate nerve cells and cause some light and dark perceptions, but that's like shocking an amputated arm with electricity. We can make it jump, but it's never going to function again. Same thing is happening with the stimulation of the brain. It won't work. So, to actually make them see, I discovered I needed to go deeper."

Doc shook his head. "How do you mean?"

"Since the optical part of their brain is broken, there's no way to make a patient truly see again via our current efforts with the brain. I concluded the only way to make them see is to feed the visual signal directly to the person's consciousness. As you might expect, this redirection was a dramatic turning point."

"I'm sure it was." He tamped the ashes of his pipe, then sucked hard to keep the fire alive. Between puffs he said, "Not sure I what you mean by that, though."

"It means I'm not focusing on the brain anymore. Because of that failure, I started working on finding the origin of consciousness and feed the signal directly to that. I wasted my time analyzing neurons. There is nothing living inside a brain cell. There can't be. Sure, it's special. And it plays an important part in manifesting our consciousness to the atomic world, but the brain is not the source of consciousness. It's not the source of *self*. From a purely objective point of view, the brain is a bunch of specialized nerves dancing in coordinated chemical concert. That's it. Beyond that, it's just a dead lump of flesh."

Doctor Lazlow gave the young man a harsh look. "Listen, John, I've written a dozen books on this and read hundreds more. My whole life has been devoted to studying the human mind. That's to say I know what I'm talking about. Believe me, the brain is the source of consciousness."

John shook his head. "No, Doc. You're wrong."

Doc's head snapped up, those sharp eyes glaring.

"No disrespect, Doc, but the brain is no different than your arm or leg. If I cut off your arms and legs, we both agree they're going to lay there. But are you now partially dead? No. I've just removed the way you move around. The body means nothing to the real source of life.

"The same thing goes for the brain. It's part of the body. It's made of the same atoms as your arm. It means nothing to the real origin of life, either. When the source of power leaves the brain, the brain becomes just another lump of dormant flesh, just like your arm or leg.

"You say the brain is the source of consciousness, but what happens if you take a bullet to the head? Are you now partially dead? Is part of your life now gone? Or would it be that what really makes up Frank Lazlow would now be trapped within a damaged processor?

"You're a psychiatrist. Think about it. If the neural circuits of the brain are damaged, isn't it possible that your consciousness would be whole and untouched, only now you'd find it difficult to express your thoughts and feelings to the outside world?"

Doctor Lazlow didn't say a word.

The young John continued, "Let me put it this way. Let's say I'm listening to a radio. If I wanted to find the musician, would I open the receiver simply because that's where I hear the sound coming from? No, of course not! A monkey might try because a monkey wouldn't know better. But everyone knows looking for the musician inside a radio is ridiculous."

"Well, of course it is!" Doc said. "What's your point?"

"My point is that's what we're doing with the brain. Science has been sifting through inanimate tissue trying to find the source of human life for hundreds of years. And in all this time we've come up empty. We've gotten nowhere because we thought the brain was the source of life. That's where we went wrong. The role of the brain is to manifest our true consciousness to the atomic level of reality, just like a radio. Nothing more."

"You're losing me, John," Doc played with a

box of matches with an intellectually bored hand. "If you have something to say, then just say it."

"I'm saying the brain is not the origin of life. The source of life, the origin of our being is the *soul*. For my experiment to work, I need to feed the optical signals directly to the soul. If I can do that, I can do a lot more. Making blind people see is just the first step. Once I connect with the soul, there's no limit to what I can do!"

Doc stopped playing with the matches. His eyes lifted with an I-can't-believe-you-just-said-that look on his face. He didn't say a word, but he didn't have to. His expression was loud enough.

He took the pipe from his mouth, but before he mustered a response John said, "The miracle of human life cannot be totally and wholly defined as bunch of brain cells working in coordinated electro-chemical activity."

John pumped his fist. "As I said, these specialized neural networks are *part* of the equation but not all of it. Life is more than that. *Human life is the state of being not just being aware.* The atomic brain resonates our awareness, providing the soul a link to this world, manifesting our being to this atomic level of reality—but there is more to reality than what we can see, hear, taste, and feel. I can show you that the brain does not define the totality of our existence. We are more than a brain inside a skull, our soul more than a genie in a bottle."

"Okay," Doc said. "You've got my attention, but I find it hard to believe the soul is the source of life."

"What's so hard to believe? Everything is made

of energy in one form or another. If the soul is real, it must be made of energy as well—only it's not atomic-energy we're dealing with."

"Are you saying there's another form of energy?"

John nodded. "There is a different form of energy in the Universe, one science has yet to fully explore. It's called dark-energy. It's energy, but it is *not* atomic in nature. I now know the soul is not only real but made from dark-energy."

Doc stopped dead still. "You can prove that?"

John straightened in his chair. "Of course. Do you think I'd be sitting here right now if I didn't have evidence of what I've been saying? You taught me long ago to speak with facts, not conjecture. And that's what I'm doing now."

Doc didn't say a word. He sat back on the couch, puffing his pipe with a noncommittal expression.

"Look, Doc, I know you never studied Physics. So big equations and scientific jargon wouldn't mean a thing to you, so trust me on this. Thinking of dark-energy as a new form of energy makes sense of the currently confounding Quantum Mechanics. I can show that by a process using what I call 'location nodes' dark-energy determines what locations atomic particles can have. The explanation involves matter waves, another ingredient of Nature that has been known to science but has to date been a mystery—but not anymore.

"Anyway, since electrons are particles, they respond to the presence of dark-energy's matter waves.

Thus, the electrical activity inside the brain is driven by these dark-energy matter waves. In short, the soul's dark-energy fluctuates, driving the neural activity within the brain. The dark-energy makes up the soul. The brain is made of atomic-energy. They're intimately integrated, tightly bonded."

"Uh, dark-energy?"

"Dark-energy is something that has been known to science for ages, yet it wasn't proven to exist until 1999. Now, before you get all amped up about dark-energy and the soul, I need to say that not all dark-energy is soul-type energy just as not all atomic-energy is rocks—but it can be conformed that way. An electron is atomic-energy but in particulate form. The spirit and soul are like dark particles—dark energy but in a different form.

"Anyway, the energy field created within a human brain is quite unique. This is due to the third and most complex part of the human three-part brain, the cerebrum. You know that much is true. And this leads us to the difference between and the need for the human soul and spirit, but let's just stick with the soul for right now.

"What we call the mind is when the atomic-energy of the brain activates a particular neural pattern, an alignment of active neurons that resonates with the dark-energy content of the soul—resonance being the key word here. It is a sympathetic entanglement of the energy within the brain and the ethereal frequencies of the soul. They sort of vibrate in tandem. The degree of resonance determines what a person can perceive, sense, or even consciously think. As you might guess, the mind is related but its definition is distinctly different from the brain."

John came off the recliner to kneel by the glass coffee table. Snatching a napkin and pen, he drew two intersecting circles. In the left circle, he wrote the word '*brain*' and in the right, the word '*soul*'. The intersection of the two, he labeled '*the mind.*'

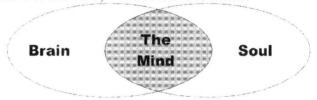

John said, "The brain, the mind, and the soul. What we used to think as synonyms actually refer to tightly integrated but three distinct parts that comprise human awareness of consciousness. The mind is what we are able to think of at a particular point in time.

"It's like turning the dial on a radio when we want to listen to another channel. Only when there is resonance between soul and the brain's neural network, signal and receiver, can one have a conscious thought."

"Am I hearing you right?" Doc leaned forward, both elbows on his knees. "Are you saying the brain is some kind of radio for the soul?"

John nodded. "Sort of. Actually, the radio analogy works quite well. Consider the soul as the station's broadcast signal. Your brain's 'radio' must align or tune the proper neuron circuits and activate them in order to manifest the soul's ethereal signal.

"And consider this, which brings us back full circle, a radio signal is an energy form that cannot be seen or heard. The radio merely translates that energy into a format your ears can detect. And like the radio, the brain does that with the soul. It can only do this one station—or one thought—at a time."

"John, please tell me you're not serious. This is nonsense. The soul is a myth. A metaphor. It isn't real."

John shook his head emphatically. "But the soul is real, Doc."

"But you can't really prove that can you?"

The young man sat back with a look of surprise. "Of course I can. We know dark-energy exists. I can show it is not atomic. And since the soul is real, it is living, animate energy. Since atomic-energy is not animate, the only other candidate is dark-energy. Dark-energy and its particulate byproduct dark matter comprise 96% of all the energy in the Universe. If this type of energy so dominates the human domain, shouldn't it also dominate our own construction? *Most of what we are as humans is not atomic. Most of the human construct (atomic, soul, and spirit) is dark-energy.*

"Consciousness is not just a function the brain. It is a function of the energy within the brain. It's a smaller leap of faith to believe the soul is made of dark-energy than to believe consciousness is purely and only the result of interacting chemicals. Life is more complicated than that . . ."

The scene froze in time. Doc's stiff finger of rebuttal stopped in mid-air when the scene vanished with a rush of white light. John felt his mind shift, his thoughts moving through time and space. When the light diminished, the scene had changed.

This time, he saw a towering office building of golden glass. It loomed over a large city like a gleaming, golden mountain. Its base encompassed an entire city block. On top a sign read, *VRTechnologies.*

The view zoomed in on the top floor and John again saw himself sitting in an elaborate office overlooking the city far below.

In this vision, John's image was older than in the first, but not by much. Expensive furniture and an array of strategically lighted oil paintings adorned the dark wood paneling of the spacious office. Thick reports lined a polished Teak desk. In the vision, John's head was bent low in intense study when two men walked into the room.

One was a black man, tall and thin. His long legs moved with a loping stride that bespoke good physical conditioning. Though only in his mid-twenties, his curly black hair was streaked with premature gray. The thin rimmed spectacles gave him the intelligent look of a recent Ivy League graduate.

The other man was shorter than the first by at least a foot and yet outweighed the taller man by fifty pounds. He moved with quick, nervous steps, struggling to keep up with the taller man's space-eating strides. His crumpled clothes were also in stark contrast to the thin man's neat appearance. His shirt was rumpled, his tie slightly askew as they both approached the desk.

John watched the dream with keen interest. He had no idea who these people were and could only guess what it meant. It was like watching home movies of someone he did not know. The whole experience seemed surreal.

The tall man sat on a padded chair facing the expansive desk and said, "You wanted to see us, Boss?" Folding his hands behind his head, he stretched out his long legs and waited. It seemed obvious from his relaxed and pleasant demeanor that he and John were friends. And by looking at him, John could understand why. He seemed smart and carried himself with an air of confidence he instinctively liked.

The fat man did not sit down right away, choosing to fidget behind his chair until the image of John motioned him to a chair with an impatient wave of the hand. He sat down quickly.

"We came soon as we could, Mr. Neumann." The frumpy man ran his words together. "You said to be here at seven o'clock and here we are. But why so early? Why the big secret? You said to tell no one, and we didn't. I swear it. At least, I didn't."

"That's good, George. Now just take a deep breath and calm down."

John tossed his pen on the desk and looked up. "I chose the two of you for a special assignment. But before I tell you what it is, I must stress that this job requires absolute secrecy. Everything said here today stays inside this room. Is that clear?"

They both nodded. Even Tom sat up straight and leaned forward to rest both elbows on bony knees.

George whined. "What's wrong with the job I have? I'm doing good, aren't I? Is that why you brought me up here? To demote me? That's not fair! My 3-D project is right on schedule."

"Relax, George. Your project is doing fine. In fact, our three-dimensional operating system is doing quite well. We've practically obliterated all competition. With its open architecture and vast performance improvement over the old binary logic of PC algorithms, our products are firmly rooted at the top of the sales charts, and probably will be for some time. With our worldwide distribution and government contracts, we've become the biggest business on the planet. As of today, we're now the number one company in the Fortune 500."

"That's great, Boss," Tom said. "But that's not why you brought us here."

"You're right. Over the last few years, our company has done a lot, but there's more to my plan than creating computers and lifelike displays. In fact, everything we've accomplished to date has been but a means to achieve my ultimate goal."

"And that is?"

"While I was in college, I had a dream, a desire to build something that would help the less fortunate people of the world. At the time, the dark-energy concept wasn't complete. I didn't understand all I needed to know. Nor did I have the money to do anything about it if I did. I had a lot of great ideas, but no way to make those dreams come true, so I kept the dream to myself. I didn't want someone else using my energy discovery to make a better bomb."

"Like they did with Einstein?" Tom said.

John nodded with grave concern. "Exactly. Obviously, things have changed. I now not only have the details, but enough money to make my dream a reality. In fact, I have already developed the architecture for this special type of computer I'll need.

I've even laid out the basic design for a new breed of object oriented processors we'll need to make the thing work. I've even given it a name. I call it 'The Genesis Machine' for reasons you'll find out shortly. The planning stage is complete. Now all I need are two open-minded individuals who can help me build it."

"And that's where we come in," the tall man said. "You want us to help you build this sucker. That's fine by me, but why? What's this all about?"

John leaned forward eagerly. "I want to make a virtual world."

"A virtual world?" George laughed. "We've got dozens of them already. Our game department has a really cool virtual reality chip called 'Space Renegades' with awesome graphics! I should know. I designed the chip myself. But the market is flooded with that sort of thing. Why do you want to make another one?"

"I'm not talking about a game, George." John's look made him shrink into the cushions. "There won't be any goggles, joysticks, or helmets. This is not a toy or illusion. I'm talking about actually forming a new boundary on the ethereal plane where we can place the spirits of real people—particularly those who are sick or dying.

"The Genesis Machine will construct a virtual world on the ethereal plane. Like I said, this is no simulation. If all goes according to plan, we'll be creating a new world on a different level of reality!

"I've been conducting some experiments on my own over the last few years and I'm convinced we can extract a person's ethereal spirit from their soul and insert this consciousness into a virtual body we'll create for them inside the Genesis World. There, they can live the remainder of their lives in peace and comfort, free of the pain and hardships that plague their bodies now."

"Okay." Tom contemplated him with a steady eye. "But why us? Why the secrecy? Why not tell everyone what you want to do? After all, you're the boss. You own the place. Just tell people what you want."

John shook his head. "Let's just say I have my reasons for not trusting my vice-president or the Board and leave it at that."

"You don't trust Mr. Lokitus?" George's eyebrows reached for his receding hairline.

John shook his head. "Not for a long time now. When it comes to the future of VRTechnologies, Jack has his own personal agenda. He's into making money, and that's all fine and good, but that's why he's fighting me on this. This project isn't about money. It's about helping people live again, to have a new beginning in life.

"Don't get me wrong. I fully expect us to regain all our capital. We could make a lot more if I let Lokitus lease the patent to the military, but I won't do that. No bombs. No weaponry. Nor will I allow the Board of Directors to force me, either. And if they found out about the Genesis Project, the whole thing would just get bogged down in dissension and controversy. I want to do things my way that doesn't require a bunch of delaying politics. Therefore, until I can prove the concept works and is absolutely safe, we must work in secret. Once we have an operational model, we'll go public."

"You're afraid of a hostile takeover," Tom said, his expression firm. "You think if they find out the truth of what you're doing, they'll find a way to take your company to stop you." He leaned forward. "How much money are we talking about?"

John shrugged. "As much as it takes. Fifty billion maybe? I admit it's high risk and that's why I don't want the Board to find out about it. I really don't care about the money. Like I said, this project is about helping people. I've allowed Lokitus to lead me down the money path too long. Admittedly, I've made more than I can count, but somewhere along the line I lost sight of my goal and started playing the corporate game. I got rich and powerful, the richest man in the world. My computers control more systems and businesses than any other company in history.

"But then I woke up to find I had become something I never wanted to be. I've made billions from my inventions that came from the people buying them. Now it's time to start giving it back, but give it back in a way that will help them more than they could ever imagine."

"You're serious about this, aren't you?" Tom stated, his face a mask of somber thought.

"You're willing to give up everything you've got, your money, your business, even your house. One wrong move and you're living on the street. And yet you still want to go through with it? I don't get it. That's an awful lot to risk."

John nodded. "It's not a matter of wanting to, Tom. It's something I *have* to do. The way I see it, the knowledge I've been given is a gift. Using that knowledge for the good is a responsibility. It's my purpose in life. This is my assignment that I must complete.

"Millions of people are wasting their lives lying in some hospital bed. There are hundreds of millions more paralyzed or otherwise incapacitated. They exist through each and every day strapped to a wheelchair, lying on a bed, their deformed bodies wracked with pain. It's a crime for me to sit on top of a technology that can help them and not do anything about it and I refuse to ignore them any longer. The time has come for me to act. I need you to help me . . ."

Suddenly, the dream once again vanished with intense light while John moved through time. When the vision cleared, he observed a warehouse-sized room with walls of painted cinder block. There were no windows, only rows of fluorescent lights overhead, giving the impression that I was in some kind of massive, under ground laboratory.

This was confirmed by a towering, gleaming, metallic structure in the exact middle of the room. It was cylindrical, rising almost thirty-feet tall and spanning that much at its base. Insulated cooling tubes penetrated the monolith's steel casing. Evaporation rising from these frosted tubes masked the air with a faint mist, lending an ominous and almost lifelike power to the machine. It was a computer. John surmised, like the other visions, that this too was from his past, but the machine was unlike anything he could remember.

There were two work stations, each containing a dozen monitors. On the far wall, a flat screen monitor stretched thirty-feet wide and twenty-feet tall. Tom sat at one of the control stations frantically pushing buttons and turning knobs while flashing alarms and blaring sirens echoed throughout the cavernous room. His curly hair matted against his forehead, glistening with sweat.

In the vision, John saw himself push through a set of elevator doors and race into the lab. At his side was a giant of a man, his huge, rolling muscles flexing mightily with incredible power. His short cropped hair was flaming red, a color reflected by the burning fire in his steel-gray eyes. When he passed, John noticed blood soaking the right side of his sport shirt.

"We've got a problem!" Tom yelled above the deafening din.

"What is it?" John shouted back. "What's gone wrong?"

"Someone inserted a virus into the Genesis Machine. Right now, it's ripping through the energy matrix, disrupting the entire virtual planet—including the people themselves. Everyone's spirit has been corrupted, and there's nothing we can do to stop it. The whole thing is ruined. Everything we've created is being destroyed!"

"Calm down!" John silenced the irritating noise and faced him. "Now, tell me how this happened."

Tom gave him a quick glance and said, "If you want my opinion, after you fired Lokitus, he found a way to hack into our system. I'm almost sure of it." He then returned to the difficult task of stabilizing the matrix, the energy structure on which the virtual world was built.

"Jack Lokitus?" John said. "How can you be so

sure?"

Tom motioned to another monitor with a truculent nod of the head. "Take a look at the personality tracker. I don't know how, but he's inserting his own people into our world."

"But that's impossible! We control all the connection pods. There's no way—"

"Oh, they're not real," Tom cut in. "They're artificial computer generated personalities—clones. But the people inside the Genesis world don't know that. To them, Lokitus' fake people are as real as you and me. And the kicker in all of this is one of them is the spitting image of Jack himself. His name is Logan, Jack Logan. You asked me how I'm sure? That's how!"

"Lokitus cloned himself into the virtual world?" the giant asked.

Tom nodded. "That's right, Mike. Somehow, they hacked into our scenario sequencer and set him up as governor. Now, there's a guy in our world who's as twisted as Lokitus and has a lot of military and political muscle to back him up. It's a deadly combination that spells disaster any way you look at it."

"But why?" Mike asked.

"I'll tell you why," John said. "He wants control of my empire. Lokitus wants my virtual world, the Genesis Machine, my company, everything. He knows the only way to get rid of the virus is to reboot the computer, but that would kill everyone inside. He also knows that, as of right now, by corrupting the people's soul, there's no way to get them out. So in essence, he's using them as hostages. I give him my company or he kills them all. It's that simple.

"But there's no need to panic. Jack's not about to destroy the virtual world, not now at least. He wants Genesis too much. This virus is a time bomb. These effects are just the beginning. They will get worse over time, the planet growing more unstable, the people more corrupt. It's his way of pressuring me into giving up."

Tom pointed to a monitor above John's head. "You may be right, Boss. See those anomalies, undulations in the matrix? His virus is not that aggressive, just persistent. If we could only find a way to get the people out of there."

There was a long, sobering silence, the only sound a gentle hiss from the cooling coils.

"I know how to get them out," John said.

"You do?"

"I have an upgrade program for the Genesis Machine. It won't eradicate the virus, which means the Genesis world will still eventually explode, but it will slow its degradation. The new code will enable the Genesis Machine to repair the damage his virus inflicted on the people's spirit. But there's a catch. I have to make the changes from the inside."

"Are you nuts?" Tom turned on him. "You can't go in there. The insertion process is a one-way ticket. If you go inside, there is no coming back. You know that better than anybody."

"Yes, but things are different now. I've known from the beginning that I'd have to go inside at some point. I haven't done it yet because of what's involved, but he's forced my hand. We're out of time.

"Believe me, I've tried to find another way. Now the virus has shifted the people's spirit out of phase with their soul. There's only one solution that can realign them—and they must be realigned. If they aren't an exact match with their real bodies, there's no chance of them coming back. I can fix that. I know I can."

"So what's your plan?"

"The computer needs a pattern, a blueprint for first repairing and then recombining the people's spirit to their soul. But the sample needs to be perfect—a real soul and a real spirit that's not been tainted by his virus.

"That means I have to go inside the world. By loading my atomic and both ethereal signatures into the matrix, the Genesis Machine will have all the information it needs for re-calibrating the people as well as repairing their real bodies in this world."

Both Tom and Mike objected at once.

John put up both hands. "I can't ask anybody else to do it," he said. "This was my idea. I created the world. I put those people in there. Now it's up to me to fix this. I've got to go in there. It's the only way."

"But why connect the body?" Tom insisted. "No one has done that before."

"My real body will stay here in this world like everyone else's. All the computer needs is a sample of my DNA. Injecting my genetic code into the main program will give the Genesis Machine a blueprint to follow. It will use this map with the power of dark-energy to repair people's defective bodies.

"Don't you see? Their consciousness may be in

the virtual world, but their real bodies are still here hooked up to the Genesis computer. If I'm successful, not only can their re-adjusted spirit pass through the barrier, the Genesis Machine can return them to a body that's been cured of whatever infirmity that forced them to the virtual world. They can return to perfected bodies."

"Don't do it, John!" Tom pleaded. "Look at the blood on LeGuerre's shirt. Those weren't Boy Scouts who just tried to kill him. They were assassins, trained killers. The next target is you. If you go inside the virtual world, you know Jack's going to program Logan to finish the job. They'll be waiting for you.

"Plus, let's remember the fact that inserting yourself into the machine will totally wipe your memory. With your memory blocked, you won't know what to do to correct Lazlow's machine. I doubt you'll even know to find him. You'll be lost."

"I've already taken care of that. I programmed Doc's alpha machine to download pertinent data—"

"Stop!" A distant voice echoed through John's mind.

Instantly, the dream faded to black. John looked around, wondering what happened. And then he realized it was Doctor Lazlow, speaking to him through his drug induced trance.

"How did you find out about my soul project?" His commands drifted through the darkness. His tone held the hard edge of suspicion. "My work on a special energy is classified top secret."

John felt compelled to obey. There was another burst of light, accompanied by the incessant, piercing drone of his alpha machine that continued to probe his thoughts. Slowly, the scene came back into view. Doc was still on the couch, pointing at John across the glass coffee table.

The movie was reset . . . a slight pause . . . and then it played.

". . . John, please tell me you're not serious. This is nonsense. The soul is a myth. A metaphor. It isn't real."

John shook his head emphatically. "We've gone over this, Doc. The soul is real."

"But you haven't proved that."

"I can prove dark-energy exists. I know that since atomic-energy is not animate, the only other candidate is dark-energy. So, if dark-energy is sentient, it is the energy that makes up the soul and spirit.

"I still say—"

"Doc," John's youthful excitement cut off his interruption. He picked up a book and waved it in front of him. "You really do need to read this. In my book, *The Dual Energy Concept*, I show example after example of how considering dark-energy as a new source of energy answers every question in Quantum Mechanics and Relativity scientists have today. Like, how do two particles interact? Right now, their only answer violates the Law of Energy Conservation. My theory answers it without having to break any laws— and it does so in logical, easy to understand terms. It is the first time in history anyone has done so. Read it and you will be as convinced as I am. Dark-energy is another form of energy."

Doc picked up the book and started flipping pages, stopping occasionally to read a section.

The young John said, "You'll see I don't employ long derivations for the primary reason that the equations I reference have already been derived. They were right. The physicists of the time just didn't understand them. My only effort, what I bring to the party is to finally provide *physical* descriptions using dark-energy as my premise. To date, Quantum Mechanics only provides mathematics to state the probability of something happening. No quantum physicist today can explain to you in physical, logical terms what is going on at the atomic level. They lean on the phrase 'quantum weirdness'—meaning they don't know the answer. However, I can and I do.

"I've also reached the conclusion there is a difference between spirit and soul. The spirit and soul are two different dark-energy particles, or darkons— what I call dark-energy photons. Most people take spirit and soul to mean the same thing, but they're not. The spirit is of a higher order than the soul. The spirit is what makes us human, what separates us from the rest of the animal kingdom. Thus, the spirit is my real goal to connect with because therein lies the root of *human* awareness."

At that time, a stately woman entered the room carrying a pot of coffee and a silver tray full of cookies. She was slender, in good shape, and moved with an athletic grace that bespoke a life of noble culture. Her face was not pretty, but yet it held a quality that most men admired. Her large, compassionate brown eyes possessed a look that had seen the world in all its horrors and yet still managed to love.

The lines in her face were testimony to the

severe hardship endured during her fifty years of life. Trials she conquered simply by surviving them. This remarkable woman walked bare foot through the plush carpet. Her pleated dress flowed delicately in her wake.

"Hello, Alice," the young John called cheerfully, eyeing the cookie tray with unveiled lust.

Alice Lazlow gave him a playful wink and then deliberately stood between them.

"If you boys are going to be up all night with another one of your silly arguments, you might as well have this to keep you going."

She laid the tray on the coffee table and glanced up at her husband.

"Don't stay up too late, Pudgy," she said, playfully tweaking his doughnut middle.

She stooped in from of him with a seductive glint in her eyes. Doc's face flushed. Alice then rose and almost danced from the room, swaying to some whispered melody. At the door, she turned back to blow Doc a soft kiss.

John was reaching for another cookie when the dream suddenly ended. The image of Alice's loving smile froze like a stop action film before evaporating from view . . .

Everything went completely dark. John looked around, expecting to see another vision of the real world that seemed to possess so many answers. But there was nothing, nothing at all.

And then slowly, gradually the aged voice of Doctor Lazlow echoed through the blackness. He followed the disembodied voice until Doc's haggard face emerged from the night, peering close to his.

John was back in Doc's darkened study. He wasn't quite awake yet, still under the effects of the serum and drone of the alpha machine. Doc was yelling something, but the words came to him slow and laborious. It took a concentrated effort to understand.

"Who are you?" Doc repeated, screaming through John's mental fog. "How do you know about Alice? My wife has been dead for years! And my computer. How did you find out about my project?"

John reasoned he must have talked out loud during his trance. His description of Alice seemed to have revived bittersweet memories that had long been dead. His response surprised even himself.

"My name is John Neumann," he muttered through half-opened eyes.

John spoke like a robot. He said the words, but the thoughts were not his. They came unbidden, as if something had attached itself to his mind and was now controlling what he said. The words played like a recorded message.

While he spoke, numbers, equations, and scores of fantastic concepts continued to fill his mind, blurred together in a continuous stream of seemingly unending data.

"This world is not real," he said. "What you see is a virtual existence, an artificial environment created by a computer I invented. The Genesis Machine sustains your spirit and this world while you are held captive here."

"That's preposterous!" Doc stiffened. "Stop this nonsense and tell me how you know so much about me! My project with the soul is top-secret. No one knows about it. No one! Why have you come here?"

John again spoke as if not hearing him. He had no control. "When a person's spirit is inserted into this virtual world, my machine blocks all memory of the outside world and implants virtual memories of a life in this world. I did this to spare you the pain of separation from those you love. By making you believe you've lived here your whole life, I made it possible for you to be happy. Knowing there were others outside this plane of existence waiting for you would have caused unbearable sorrow. That is why you don't remember me, your programmed memories are only of this world.

"In the real world, your body was dying, so I extracted your spirit and placed it here in this virtual domain. Even now, your real body survives in the outside world, kept alive by my machine. But the consciousness within your spirit lives here, unaware of the world beyond your programmed level of perception."

There was a slight pause in which countless more images flooded his mind, millions of bits of data poured in from the outside world via the alpha device. When this particularly intensive surge finished, he continued reciting the recorded monolog.

"Doc, you must believe me. I need your help."

"Help you do what?" His voice seemed despondent.

"I came into this world to get you people out of here. To do so, I need to establish an ethereal link with the Genesis Machine. That is why I need your computer. Without the power your machine can provide, my spirit cannot breach the energy barrier that separates us from the real world."

"A computer to connect with the spirit?" Doc shifted uneasily, his eyes averted. "I don't have any such computer. I don't know what you're talking about."

"I gave you the design years ago because I knew I would need it once I arrived. However, you are struggling with its development. You've allowed another to adulterate my original design. Though I provided someone to help, you still do not fully understand its principle. That's why I have come here myself, to help you understand the truth and complete your project in time."

"My project—"

"Unlike yours, my mind was not programmed with a virtual past, hence my apparent loss of memory. This was deliberate for technical reasons. But I anticipated your use of this alpha device. Once you connected me, the Genesis Machine began downloading tons of information into my mind. With this data, I can repair your computer and get you back on schedule.

"But we must hurry. The Genesis Machine is set to begin assimilating my energy data exactly forty days from my advent here. There is no room for error. If I do not establish contact on the fortieth day, the computer will assume I failed."

"Oh, yeah?" His voice quivered, his eyes unfocused. "And what happens then?"

"There are others vying for this world, people of ill intent. I cannot allow the power of Genesis to fall into their hands. If I am captured, killed, or otherwise unable to upload my data on time, the Genesis Machine is programmed to self destruct. This virtual reality, and all who live in it, will then cease to exist."

Doc ran pudgy fingers through his hair, leaning back and moaning. He cried, emotions pouring from a tortured mind. He buried his face in age spotted hands and slowly rubbed his eyes.

"Virtual world?" he mumbled absently. "Dark-energy? Alice? My sweet Alice. I don't know. It's just too much to deal with."

He remained like that for some time, face buried in both hands. As time passed, John emerged from the sedative's effects. He struggled against the interminable droning of the strange machine by his side, straining to regain command of his own thoughts. He looked at Doctor Lazlow. From the tears welling in his eyes, he knew he was thinking of his beloved Alice again. John recalled the mention of her name was what distracted him from their session. Doc knelt by his side, silently sobbing the lonely cry of lost love.

Doc looked up, his eyes bleary with torment, and pleaded in the voice of a broken heart, "Tell me, please. How do you know my Alice? Who are you?"

There was a pause in which John fought the impulse to respond. But something inside forced his arm toward the concealing shadows of the ceiling. "I come from out there, beyond the darkness, from a realm you cannot see. Alice is there, in the real world. She visits you every day. She talks to you, praying you will come back to her."

Doc immediately turned off the machine with a

99

violent swipe. The drone-like state ended and John regained full control of his shifting mental focus.

"What happened?" He blinked rapidly, coming out of his trance. He saw Doc crying. "Are you all right, Doctor?"

Doc stiffened, pasting a thin smile on a tired and drawn face, but it was a hopeless effort. His emotions were naked. John could almost feel the pain trickling down his cheek. Doc choked out the words, "Pudgy, that was what Alice used to call me when we were alone. How did you know that? No one ever knew that."

Without waiting for an answer, he rambled on. "She always brought me cookies whenever I worked late at night. That's how I got this big middle, you know." He grabbed his rolling mid-section with both hands.

He nodded, looking John in the eye. "You say she talks to me. I must admit when it's still and quiet, there are times I can almost hear her voice."

John rose on one elbow, removing the helmet. "Uh, Doc? I don't know what to say. I'm sorry if I disturbed you . . . Doc? Doc, where are you going?"

But he was talking to a receding shadow. Doc opened the back door to a pitch black night. The session, short as it seemed, had lasted hours. Without a word, he closed the door behind him and disappeared into the darkness.

John flopped back on the couch, trying to recall details of his vision. He wondered at the amazing facts now filling his head and what they all meant. He was disappointed that, except for those few scenes in his dream, his past was still a large blank. However, along with the scientific concepts, he now knew his mission. That haunting feeling of not knowing his purpose, wondering why Logan was trying to kill him, was gone. This was critical.

He now remembered Logan was a clone, a replica of Jack Lokitus. Lokitus had found a way to communicate with him somehow. That was how Logan knew to look for him atop Rock Hill. That was why he was trying to kill him. If he succeeded, then everything would be lost.

He had to find a way to get these people out, and the first step was to use Doc Lazlow's machine. To do that, he had to convince him of the correct relation of soul and spirit. All he had to do was connect his mind to Doc's computer. Then everything would be okay. The Genesis Machine would do the rest.

John's mind spun with effort to make sense of the myriad of fascinating thoughts and ideas coursing through his mind. Gradually, he drifted off to sleep, gazing at the ceiling, wondering at the secrets the darkness concealed.

Chapter 8

An Army helicopter roared overhead then out to sea. In a secluded clearing outside of town, the members of Logan's Special Force Unit were gearing up for the search and destroy mission in the surrounding woods. Fishetti and Corporal Miller looked up from strapping the laces of their hiking boots and watched the bulky green machine disappear behind a thick stand of trees.

"I see they've called in the big guns," Miller said. "I don't know why they need us pounding the ground when they got choppers. Seems they could find this guy faster than we can on foot."

"Because Army birds can't see past the tree tops." Fishetti knotted his bootlace with an agitated jerk. "They need us grunts to beat the bushes and drive him in the open so those guys can nail them. It was the same during the war. Fly boys get the glory while grunts get the gory."

"Yeah, well I still don't understand why we need this many people. I mean, regular army? This looks more like an invasion than a manhunt. That was no ordinary chopper. That was a gunship. Fifty-caliber machine guns, air-to-ground missiles. How much firepower do they need to kill one guy?"

"I don't know about them, but I just need one

more shot," Fishetti said with a grim face. "We better
get moving. If he is out there, I want to find him before
someone else does. With the million dollar reward
Logan put up, we're going to have every kid with a
popgun looking for this guy."

"That's what I don't understand," Tony rose,
adjusting his belt. "Why is this guy so important?"

A man passing by heard the comment and
joined the conversation, a cup of steaming coffee in his
hand. The insignia patch on his shirt identified him
from the Police Department. His fresh crew cut
glistened in the morning sun.

"I heard he's an assassin." He sipped his coffee.
"He's a member of some militant group from the
Middle East. There's supposed to be a bunch of them
in this country. From what I hear, this one's here to kill
the governor. Already killed a farmer by the name of
McCain."

Fishetti turned away with a disgusted sneer.
"Oh, give me a break!"

The officer said, "No, it's true. My captain says
this guy's been linked to half a dozen murders. That's
why Logan called in the big guns. For all we know,
there may be more out there."

"Oh, so now he's a terrorist?" Fishetti's raised
eyebrows emphasized his condescending tone. "You
mind telling me why a terrorist would come half way
around the world just to kill a two-bit farmer like
McCain?"

"I don't know." The young officer shrugged.
"Maybe he's a mental case that gets his jollies
knocking off two-bit farmers. I really don't care. All

that matters is that we stop him. There's too much ground to cover for one unit. That's why a bunch of guys from my precinct were assigned to help in the search."

Fishetti said nothing. He finished lacing up his boot and turned away when he noticed a group of men coming his way.

"Hey, Fishetti!" one of them called out.

Nick recognized Sergeant Bob Vance right away. Vance was Fishetti's counterpart on the city's police squad, a sniper. A tall, fit man who took great pride in his appearance—the exact opposite to Fishetti's delinquent slouch.

Three other patrolmen from Vance's squad trailed close behind their sergeant, eager to witness the coming exchange. Broad grins spread each man's rugged features in anticipation of the coming sharp barbs between these two. There was an inter-office rivalry that was nothing if not competitive.

Fishetti frowned. "What is it, Vance? Can't you see I'm busy?"

"Yeah, I'm sure for someone of your intelligence, tying a shoe must be pretty hard work." He jerked a thumb at Miller. "Why don't you let your new boy toy help you?"

Fishetti's face burned red, his voice cold. "Get out of my face. I'm not in the mood today."

Vance snapped Fishetti's Swiss-style suspender. "Not until I complement you on how pretty you look." A howl of laughter erupted from his friends. "Since when did you Special Force guys start wearing those cute little shorts?"

Miller stepped between them. "It was our

captain's idea of a low profile. This way, we don't look like cops. We need to get close enough for positive ID."

Vance brushed Miller out of the way, his eyes fixed on Fishetti. "I always did take you to be gay. Now I guess we all know for sure. Seems like you should be wearing a skirt instead of them shorts."

Fishetti stepped toward Vance. His deadpan expression revealed eyes glowing with malignant glare. Tony Miller took a few steps back, distancing himself from the altercation.

As the city officers laughed, Vance said. "The real reason I came over was to find out why you can't shoot your rifle as well as you do your mouth."

Fishetti's voice was low and ominous, his eyes mere slits. A final step brought him nose to nose with the smirking sergeant.

"Say that again," he said.

The laughter died quickly to tense silence. The joking was over.

"What's the matter? Are you deaf, too?" Vance faced the challenge head on. "For years you've been mouthing off how good you are at this, how great you are at that: martial arts, knives, fists, and guns. You're supposed to be the best there ever was." He turned to his compatriots. "Oh, and what's that record he keeps spouting off about?"

"One hundred kills, one shot," a friend said.

"Yeah, that's it. Some sort of super sniper you turned out to be. Well, I don't see no big red 'S' on your chest. In fact, the way I heard it, you had an open field shot at this guy. What was it, twenty, thirty yards max? My five-year-old daughter could have hit him at that range. Surely, the best sniper in the world couldn't possibly miss."

He pushed Fishetti's shoulder.

Miller took another step back.

"So the way I figure it, you've been lying about your so-called one shot world record." Vance jerked a thumb at the man to his left. "Joe here thinks you're a psycho. Personally, I think you're a liar who wouldn't know the wrong end of a gun if you sucked the barrel. So tell me, Sergeant Sloucho, which one of us is right?"

Vance stood with hands on hips, his head turned in a laughing exchange with his friends.

Fishetti's answer came swift and brutal. He threw a hard right into Vance's stomach, doubling him over. As Vance gasped for air, Fishetti lifted a knee, viciously smashing the man's unprotected face.

The blow jerked Vance upright and Fishetti hit him with a swinging left-right combination that rocked Vance back on his heels. Already out on his feet, Vance would have fallen had Fishetti not grabbed him by the shirt and pulled him forward into a straight jab to the face. With that, Vance collapsed, sprawled onto the grass where he remained still and unmoving.

The other officers gawked at their fallen comrade and then looked at each other in shocked disbelief. Everything happened so fast, no one had time to respond. The smiles were gone. Moving as one, they approached Fishetti, faces grim with anger.

"I was right," Joe said. "You are a psycho."

Fishetti let them come, a slight smile stretching his thick lips.

The three men surrounded him, each taking a separate front. They attacked as one unit. The man on Fishetti's left threw a right hook at his head. Fishetti ducked. The man's fist whisked open air. Fishetti then snapped a sidekick from his squatting position, powering through the man's knee. The officer's scream of agony covered the wet ripping sound of tearing ligaments as the joint broke backward. He collapsed holding his deformed leg, writhing in pain.

Fishetti was already leaping high into the air, whipping one leg in a blinding, roundhouse kick that crushed the second man's cheek, snapping his head hard right. The man reflexed lazily, one arm flopping in an unconscious loopy swing as he fell face first into the dirt.

Fishetti landed in a wide-legged crouch. The third man stood over him, hands clenched, waiting for his foe to rise. But Nick Fishetti did not fight fair. He fought to win, and by any means possible. From his squatting position, he lanced a fist to the man's groin. The officer dropped to his knees, both hands holding his crotch. Fishetti rose, took a step back, and smashed a side kick into the man's face. The blow rocked him to the ground where he lay dazed, moaning through a bleeding nose and broken teeth.

Miller's wide eyes stared at the destructive scene. He shook his head and stared. Fishetti simply walked away as if nothing happened, absolutely no sign of remorse.

A high-pitched voice shouted, "Fishetti, halt! That's an order!"

Fishetti ignored Lieutenant Carpenter running

up to the scene.

"What do you think you're doing?" the lieutenant said. He grabbed Fishetti's arm and spun him around.

Fishetti jerked his arm away, his eyes flashing venomous insanity, but Carpenter either did not see the warning or ignored it. He stepped close to his bulky sergeant, challenging the bigger man's lethal glare.

Tony Miller grabbed Fishetti's raised arm. He strained, pulling back hard. "Nick!" he yelled. "Snap out of it, man. It's our LT. Let it go, man. Let it go!"

Fishetti glared at his commanding officer a brief moment before ripping his arm from Miller's grip. Without a word, he walked off to gather his gear.

Four men lay moaning around them, two of them seriously injured. Fishetti picked up his backpack, stepped over one of the writhing bodies, and headed for the dense forest.

Lieutenant Carpenter looked at Miller with a nod toward Fishetti. "You better keep an eye on him, Miller. For some reason, he likes you, though only God knows why. See what you can do to keep him in line."

"What about these guys?" Miller asked, rushing to gather his equipment.

"Don't worry about them. I'll have Petra smooth it out with their captain. They had it coming. They should have known better than to razz Fishetti when he's on edge. It's eating him alive everyone knows he missed that shot. Messes up his perfect record. Riding him about it just pushed him over the edge. And for Fishetti, that doesn't take much."

He unfolded a map and indicated a region along

the ocean. "You two will be part of a reconnaissance team assigned to quadrant four north of Rock Hill. There's about a dozen houses scattered up the coast there. I don't care if we searched them before. Search them again. Report back every hour."

He turned to address the group who had gathered to witness the results of the brief brawl. "The same goes for all of you. I want everyone in groups of two. Remember, the guy we want is armed and dangerous. Do not, I repeat, do not take any unnecessary chances on apprehending him.

"Once you make positive identification, you will call for back up. I want this done by the numbers, people. We don't want any dead heroes. Your orders are to bring him in alive. Logan wants him for questioning."

"But what if he resists arrest?" a soldier asked. "A man like that is bound to put up a fight."

Carpenter regarded the soldier with a steady gaze. "On the record, your orders came from Governor Logan. Personally, I'd rather you shoot him and be done with it. If you do, just make sure you make it clean. I don't want any more screw ups. I'm still cleaning up the mess from last week with McCain."

Carpenter ignored the questioning looks exchanged by two city cops standing beside him. He dismissed his squad with an aggressive wave toward the surrounding forest. "Okay, you've got your orders, now get going. We'll rendezvous back here at 1800 hours."

Chapter 9

John Neumann awoke with a start. It took a moment to realize he was still on the couch in Doc's study, only now covered with a woolen blanket. A bright band of morning gold streamed through a gap in the dark curtains behind Doc's desk, falling gently on a woman sitting in the chair.

The sunlight shimmered through her long, auburn hair, transforming her face into that of a radiant angel. She was slender, but not skinny, wearing a white cotton sun dress—the same one he saw in his dream on the way to the house.

She leaned forward, resting her chin in both hands as she stared at him with the most captivating pair of brown eyes he had ever seen. They were soft, pouring with heartfelt tenderness. Yet they also held intensity, a fire that bespoke determination and intelligence. This was Mary, Doctor Lazlow's daughter.

John flushed at the attention and sat up. But when he rose, her eyes remained fixed straight ahead. That was when he noticed the tiny earpiece. A thin cord led to the recorder on the desk and he realized she had not been watching him at all. She was merely concentrating on the space in front of her, listening to the recorder by her side.

John's immediate suspicion was her father had recorded his subconscious rambling and she was eavesdropping on what he said. For a moment, he got mad at the thought, but then her enchanting gaze shifted to engulf him. When she smiled, her warmth instantly melted any resentment he may have had.

"Don't be upset," she said. "My father always records his sessions. Most of the time, his patients don't remember anything they said and so he plays it back to help them remember their dreams.

"I can tell you're upset. Please, don't be. The only reason I'm listening to it now is because he asked me to. Your trance was the first time he used his Alpha machine and he wanted my opinion on what you said. You were quite detailed."

"Why would you be interested in anything I said?" John tried to sound offended but could not pull it off, not with that smile and those magical brown eyes focused on him.

"I have a Master's Degree in Engineering Physics." Her tone was matter of fact. "Over the years, I helped my father with many of his projects—especially this last one. He was disturbed by some things you said about something you called dark-energy and the soul. And since he's not a scientist, he wanted my opinion on your new type of energy concept. Which I might add is quite intriguing. It's somewhat like our own, but there are a lot of differences. You seem to possess more detail and accuracy we haven't thought of."

"No way! You're a physicist?" he said, sitting up straight.

She groaned through clenched teeth. "Why does that always come as a shock to you men? You're all the same. Just because I'm a woman you think I can't do anything but cook, clean house, and have babies!"

"No! No, it's not that at all!" John stammered, coming to the edge of his seat. "It's just . . . I mean, I was wondering . . . I'm glad you're here. Really I am. I just wasn't expecting to find someone who knows physics—man or woman. I was surprised, yes, but it's a pleasant surprise. Honest, I didn't mean to sound degrading. I need someone like you to talk to. I have bits and pieces of science data going through my mind. I need someone to help me figure it all out."

She looked at him a long, withering moment. Her eyes, once soft and caressing, now flashed that withering fire. Her auburn hair flared in the morning sun. The thick, flowing mass fell across one cheek. In the silence, John could hear a faint, thin voice still playing through the earpiece now lying on the desk.

Mary's anger did not last long. Deciding no offense was meant, she tossed back the shock of hair and smiled. "Sorry. I didn't mean to snap at you like that, but male chauvinism is all I get around here. I guess I'm just a bit oversensitive this morning."

She changed the subject. "Are you hungry?"

"Starved," he said, relieved to be off the hook. His mending body craved food.

She picked up her father's recorder and notepad and preceded John up the stairs to the kitchen. She did not say much on the way up, choosing to scan the handwritten pages while she walked. In the kitchen, still reading the scribbled notes, she opened a cupboard with one hand, took out a box of cereal, and placed it on the counter. She then sat at the table, adjusting the earpiece while turning another page.

John grinned at a mental comparison with her father. He opened the refrigerator to get the milk himself. No cooking, no pancakes, no fuss. Do it yourself or not at all. This was one independent woman who knew how to make a statement!

He sat across from her and began eating. Mary never looked up, concentrating on circling data and scribbling her own notes beside those of her father's.

John just started his second bowl when David shuffled into the room, rubbing sleepy eyes and yawning deeply.

"Heeeey, David!" John said. "Do you want some cereal?"

"Yes, sir. That's my favorite kind." He slumped into a chair.

John rose to get him a bowl and a glass of milk.

Mary seemed oblivious to all but the recorder and Doc's manuscript. John took the opportunity to talk with her son. "So, what are you doing today?"

"I don't know." He shrugged. "I guess watch TV. It's so boring here. I wish there was somebody I could play with."

John felt sorry for the little guy. The kid was lonely, but John's heart went out to him for reasons that are more selfish. There was something familiar about him, something vital, but he could not quite place what it was.

David only nodded or shook his head whenever John asked a question. That is when John thought playing with him might get him to open up.

"Would you like it if I played football with you?" John said

David's head snapped up, his eyes wide. "Yeah! That would be great!"

Mary looked up with a stern look of quiet and went back to work.

"Yeah, that would be great," David repeated in an excited whisper. "When can we play?"

"How about now?"

He grabbed David's arm when he jumped out of his chair. "I meant after breakfast. Ask your mom if it's all right."

After repeated begging, Mary finally gave a half-hearted nod.

"All right!" David shouted and hurried to fill his bowl.

John once again marveled how a child's temperament could flip from one end of the emotional spectrum to the other in a heartbeat.

In his haste, David splashed milk onto the table and had to be reminded on several occasions to slow down. When he finished, he dashed up the stairs, leaving his forgotten dishes on the table.

Mary looked up from her notes long enough to yell, "David! I washed your jeans and laid them on your chair. Try to stay out of the mud this time."

"Okay," his tiny words floated down the stairway.

"I'd better go freshen up as well," John said. He excused himself to get a quick shower and shave. It had been days since his last bath and he was ripe for another.

In his room, he removed his left arm from the

sling and gingerly tested its motion. Other than being a
little sore, his shoulder and leg felt normal. It amazed
him how quickly he recovered from the terrible
beating less than a week before. The swelling and
discoloration of his cuts and bruises were almost gone.
It was miraculous, to say the least.

By the time he finished dressing, David was
already in the kitchen, tossing the football in anxious
anticipation. Mary was still at the table, her head bent
in deep study.

"You're sure you don't mind if we get out of
your way for a little while?" John asked.

Her head lifted slightly, but her lingering eyes
finished their assigned sentence before looking up. She
flashed a polite smile. "No, I guess it's okay. Just
make sure you stay in the back yard. Don't go into the
woods. I don't want you taking chances."

John was on his way out the door and stopped
to look back at her. *What did she mean by that*? But
she was already absorbed in her work and he decided
not to bother her again. And so he stepped into the
bright sunshine outside.

Chapter 10

Tony Miller's breathing came hard and fast. Since leaving camp, Fishetti maintained a rapid, space-eating stride and it was all Miller could do to keep up. The rising sun baked away the early chill and now burned hot in a cloudless sky. With a bullet proof vest beneath his shirt, he was sweating profusely.

To his left and right, other two-man teams struggled through the brush. All of them scoured the ground, searching for clues—footprints, broken limbs, anything to suggest a man had been there. Most of the men had been on the mountain with him and Fishetti that first night, so they had some idea of what their quarry looked like. This was why Logan's Special Forces Unit had been pulled from the citywide search and assigned the forest area. The National Guard and off-duty Police patrolled the metropolitan areas.

Not a breath of air. His shirt clung to his skin. Not far away, the ocean surf rolled against the rocky cliff. Miller shook his head. Despite the heat, the scene was beautiful, so peaceful. It was hard to believe they were there to kill a man. Logan demanded his capture, but there was no stopping Fishetti. If they found him, the man was good as dead.

He gulped water from his canteen when Fishetti stopped to check his map. Sweat trickled in his eyes.

"How much farther?" he said, wiping his brow with a free hand.

Fishetti nodded straight ahead. "Not far. The first house is about a mile down this trail."

He turned the map slightly, aligning it north and south, and then looked around to get his bearings. Spotting the crest of Rock Hill, he returned his attention to the map. Satisfied, he folded the paper and stuffed it inside his shirt.

A gunshot cracked the stillness.

Excited shouts rose all around. Men started running, everyone pushing through the matted shrubs to converge on the spot.

Fishetti and Miller exchanged looks. Without a word, they broke into a run, arriving in time to see half a dozen soldiers already gathered around the prone figure of a man. He was lying on his back, bleeding from a chest wound, his heart destroyed.

Fishetti broke through the circle and stood over the man whose wide eyes danced with the fright of impending death. He tried to speak. His mouth moved but only the sound of gurgling blood flowed from his quivering lips.

Nick kicked the man's hand off the bullet wound with his boot. The man looked at him, silently begging for help. But if Fishetti cared, he never showed it as the man suddenly stiffened and then slowly exhaled his last breath.

"Who shot him?" Fishetti demanded, scanning the crowd.

"I did!" A young officer stepped forward with obvious pride. "Private Davis. I got him clean, too.

One shot, just like you, Sarge." He punched a buddy in the arm. "And at fifty yards! Let's see you try that through this stand of trees—and with a pistol, no less."

Fishetti knelt beside the corpse and examined the man's body. He had dark hair and was of medium build, matching the general description. He ripped open the man's T-shirt, revealing a smooth, hairless chest. He rose quickly with barely controlled rage. Bloodshot eyes pierced Davis.

"You shot the wrong guy!"

The men fell quiet, the shouts of celebration replaced by the lonely sound of the ocean.

"W-what do you mean?" The soldier's voice quivered. "It has to be him. It looks like him. Who else would be out here in the middle of nowhere?"

Fishetti stepped within inches of his face.

"What's the matter with you, Davis? You were on the mountain. You saw him just like the rest of us. He was shot. He fell off the cliff. Did you ever think to check this man for bruises or contusions before you killed him? Or do you just never think at all?"

The young man shrank from Fishetti's threatening approach.

"There are dozens of hikers up here, Davis. This is after all a State Park. But you were so eager to collect the reward money that you never bothered to find out who you were killing."

He shoved a stiff finger into the smaller man's chest, pushing him back another step. "You let greed interfere with your judgment. Now you're going to pay because of it."

The crowd of men who had been clapping Davis on the back quietly distanced themselves, leaving the rookie to stand alone. Fishetti spun on his heel, cursing the incompetence of cocky youth. He paced back and forth, thinking. It didn't take long to come up with a plan.

"Tell you what we're going to do," he said.

Extracting a knife from his belt, he knelt beside the corpse and plunged the blade into the dead man's chest. He turned and twisted hard, digging around until he found the bullet, which he pried out with cruel disregard. He wiped the bloody knife on the man's leg and tossed the disfigured slug at a very sullen Private Davis, who caught the lump of lead with two shaking hands.

"What are you doing?" he asked.

"I'm saving your life. If Logan finds out about this, you're dead meat. First thing is put that bullet where no one will find it. Then I want you to throw this guy's body off the cliff. Be sure to scuff the edge a bit. Whoever finds him will think he got too close and the ground gave way beneath him."

He took a step toward the cliff's edge and indicated the jagged rocks fifty feet below. "If you drop him on those rocks, the waves will cut him to shreds in a matter of hours. There'll be no way anyone can prove he was shot. Being this far from town, it's not likely anyone will find his body for a few days. So we're safe."

Fishetti turned to Davis. "I want *you* to dump the body. It's your mess, you clean it up."

He jerked a thumb at two others standing nearby. "Shantzen, Thomas, you two stay here and make sure he does it right. Erase our tracks and all signs of blood. Make it look natural. The rest of us will continue our assigned search pattern."

Davis stood transfixed, staring at the dead man. Fishetti stepped toward him and smashed a hard fist into the rookie's face. Davis sprawled awkwardly, landing on his back. Fishetti stepped forward, knife still in hand. Davis crab-crawled away, staring at the muscular sergeant standing over him.

Fishetti said, "If you ever do something like this again, I will kill you. You got that?"

Davis gave a hurried nod and Fishetti turned around, spitting a stream of tobacco on the bloody corpse.

He addressed the rest of the group and said, "Let's get this straight. I'm not your mother and I don't have time to wet nurse you. So let me make this clear. Nobody kills this guy but me. If you find him, you retain him until I get there. I swear to God I'll kill the man who even thinks about firing another shot."

The men gave a unified nod. Davis wiped blood from the corner of his mouth, still cowering in the dusty trail. Fishetti lingered over him for some time. His eyes glared, fingers gently rolling along the rubberized hilt of the knife.

He took a step forward. Davis gasped in horror and stared into the madman's eyes. Miller grabbed Nick by the shoulder and pulled gently, shaking his head with a discouraging frown. Angrily, Fishetti shoved the blade back into its sheath and marched up the trail, heading north.

"Come on!" he called for Miller. "Let's go check out that house."

Chapter 11

David bolted out the back door, leaping across all three steps to land at a full gallop in the plush grass below. John followed him outside. David wheeled and tossed him the football.

"Throw me a long one!" he yelled over his shoulder.

John threw him a soft lob, the ball floating in a high arch. David was thirty yards away when he caught up to it, but snagged the ball with ease. He dodged left and right, fending off imaginary players before he fell, rolling in the grass as if being gang tackled.

Smiling broadly, he scrambled to his feet and ran back to John, the ball tucked under one arm. "Wow! That was fun. Can you throw me some more?"

"Sure. Why do you think I came out here?" He took the ball from David's extended hand and said, "Do a down and out."

"What's that?" A curious frown wrinkled his face.

"You don't know what a 'down and out' is?"

He shook his head.

"Do you know any pass patterns?"

Another shake told John the whole sad story of the boy's lonely life. Without a father and Doc busy in his lab, he had no male role model to teach him sports, how to build a bird house, wrestling in the open field—the simple joys of a man and his son. And so for the rest of that morning he showed him how to plant a foot when making a turn, how to look a defender off when running a route, and other fundamentals of an organized game. David absorbed every word, and did most of them fairly well before the morning was through.

After an hour, they were both tired. John sent him on a long bomb in which he was to run far and as fast he could while John threw the ball down the field. John misjudged David's speed and overthrew him. The ball slipped through David's tired arms and bounced haphazardly into the heavy brush surrounding the back yard.

David hesitated to go in, but John strolled into the brush and eventually found the ball at the bottom of a small gully. He slid down the incline and picked it up. That's when he noticed a creek running nearby.

He looked up at David, who still obediently remained in the back yard.

"You want to take a break?"

The boy's heavy breathing said "yes" before his silent nod. David looked back at the house then followed John down the bank. They sat on the rocks lining the creek, sipping the cool water in the shade of overhanging trees. It was nice there. The shade was nice and the sound of the ocean surf provided a soothing cover. Not a breath of air moved beneath the broad leaves. Above them, a few wisps of thin clouds marred the otherwise perfect blue sky. John did not remember feeling so good, so much at home.

Off in the distance, the muffled crack of a gun shot echoed through the woods. John jerked and looked around.

"Probably hunters," David said. "Mom says they shouldn't be here because these woods are a state park, but I hear gunshots all the time."

John did not like it, but decided not to alarm the boy. Instead, he prompted David to tell him about life with his mother and grandfather. Yes, he liked school. He liked reading and taking things apart to figure out how they worked. No, his mother did not have any boyfriends. She was busy most of the time. She substituted teaching at the University, but most of the time she helped his grandfather work on some big computer hidden in his office. His mother did things with David as much as she could. Sometimes, they took long walks through the woods where she pointed out and explained all sorts of bugs, birds, trees, and plants.

He fell silent for a while watching the stream flow by. John prompted him to tell him more, prying the boy with questions about his school and friends. He learned about Ryan and Tony and how they would have a great time playing practical jokes on each other during class.

Ryan was the chubby one who could burp on command. For some reason, David thought this was extremely funny and delighted in repeating many incidents about that in the school cafeteria. However, when he came home, he was usually alone the rest of the day. His grandfather and mother were normally in the lab and although Ryan lived but a few miles away, it was rare when they got together.

"Why not?" John said.

"Because of the bad men around here." He picked up some pebbles and began tossing them into the stream. "My mom doesn't like the idea of me riding my bike to Ryan's. She says it's too far. She's afraid they might grab me if I was by myself. She doesn't even like me getting out of the back yard."

"She's probably right," John said. "You can't be too careful these days."

The conversation over, they strolled back the kitchen for something cold to drink. John opened the refrigerator and got David the cola he requested. John opted for a large glass of lemonade. He poured the glass and glimpsed Mary sneaking behind David. Springing around the corner, she wrapped both arms around him with a playful hug. "I love you!" she said, kissing him with exaggerated smacks.

"Aw, Mom!" David wriggled from her arms. He ducked the kisses like all adolescent boys. He walked into the family room to watch a movie, but when he looked back, John noticed the twinkle of appreciation in his eyes.

The boy plopped onto the sofa and grabbed the remote control. The TV came on and his attention instantly riveted on the screen, leaving Mary and John practically alone.

"Thank you for playing with him." Loving eyes lingered on her son. "It's not often he gets to play with others with my father being so busy and all. I'm sure David appreciated it very much."

She turned and examined John's grass stained clothes. If she recognized them as belonging to her late husband, she did not say a word. Smiling, she pronounced with satisfaction, "You're obviously feeling better. It's hard to believe you're the same man you were a few days ago."

"Well, it's all because of you," he said. He stepped close and took her hands in his. "I haven't thanked you for what you did, but I do, thank you that is. I owe you my life."

She looked up, pouring those deep, brown eyes directly into his, searching for something unspoken, something unknown. John's heart thrilled, leaping with joy at being the subject of her deep attention. For him, time seemed to stop as all other sight and sound drifted away.

She suddenly stepped back, pulling her hands from his with a nervous glance at the table. "Well," she said, wiping an unseen speck, "you're a good healer."

With that, she sat at the table and changed the subject. "The vision you described last night was most fascinating. I've never heard of a trance like that. Usually, people recount their repressed childhood, which are at best scattered bits and pictures.

"It was the first time Father used his alpha device. Maybe that was why yours were so vivid. And this energy you spoke of is awesome. The scenes you described was as if they were from another place a long time ago. I checked Father's alpha equipment but all indications verified you were telling the truth. You honestly believe you came from . . . how did you say it? Beyond the darkness, whatever that means."

She examined him a thoughtful moment.

"Would you mind answering some personal questions? Father was a bit disturbed with your comments about that Genesis computer. Our brain and soul research is top-secret and yet you described it very well."

"Mary, I —"

She held up a hand. "I'm just warning you the next time you see my father, you better be prepared to answer a lot of questions. He demands how you know so much about what we're doing."

"But that's my point," he said. "I don't know how I know. Everything I saw was just as much a surprise to me as it is to you."

"Well, that may be true. Personally, I could care less about secrecy. I'm a physicist. I'm more interested in this other form of energy than how you know what we're doing. If what you said is true about this new energy concept, the difference between soul and spirit could be just the break we need. That is why I need more information. I want to know how this dark-energy interacts with the brain. You never did get to that. After you mentioned my mother, Father ended the session rather abruptly."

"Yes, I'm sorry about that. I didn't mean to upset him. I actually wasn't aware what I was saying at the time. It was weird, like someone—or some*thing*— had taken over my mind, as if I was watching movies of people I didn't know. During the entire session, my mind was being inundated with a data, much more than what I actually saw. Raw facts of energy and computer technology faster than I could assimilate at the time. It's going to take me days to sift through it all, but I know it has something to do with your computer. I'm not sure if I can answer all your questions now, but I will try. Ask me what you want to know."

He sat across the table from her, watching her pick at unseen specks.

When she continued hesitating, he said, "Mary, before you start, can I ask you something?"

"Well, I guess that would only be fair. What would you like to know?"

"Why don't we start by telling me something about yourself? Right now, I know your name and that you're beautiful and smart, but that's it. I don't know where you're from, your hobbies, what you believe, none of the important things. Let's talk about you for a while. If you do that, I promise I'll tell you everything I know."

She looked at him with a shy shrug, her face flushing red. "Why would you want to know anything about me?"

He leaned both elbows on the table, stirred by his strong feelings for her. It wasn't just physical attraction, although there was plenty justification for that. What he felt was something else, something deeper.

"I'm interested in what you know, what you have to say about everything. I want to know what motivates you, your likes and dislikes. There's something about you I can't escape. It's like we've met before. I know you from somewhere."

"Oh, come on, John," she smiled. "That's an old line."

"I know, but I didn't mean it that way." He reached across the table to touch her hand. "Mary, I saw you in a vision while on my way here. Twice."

That stopped her cold. Her shy smile faded, the imaginary specks of dust forgotten. She sat motionless, watching him with intense interest as he leaned back and sighed.

"It was definitely you. Clear as day. You had this same white summer dress you're wearing now. You kept beckoning me to this house."

He paused a moment, unsure how to phrase his thoughts.

She leaned forward. Her dark brown eyes enveloped him. "Tell me more."

"All I can add is that it definitely was not a dream. And then there was the picture of you and Doc on his boat with a sailfish. I was there. I can't explain it, but I know I was there. It was like I took that picture."

He shook his head. "I can't shake the feeling you and your family hold the key to unlocking my past—and my future. I was thinking, hoping really, that you might bring back other memories that could connect the fragmented pieces of my mind.

"The session with your father helped, to be sure. But I still don't know who I am any more than what I saw. All I have is a bunch of facts and data running through my mind like a computer compiling a gigantic program. A lot of it is physics stuff, but what does science have to do with anything?"

"So you still have no idea who you are?"

He shrugged, pointing to the ceiling. "I know I am from out there, beyond the darkness of space. I know it sounds crazy, but I know I'm not from here. The only things I know for certain are there is a form of energy beyond what the eye can see. And I know I have to connect my mind with a super-computer your father is working on. Beyond that, I'm not certain how—or why. But there's something I should be doing. Something important, and not knowing what it is is driving me nuts."

"How did you know about our computer? No one is supposed to know about that."

"I didn't know you had one until Doc mentioned it last night."

He reached across the table to hold her folded hands. "Do you see what I mean? The trance meant something. The science means something. I think it has to do with your research, but how? That's why I need to talk with you. I believe that by talking, you can help me figure all this out.

"The vision of you on the trail is one of the few memories that I can truly call my own. I know you from somewhere. I got the same feeling when I first saw Doc in the doorway and now when I was with David. There's something about your family. It's important that I know. So what do you say? Can we talk about you first?"

Mary slowly withdrew her hands and bit her lower lip, looking at him with a shy frown. At one point, she opened her mouth as if to say something, only to drop her eyes and wring both hands in her lap.

After a couple of iterations of this self-conscious debate, she sat bolt upright and said, "Okay. What do you want to know?"

They sat in the kitchen for over an hour. They talked about a lot about of things, big and small. At first, John had to ask direct questions just to get a short nod or shake of the head, but she soon began to relax and open up. He got the impression this was a part of Mary few people ever saw. She seemed guarded, as if she did not trust anybody with her true feelings. As time went on, however, she seemed to trust him.

She told him of a relatively happy youth. She was an only child with many warm memories of her mother and their wonderful life before she died. She described sweet bedtime stories her mom read and the Saturday afternoons when they would cook cakes and pies.

On weekends, the family often went on fishing trips. They would pack coolers with sandwiches, sliced tomatoes, and iced tea. Mary loved the picnic more than anything else. While her father and mother fished, she usually just sat on the shore and read a book or just watched Nature breathe around her.

She liked lying still, looking up into the sky, blocking out all thought in a silent effort to hear the world, to smell its fragrance, to touch the newborn grass. She loved feeling at one with Nature. Not just living in it, but being an integral part of the Universe.

She told him of other little things, like when she fell out of a tree when she was nine, landing on a piece of glass that cut her knee so bad she could hardly walk for a week. John visualized her leg wrapped stiff in white surgical gauze. She must have limped heavily, her ponytail swaying wildly from the ungainly effort.

Classmates teased her relentlessly throughout her life. Mary said it was because she wasn't attractive, though John found that hard to accept. He suspected the real reason was that her high grades always blew the bell curve. She was also very religious, possessing a strong moral fiber that refused to bend to the destructive pressures of the teenage crowd. Because of this, there were but few she could call a true friend.

Some of the stories he already heard while on his tour of the house with her father—only this time John found out that it was she, not David, who threw the baseball through the window the night of the governor's dinner. He did not understand the reason for her mischievous smile until he learned it happened just one year ago. She made it very clear she did not like Governor Logan. And that pleased him.

As she serenaded him with more memories, she would stand to reenact her days of playing softball or free climbing the cliff walls by the shore. John loved how her eyes sparkled when she laughed and he sat there, drinking her in, absorbing all he could. Her voice, her thoughts, her aroma, everything about her made him feel warm and comfortable inside.

She stopped in mid-sentence. "Am I boring you?" She bowed her head and sat down quickly.

"No! No, not at all!" he said, finally aware he had not said a word for some time. He shook himself from his peaceful reverie. "On the contrary, this has been most interesting. I loved it. I was just imagining you as a tomboy, climbing rocks and trees. And now you're a Physical Engineer. I'd say you've done pretty well for yourself."

She averted her eyes and blushed at the compliment. "Oh, I don't know about that. I normally don't go on about myself like this and I feel a little weird telling you all these things. But there's something about you that makes it so easy. I want to tell you everything I ever thought of, and yet I hardly know you. Yet at the same time, I feel like I've known you all my life. Isn't that strange?"

He shook his head. "No. I feel the same way."

She studied him with anxious scrutiny. "You mentioned that vision of me on the trail. I had that same dream a few days ago, beckoning a man to follow me. Except, when I woke up, I couldn't remember what he looked like."

She stopped, those alluring brown eyes boring into his. "I never told anyone about that dream. No one. But I have no problem telling it to you. What does that mean?"

John didn't answer her. He couldn't. What could he say? He could only sit and stare into her eyes. He suddenly wanted to kiss her, to feel her soft warmth. He settled for reaching across the table to place his hand on hers.

"Thank you," he said. "You've helped me more than you know."

She blinked a relieved smile and squeezed his hand in appreciation. "And what about you, John Neumann? Who are you?"

"I honestly can't remember it all. I've got pieces to the puzzle, but I just can't seem to fit them into a meaningful picture. The Dual Energy Concept is something that came to me during my trance. I know what I said in the trance, but I'm still not sure exactly how it fits with the soul, but I'm working on it. That part is coming together, at least, and I would like to run it past you."

"Well, you did say this Genesis Machine blocks

one's natural memory and that you programmed a fake memory for everyone here. Since you don't have one, you obviously didn't program a memory for yourself for a reason."

"So you believe me on that?"

She nodded. "Like I said, the machine proved you were telling the truth. I may not understand it, but for some reason I just believe in you."

He nodded. "Thank you. That means a lot to me. As for my lack of memory, I think it has something to do with connecting my mind with your father's computer. I think my mind needs to be clean, the way it was when I came in, but again I don't know why."

"So," She paused. "So, you don't remember anything about your real past, like your family? I mean . . . are you married, or, well, anything like that?"

"Mary?"

"Yes?" Her head came up. Her eyes danced, searching his.

John took a deep breath, searching for the right words. At the last moment he opted for, "Would you like to go for a walk?"

She blinked. Her shoulders sagged with a heavy sigh. "Sure. Let me get David. He should go with us."

David, always eager for a trek outside his own yard, immediately turned off the TV when she called. He grabbed his football and trotted into the kitchen. Mary picked up her sweater and they headed out the front door. David characteristically jumped all seven steps in one giant leap. He hit and rolled on the stone walkway like a paratrooper before springing to his feet and tossing John the ball, begging him to throw him a pass.

That was the first of many times Mary and John walked side by side while he threw imaginary touchdowns to her son. David would often see something of interest and dart through the bushes like a football running back, disappearing into the dense foliage to explore its many mysteries. A few minutes later, sneakers pounded the dirt as he ran to catch up with them, little clouds of dust marking his path.

Time and again he would then race by, begging John to throw him the ball. No sooner would he catch the pass than he would see something else on the hillside that needed exploring and knife through the brush once more, leaving John alone with Mary. They spent the rest of that morning talking with growing intimacy.

They rounded a bend in the trail and John recognized the place where he collapsed on his way to their house. He commented as much to Mary.

"I know," she said.

His head snapped up. "You do? How could you know that?"

"I back-trailed you the other day." Seeing his expression, she added quickly, "I didn't do it on purpose. I mean, I didn't come out here to check up on you. Your fever had broken, you were out of danger, and were sleeping well. After being cooped up in the house so long, I needed some fresh air.

"Anyway, your shuffled footprints were easy to follow, and so I spent the morning brushing them out in case anyone might follow you. That's how I found this spot. With all the blood, I knew you must have fallen here.

"You know it's a miracle you're still alive. The fall off Rock Hill should have killed you. And I'll never understand how that boulder landed on top of you like it did. It had to have been an act of God. That's the only way to explain it."

"You saw all that, too? You trailed me from Rock Hill?"

"Well, no. I didn't actually track you, per se. Your trail disappeared in the woods not far off from here. Father told me about your fall. I just decided to see for myself what happened on the plateau."

John crossed his arms with deep concern.

"The boulder wasn't that obvious," she added quickly. "But the hole at its base and the drag marks where you crawled out were. There was a bloody handprint on the rock. It was clear it was yours. But don't worry. I covered it all up."

She stopped, looking at his deep frown. "What's wrong, John? Are you upset with me?"

He looked up and tried to appear relaxed, wrapping an arm around her shoulders with an affectionate hug. "How can I be mad at you? I'm just concerned, that's all. I was just wondering if you can trail me, those men can track me, too. And when they do, they'll find me in your house. I fear I'm endangering your lives by staying here."

"I told you, don't worry about it. I brushed up all the tracks and camouflaged the hole where you hid. We'll be fine . . . I think."

They stopped walking and John took a deep breath, reliving the violence with which those men searched for him that rain swept night. He spoke openly, feeling she had a right to know.

"Mary, these men mean business. Believe me, they'll stop at nothing to kill me even if that means killing your family in the process."

"Who are 'they?' Is it the gang my father spoke of?"

John shook his head. "This was no gang. They were definitely military. Black camo-fatigues and army issue boots. I can't imagine what I could have done to warrant such a manhunt, but it's a sure bet they won't stop looking till they find me. I overheard they've got orders to search every house from Rock Hill to the city. I'm surprised they haven't ransacked yours already."

"That's because town is that way." She pointed south, the opposite direction of her home. She cocked her head, eyes squinting. "You say the men wore black fatigues?"

When he nodded she said, "It sounds like Jack Logan's Special Force Unit. That's their normal attire. He's a despicable snake and I wouldn't put it past him to do something like that. If Logan is after you, then I'm certain you did nothing wrong. My guess is that you've probably got some dirt on him and he just wants you out of the way. That's his motif."

"I heard one of the men call him General Logan. Do you know him?"

She rolled her eyes and answered with an exasperated groan. "Oh, do I ever! He was a General in the Army during the war. He's our Governor now, but when he's with his Special Force Unit, he likes to wear his military uniform and be called General. It strokes his ego."

Another piece of the puzzle fell into place.

"Tell me more about this Logan," John said. "Your father seems really taken in by him. As I understand it, Logan puts up the money for your research. Is this true?"

She nodded.

"Your father told me a lot of other things as well." John paused a moment, uncertain how to phrase the question. "Can I ask what, uh, relation he has with you?"

Her eyes flashed. "Jack Logan means nothing to me! It was only after Paul died that Logan started funding our computer project. He keeps pressing my father to make me marry him. He comes over to the house a lot.

"He says he's there to check our progress, but he spends more time trying to woo me than inspecting the lab. He thinks he can sway me with his charm, money, and by showing favor to my father. But I don't care what he does or how much money he gives us, that man is despicable. I'd rather die than marry him!" The flare of her nostrils and stormy flash in her eyes proved she meant it.

"My father is normally a sweet, loving, and intelligent man. But ever since he started working for Logan, he's changed. It's like Logan has some type of mind control over him."

Her face flushed red. "Jack doesn't know half of what he wants us to believe he does about computers, but Father lets him direct the project. Father knows something is wrong with Logan's design, but he does whatever he says anyway.

"You've talked with my father. He refuses to accept anything negative about Jack Logan. He reveres him like a saint—probably for saving his career after he was let go by the University. I guess for that reason, Father just cannot see Logan for what he really is."

She went on to relate details leading to her husband's death, the accusation concerning the murdered girl and how the mob stormed the house and drug him outside. They later proved he was a victim of mistaken identity, but that apology didn't bring him back did it?

She blamed Logan for the whole thing, claiming he bribed some dubious witnesses to lie in order to convince the mob. She tried to defend him that night, saying it was illegal, but no matter what she said, no one would listen to her—not even Logan. And so she watched in helpless horror as they hung him. Ever since then, despite all her protests and accusations against Logan, nothing was ever proved.

As she relived that fateful evening, tears streamed down her cheeks. John's heart went out to her. He could not imagine the emotional pain-filled life she endured. The death of her husband, the advances of a hated man, a lonely life of forced isolation, each day spent in silent desperation.

A silent tear trickled to the dusty ground below, splattering a tiny spot of mud on her shoe. She turned her head in shame, not wanting him to see her cry.

With sympathetic instinct, John touched her on the shoulder and was surprised when she immediately turned and fell into his arms, sobbing heavily. He did not say a word. He simply wrapped both arms around her, allowing her to vent emotions she had bottled up for years.

The bitterness she felt toward Jack Logan pleased John. The fact she trusted him with her feelings pleased him even more. She allowed him into her heart and soul, a place few, if any, ever knew. That is when John fell in love with Mary Lazlow.

Her shoulders heaved with deep, shuddering sobs, her tears wetting the front of his shirt. They stood atop the cliff overlooking the ebbing sea. She snuggled deeper into his supporting arms, crying until her emotional flood was spent.

Chapter 12

Nick Fishetti knelt beside the dirt trail and touched a boot print. "It's a fresh track."

Miller, sweating profusely, took another long pull from his canteen.

Nick lifted his eyes and looked down the trail. "He's close."

Miller breathed heavily, wiping his mouth. "How can you be sure it's him? There's no telling how many people have walked the trail this week. That footprint could have been made by anybody."

Fishetti shook his head. "It's him." He rose and adjusted his gun concealed in the waistband behind his back. "I know it's him."

Miller shook his head. "But I still don't know how you can be sure. To me, a footprint is a footprint. They all look alike."

Fishetti lifted steady eyes at his young partner. "I'm sure." His tone carried a sense of finality. The topic was closed.

"Well, what are those other footprints then?" Miller pointed with a skeptical sneer.

"It's a woman and a small boy—although it may be a girl." Fishetti turned to study the trail a while longer before nodding. "No, I was right. See the way the kid's prints jumble and turn? A boy made this track. Girls tend to walk in a straight line."

Fishetti looked up, his nostrils flaring as he sniffed the ocean breeze. "He's close, all right. I can feel it."

Miller surveyed the map and then pointed down the trail. "There's another house just around the bend up there. You want to check it out?"

Fishetti shook his head. "These tracks lead away. Besides, I know that house. I've pulled escort duty when Logan visited there. There's a girl there, Mary Lazlow. Logan's sweet on her. Her old man lives there, too, but these prints were not made by any old man." He looked up the trail. "Come on. We can check the house later. The prints head toward the mountain. Let's follow them and see what we can find."

Fishetti's phone rang. "No! No, not now!" Quickly, he mashed the button. "Yeah, what is it?"

"Fishetti? General Logan. What's your status?"

"Sir, I think that would be best answered by Lieutenant Carpenter or Captain Petra. We've been checking in per our orders."

"Forget your orders!" Logan shouted. "I just talked to both of them and they've got nothing. You're my best tracker. If anyone can find this man it's you. Now tell me what you've got."

"I've just found some tracks leading out to Rock Hill. A man, woman, and a boy. Miller and I were just on our way to check it out when you called."

"Rock Hill, you say? Are you sure?"

Fishetti stifled his chagrin, his tone curt. "That's what I said."

"Don't take that tone with me, Sergeant!

141

Remember who you're talking to here."

"Yes, sir."

"Are you sure it's him?"

"Not positive, but I'm willing to bet on it. He's here, alright. He's close. I know he his."

"Oh, I can't believe this." Logan seemed emphatic. "Listen, you make sure. You hear me? You make real sure and get back to me the second you know anything. If it really him that far north, that can only mean . . ."

Fishetti waited. After a long pause, he said, "Sir? Mean what?"

Logan snapped, "Never mind. It's impossible. Besides, it doesn't concern you. Just check out that lead and let me know. Call me direct."

The phone went dead.

Miller looked at Fishetti who looked like he was about to throw his phone into the woods. "What's up with him?"

"Who knows? Here we are in the middle of the hunt and he has to call me now. For all I know, the ring may have spooked our man. Right now, I'd rather shoot Logan."

Fishetti turned in tight circles, pulling his hair, cursing. Finally, he stopped in mid-turn and said, "Oh well. Can't do anything about it now. Let's get to it. If that call sent our man underground, we'll have a hard time finding him among those rocks. So if you think you're tired now, you better suck it up. Double time it, Corporal. We've got a job to do."

Enlightenment

Chapter 13

Mary pulled away from John's embrace, drying her tear-streaked face with aggravated swipes from both hands.

"I'm sorry." She sniffed. "I haven't been able to say what I've truly felt for a long time. Every time I tried, it just made things worse than before. My own father won't even listen to me! He treats me like an insolent, ungrateful little girl when I do."

She stamped her foot on the trail, raising a small dust cloud. Once again, she turned to face the surging ocean tide, trying to hide her swelling tears. "Why? Why won't anyone believe me?"

John wanted to reach out to her, hold her in his arms again, but he didn't. Each moment of awkward silence was punctuated by the crash of another rolling wave. Many times he started to say something only to stop at the last moment, uncertain whether it was the right thing to do. In the end, he did not know what he should do, and so he did nothing at all. He just stood there, wishing he could do more.

She suddenly turned on him. "Why do you care about this? What's it to you?"

"Huh?" he said, caught off guard.

She sniffed back another tear and wiped her nose with the back of her hand. "Oh, I'm sorry. I didn't mean for it to come out like that. What I meant was that I hardly know you and yet you make me feel so, well, so comfortable. I can't explain it, but I feel like you really care. You believe me." She looked up at him through tear-filled eyes. "You do believe me, don't you, John?"

This time, John didn't hesitate. "Yes, I do believe you, Mary." He brushed her wet cheek with a gentle thumb. "You made me realize that stopping Logan is one of the reasons I'm here. I know that now."

She sniffed a relieved smile and came even closer, her misty eyes peering into his. "What is it about you, John Neumann? Why is it that I can trust you more than anyone I've ever known?"

John didn't answer her because he had no answer to give. He caressed her cheek with the palm of his hand, his eyes never leaving hers. The ocean breeze blew a lock of hair across her face and he smoothed it back in place. He felt the softness of her neck before moving up to catch a lingering teardrop. All this time she never moved, welcoming his gentle touch.

Her brown eyes consumed him with desire. On impulse, he kissed her full lips, still wet with salty tears. Her arms immediately flung around his neck as she returned his embrace with the heated passion of a woman starving for love—and for someone to love her in return. She pressed her body hard against his as they exchanged torrid kisses. With unbridled passion, he poured himself into her, and her in him, each filling the emptiness in the other's soul.

For minutes on end, their love continued until their lips finally parted to catch a reluctant breath. Then, their breath coming in ragged gasps, she fell against him, moaning in ecstasy as he kissed her ear and the soft nape of her neck.

She closed her eyes, her moist cheek nestling his. John did not know how long they held each other like that. For him, that first embrace lingered for days.

She leaned against him, trembling softly, silently struggling against the demons of her tortured past. For years, she fought them alone. But now she had John, and he vowed she would never have to fight them alone again.

He lifted her chin and caressed her lips with his own, running his fingers through her long, auburn hair. She kissed him back, a soft meaningful gesture as she gazed into his eyes.

Something hit the ground behind them.

Mary yelped.

They turned to see David standing at the edge of the forest. He looked at them with a confused frown, the fallen football still wobbling at his feet. In that tense moment, only the gentle roar of ocean waves far below breached the awkward silence.

John's eyes went from David, to Mary, then back to her son. "Oh! Hi, David."

Mary pulled away, her flushed cheeks matching John's.

David did not say a word, nor did he move. He stared at them, arms hanging at his sides.

As Mary straightened her dress and hair, John searched for something to break the tension. He picked up the football and told David to go out for another pass. The boy hesitated, watching them with a wavering look. He glanced at his mother and then trotted off in indifferent obedience.

John purposefully threw the ball into a deep thicket, forcing David to search for it. The tactic bought them more time alone.

"We shouldn't have done that," Mary said, her breathing not yet under control. "I'm sorry. I don't know what came over me."

"Don't be sorry. We—"

"No!" She shook her head. "We came out here to talk about you and your energy concept, not to act like a couple of teenagers. What we did was nice, but it was wrong. We can't allow ourselves to get emotionally involved. If we did, well, it would just cause problems with my father, not to mention Logan. You have to trust me on that."

Running both hands through her hair, she closed her eyes and took a series of long, slow breaths. John's own mind reeled as well, his heart beating fast.

"About that theory of yours," she said. She took another cleansing breath and held it for a moment before exhaling slowly. Only then did she open her eyes. "Can we talk about that now?"

John wondered how she could control her emotions so well. If she felt as calm as she appeared, she was far stronger than he was. He wanted to hold her, to kiss her again. Instead, he settled for a heart-wrenching shrug and said, "What do you want to know?"

"I find your idea of a new form of energy intriguing. I have a feeling this is the breakthrough we've been looking for, but I need to understand it better. You mentioned the soul is made from it, but what physical evidence do you have that dark-energy even exists?"

She sat on a log in the shade of an old, moss-covered oak tree and pulled him down beside her. David returned, having finally found the football. When he saw they weren't going anywhere, he dropped the ball at John's feet and disappeared into the surrounding brush.

"Start at the beginning," she spoke softly. "I'm sure anything you can remember will be useful."

Despite her warning of getting involved, she snuggled close, seemingly oblivious to the stimulating effect of her warm breasts against his side. She wrapped both arms around him and looked up, moist lips parted. The seduction was not intentional, but all he could think about was kissing her again. He had to look away to collect his emotions.

"What's the matter?" she said. "Can't you remember anything?"

"Um, yeah," he said, his mind spinning. "Give me a minute." John shook his head. "My idea is somewhat similar to what happened a hundred years ago when a radical idea came out that everything is made of energy. This was a remarkable change in perspective that provided answers to many confusing things plaguing science at the time. That's the main thing I'm proposing here, a *change in perspective.*

"One simple concept solved the all the problems of that era. At first, not many liked the idea that everything is energy. It took a while, but the single-energy theory was ultimately accepted. That simple concept proved monumental.

"Somewhat like back then, we once again find ourselves stumped on how to explain new, more complicated observations. We can't explain them because *we have exhausted the capability of the single-energy concept* to do so, hence the many conflicting, irrational, and often illegal theories we have today. All I'm proposing is that everything is made of energy, only now let's consider there is more than atomic-energy at work in the Universe. There is a non-atomic form we must consider.

"With the single-energy theory, Quantum Mechanics has no physical meaning. Plus, theorists are plagued with ever increasing complications. It is an enigma. Everything is left to be explained by equations only, but it doesn't have to be like this. With a dual energy concept, everything we see in Quantum Mechanics, Relativity, and the Cosmos can be readily explained in logical and physical terms—something that is impossible today.

"The only way to make logical sense of it all is to once again change the way we view reality. That's why I need to introduce the Dual Energy Concept. There are at least two kinds of energy we must deal with to make sense of it all—particularly when it comes to explaining the spirit and the soul. These *definitely* are of this other form of energy."

"I already . . . oh!" Mary shouted surprise when

David bolted through the bushes roaring like a pouncing lion. Her scream brought a satisfied smile to the boy's face.

Mary turned to hug him and then suddenly stopped dead still. David casually tossed a hand grenade like a toy ball.

With a frightened shriek, she said, "David! Put that down!"

Her tone scared the boy. He fumbled the grenade, bobbling it momentarily before ultimately dropping it. Mary threw herself on top of her son, flinging him to the ground and covering him with her body.

"What's the matter, Mom?" David groaned beneath her weight. "Did I do something wrong?"

With a wondering look, Mary turned to locate the grenade. Her head dropped and she smiled sheepishly when she saw John holding it.

"What happened?"

"Apparently it takes more than a drop to set one of these things off," John said. He pointed to the pin. "However, if he had pulled this little ring here, well, let's just say none of us would be standing around to talk about it."

Mary furiously scolded David. John knew she was more frightened than angry, but he wasn't sure the boy knew the difference.

"Where did you get that thing?" she demanded. She shook him by the shoulders. "Tell me!"

"Up there." He pointed to a rocky slope behind them. The trail skirted the base of Rock Hill. "There's a really cool cave up there. It has all kinds of boxes filled with neat stuff like this."

"There is?" Worried eyes followed his finger. "Where?"

"Come on. I'll show you."

They followed him up the steep incline, winding their way through the broken shale and rocky debris. About twenty feet above the trail, an ancient ocean had carved a hole into the face of the mountain, creating a cavernous room. What made it unusual was a slap of harder stone had not eroded, shielding the slender opening. Looking at it straight on or from the trail below, the cave was invisible.

One by one they slipped into the dark, damp interior. It was larger than John expected. The main room was about fifty feet long and maybe thirty wide with dozens of wooden crates stacked along the back wall.

In the left rear, a dark hole revealed another, though smaller chamber. David called from this interior, his voice echoing through the darkness. "Here it is."

Mary and John ducked into the back room, squinting through the shadows to see what he so proudly displayed. Slowly, as their eyes adjusted to the faint light filtering from the main entrance, dozens of military munitions boxes came into view. They were everywhere, stacked end to end and to the top of the alcove.

John walked to the nearest crate and lifted a loose slat. Inside were rows of hand grenades. In that semi-darkness, their pineapple shaped surface looked deadly ominous. One was missing, the one David took. He replaced it in its foam fitted slot and closed the lid.

"Hey, this is cool!" David shouted.

John turned to see him admiring the well-oiled barrel of an M-16 rifle. He turned it over, his tiny arms straining to get a grip around the rubberized stock.

"David!" John snatched the gun from him. "That's not a toy."

A quick inspection revealed the clip was full. The safety was off. The weapon was ready to kill. He replaced the rifle inside its crate and noticed more boxes labeled "Ammunition."

"Looks like someone is stocking up for a war," John said. "There's enough stuff here to supply a small army."

When Mary didn't answer, he turned to find her pacing, her teeth gritted and both hands clenched in tight fists.

"I can't believe it," she kept repeating to herself. "I just can't believe it."

"What can't you believe? What's going on?"

"My father!" She gestured at the boxes. "He told me he got rid of this stuff, but all he did was get it out of the house to hide it from me."

She looked at him and her shoulders slumped. "Well, since you've seen this, you might as well know the rest."

She ran both hands through her long, thick hair and took a deep breath. "Paul got obsessed with wiping out Logan's Special Force Unit. We were both convinced Logan was behind all the crime around here. I still am. His Special Forces are nothing but a front. Oh, sure, they do all the normal protection detail for a governor of any state. But for Logan, they also provide muscle for his drug operations."

She looked at him. "The moment I first saw you, I knew it was Logan's men chasing you that night. That's why I hid you. But what I didn't know was why would he want you bad enough to come out himself. Logan is always careful to stay behind the scene. I've never heard of him taking an active role before. It's all part of maintaining his public image to let someone else do his dirty work. He must be desperate to want you dead to take a chance coming out like that."

John shrugged. "You said I must have something on him, but I'm beginning to think it's more about what I *know* that can stop him in a way no vigilante group can. It's something I can't quite bring into focus just yet, but it came to me in my trance. But go on. Tell me more about the men and these weapons."

She looked at him a long moment before saying a word. Finally, she turned to pace the floor and said, "At first, Paul tried the legal route to expose him, but he got stonewalled every time. Apparently, Logan owns the courts as well. And any witness either recanted their story or conveniently turned up dead. Paul finally got fed up and said if the government wouldn't do anything about Logan then he was going to do it himself.

"That was when he and a man in town started recruiting dozens of men into their group. However, when Logan found out about it." She paused, gazing into the darkness. "Well, you know what happened then. People started disappearing.

"I think that's the real reason he had Paul killed.

And when Paul died, Logan probably thought this insurrection died with him, but it seems he was wrong. Apparently, the insurgent group still exists—and it looks like my father has joined them."

"Joined them?" he said. "But I thought your father liked Logan."

Mary continued her pacing, her tone biting hard. "Oh, Father doesn't think Logan has anything to do with organized crime. He thinks these men are going to take the fight to the gangs and run them out of this place. The old fool thinks he's doing Logan a favor.

"If Paul's vigilante group is still active—and by the looks of this, they are—then it's going to be old men and shop keepers against Logan's trained killers. The only thing I don't understand is why they haven't made their move yet. They've got the weapons."

"They're waiting for something, or maybe someone," John said with a positive nod. "But no matter if they got what they're looking for, these guys can't go up against Logan's men, especially Doc. He's too old for this sort of violence. Besides, civilians against trained professionals? It would be a slaughter. Your father's group won't stand a chance."

Her rebuttal was a sarcastic, "Hello? That's what I've been saying! Oh, I'm sure when the slaughter's over Logan will make it look like the gangs did it. I wouldn't put it past him to even get some of them to participate in the fight—and then kill them himself when the time comes. That way, the press will have plenty of bodies for their newspapers and Logan will come out a hero."

She stopped pacing and glanced frantically left and right. "Where's David?"

Exiting the back cave, she found him sitting near the entrance drawing figures in the dirt. Mary stepped past him and stood in the cave mouth, staring off into the distance. Below her was a carpet of trees swaying gently, nudged by the gentle breeze.

She stood there a moment, a worried expression straining her face. "It's getting late," she said. "We'd better be getting home."

Chapter 14

Fishetti came to a sudden halt, forcing Miller to dodge nimbly to one side to avoid running into his back. He stood in the middle of the trail, staring at the mountain in front of him.

"What happened to the tracks?" Miller said, squinting against the sting of sweat. "They disappeared."

"They left the trail and went up on that rocky ridge." Fishetti pointed to his right. "They must have heard Logan's phone call and took to the high ground. There's no way to track them in those rocks."

Palming a radio, he called for a nearby team. Fishetti outlined the situation and instructed them to continue down the trail while Fishetti and Miller circumvented the base of the mountain.

"Get on the radio. I want two more teams scouting the tree line at the base of the mountain looking for tracks. If they left the shale, I want to know where. One team takes this side of the mountain. The others start on the far side and make their way around. We all meet on the other side of Rock Hill," he said. "Miller and I will be totally exposed on that rocky slope, but that's okay. I want them to see us. That way we'll either flush them toward you or to those in the forest. Either way, all you have to do is grab them."

He stepped off the trail and scrambled up the steep shelf of broken shale that skirted the mountain. Turning around, he added, "And for God's sake somebody please tell Lieutenant Carpenter what we're doing!

"And remember what I told you before. No one shoots anyone. You got that? If you find them, just detain them and call me on the radio."

Fishetti and Miller turned away when one of the men asked, "But what if it's him, Sarge?"

Nick looked back over his shoulder. "If anyone is going to kill anyone today, it's going to be me. You got that? Nobody kills that man but me!"

~~~

Mary ducked through the cave's entrance when John grabbed her arm and pulled her back from the narrow opening.

"Wait a minute!" he whispered. "I hear something."

Faintly at first then growing steadily louder they heard the sound of someone scrambling over the loose rubble of rocks. Mary peeked around the concealing flow of rock entrance to the cave and pulled back instantly, stifling a frightened gasp as two men passed by only five feet away. She retreated into the deeper shadows, thankful that neither of them bothered to look back.

"Oh, they're just hikers," John said.

"Since when do hikers carry guns?" she whispered, watching them pick their way along the uneven slope. From behind, the black grip of automatic pistols protruded from each man's belt.

"Those are Logan's men. I recognize the one in the lead. His name's Fishetti. I don't know the other, but I'm willing to bet money they're looking for you."

She pulled him deeper into the dim interior. "Oh, this is bad!" Mary said. She began pacing nervously. "Just when things couldn't get worse. First my father and now this." She held both hands to her head. "I can't handle all this."

John stepped in front of her. She stopped and he wrapped her in a reassuring hug. "Don't worry." He smiled. "Everything will be all right."

"All right?" She pulled away. "How can you say that? Those are Logan's men. They're obviously trailing us. Who knows how many more are out there searching for you? And if they find you . . ."

John shrugged and sat on a large rock, inviting her to join him. With laced fingers behind his head, he leaned back and smiled again, trying his best to appear relaxed – which, of course, was the farthest thing from his mind.

"Look at it this way," he said. "This cave is the perfect hiding place. All we have to do is wait a while. If they are trailing us, they've already missed the cave, which means they'll just keep on going. All we have to do is wait a while. We'll go home when it gets dark. We'll just stay off the trails from now on. You know, be more careful."

David stopped drawing in the sand. "What's wrong, Mom?" he asked. "Are those men really after us?"

Mary looked at him with a worried frown. "Yes, honey. And they have guns. But as long as we're quiet, and I mean completely quiet, they won't find us. So go back to playing, okay? I need to talk to Mr. Neumann for a while. That's right, go on."

David turned and said, "Don't worry. They won't find us. We'll be all right." Then he did as he was told, seemingly unconcerned as if nothing was wrong.

Mary regarded him a wondering moment. "How does he do that?"

"Do what?"

"Know things like that? It's like everything is already in the past to him. Like he's seen it before."

John turned to look at David with a new look of wonder as Mary turned to pace the floor. Apparently, she wasn't as convinced as David.

After some time, John said, "Tell you what. Why don't we talk? It will help get your mind off things."

"Talk about what?" She sat on a nearby rock but kept fidgeting, casting fearful looks at the cave's entrance. It wasn't long before she was up pacing again.

"How about I tell you more about my theory? That might help."

"How could we possibly talk about your energy theory at a time like this? Those men are trying to kill you! Don't you understand what that means?"

"Sure I do, but there's nothing we can do about it except wait them out. The way I see it, you've got a choice. You can spend your time pacing back and forth worrying and getting nowhere or we can make constructive use of our time expanding your project. Come on. Sit down. Anything to get our minds off the situation will help, might even do some good."

"I don't know if I can."

"Sure you can. You're strong. Just put your mind to it. Remember, it was your idea to talk about my concepts. That's why we went for a walk. And what better place than this? I think once you understand how dark-energy works, you'll see how to get your project back on track. That should get you going. That's what is really important, not those men. David's right. We're safe here, so let's talk."

Mary nodded and sat down while casting yet another glance at the cave opening. She then turned back to him, her face grim. "Yes, you're right. I've got to think. Think! Yes, that will help." She took a deep breath, scooted closer beside John and sighed. "Go ahead. Tell me about this Dual Energy Concept of yours. To start with, how do you know this dark-energy is not atomic?"

John said, "For one thing, I know it is not charged based, like atomic-energy is. that alone says a lot. To be complete, they each need the other. The photon needs the darkon to approximate the primordial unity they had in what I call the Absolute Energy Medium. This is the balance of the Universe, places where the Medium of space-time is undisturbed. They seek to regain that balance. Second, the Schrödinger and deBroglie-Bohm equations prove the existence of what I call 'Location nodes.' These are points in space where energies are more concentrated than others. Particles gravitate to these nodes . . ."

They talked for hours about the details of the Dual Energy Concept. The more John talked, the more data that had been streamed to his brain made sense. Speaking his thoughts out loud helped him think, and to have Mary there to talk to made it all the more easier.

When he finished, Mary said, "So that's our new approach then, to monitor the neural energy flow within the brain and thus control the soul and spirit. I mean, if I'm understanding the basic concept for dark-energy. You're saying photons need darkons to be complete, and so they attract each other like magnets. The atomic-energy photons generated by the brain attract the soul and spirit darkons and vice versa. All three attract each other to form a type of bond."

John nodded. "There's more involved, but basically you're right. The atomic-energy emanating within the brain interacts with the dark-energy of the soul. The neural energy of the brain is made of atomic-energy, or photons, and the soul is made of dark-energy, or darkons. What one does to one affects the others. If we can control the neural energy of a brain, the spirit and soul will react to that control. That's how we get your experiment to work."

They talked a few more hours about details regarding the brain and soul interactions until eventually Mary looked at her watch. She frowned and turned toward the cave entrance.

"It's getting late," she said. "Those men should be gone by now, don't you think? But let's not take chances. You wait here. David and I will make sure the coast is clear."

She led David down the rocky slope, both of them scouting the landscape in a continually turning vigilance of paranoia. At the bottom, she looked both ways along the trail three times before waving an urgent hand for John to follow.

He scrambled down, slipping on the thick shelf of broken shale while Mary continued to scan the surrounding forest. David looked around too. He did not seem as nervous as his mother but was just as intense.

They walked in silence for some time, all of them lost in their own thoughts and fears. David started jumping in and out of the tangled overgrowth with yet another game.

Mary broke the silence. "There is a way to stop him."

John shot a wondering look at David. "Oh, I think he's all right. Those men are on the other side of Rock Hill by now."

"No, I'm talking about my father! You can stop him."

He shook his head and shrugged. "If your father is involved in some kind of militant group, I'm not sure I'm the right person to talk him out of it."

"Oh, but I think you are. You know how to make his machine work. And from what you told me, I'm sure you'll figure out how to get an ethereal soul to interact with an atomic brain. My father can't, but that's what he's looking for."

She grabbed his arm. "Don't you see? Your ideas on energy are what we've been missing. You can make our system work. The only reason my father's mixed up with this vigilante group is because he wants to feel important again. There was a time when Father was world renowned. People knew who he was and looked up to him. But now he feels like a nobody, a has-been.

"This project was his last chance to prove his theories on the soul and regain his social status, maybe even get the University to take him back. But with the way things are going, it doesn't look good. And he knows that."

"What do you mean?"

"Oh, we're getting nowhere and haven't been for some time now. He's almost ready to give up on the whole thing. That's why I think he joined the vigilantes. He sees it as a way back into the spotlight, if only for a little while. With his ego, he'd do anything to get the world to notice him one more time before he dies."

She looked at him, her eyes dancing. "But you can change that. If you tell Father what you just told me, I'm sure he'll agree and drop this fighting nonsense."

They rounded the last turn in the trail and came in sight of the house. David said he was going to finish his movie and ran inside, leaving the two of them standing at the foot of the stone walkway.

"However, there is big problem," she said. "Logan is involved with our project. That's both good and bad. It's good in that we have the money, but every time Logan has one of his inspirational ideas he comes over and forces us to do what he says.

"If you ask me, we'd be better off without him. He's the reason everything is so confused. He doesn't know what he's talking about and thus he's the main reason we're not getting anywhere—but don't try telling that to my father."

"Logan, huh? That does complicate things. If we start making the changes I need, he's going to know I'm involved. We'll have to hide our modifications. Otherwise, he'll have his men here in nothing flat looking for me."

She shook her head. "Hiding your changes shouldn't be a problem. Logan's not that technical. The problem is getting Father to change his mind. Although the computer shows no sign of functionality, he's bound by honor to stay the course. He's wrong, but once he makes up his mind, well, let's just say he doesn't change it very often."

"No way!" John smiled away any offense. "Are you saying your father is hardheaded?"

"He's not hardheaded!" She squeezed his hand playfully. "He's more stubborn, obstinate, and cantankerous than that. Father's pride has always been his downfall. Normally, he would rather die than admit he's wrong. Once he makes up his mind on something, it's like God wrote it on stone. You can forget showing him any more facts because he just won't listen. I should know. I've been trying it for years." She shook her head. "With that mentality, we're bound to fail."

"If that's the case," he said, "everyone on this planet will die."

She looked up sharply. "What do you mean?" Her eyes searched his. "There's something you're not telling me. What is it?"

John looked away, trying to put his nebulous feelings into words. "Your project is, or actually should be, more than proving the soul is real. It's about connecting with the outside world. It's about convincing people there is another form of energy, that there's a realm beyond what they can see. We have to convince them the outside world exists."

"Why?" She shrugged. "Most people don't care how reality is put together. And they probably couldn't understand it if you explained it to them. All they care about is what's on TV and if there's another beer in the fridge."

"Maybe, but we've got to try. You asked about me, where I came from. I am from that outside world, the world beyond the darkness. I've come to create a way to bring you home. I know that now. If I can connect my mind to the Genesis Machine using your father's computer, I'm sure I'll remember it all. It's the first step in my plan. After that, I'll know the next step that must be done. But making that initial connection is essential.

"As for the people, taking the way out that I will create is a conscious choice. I sense the Genesis Machine needs them to give themselves up before it can work with them, their willingness to let the computer perform the necessary changes that are required. It deals with their attitude, which allows an alignment of the spirit. If their attitude is against it, then the computer can't work with them.

"They might not be able to understand it all, but they don't have to. For some, just knowing there is an answer may be enough to gain their trust to get them through. That answer they must believe is that the soul and spirit are real, and that there is another realm beyond this one we all can attain—should attain. If they can only believe, that is enough to get them through all that is to come."

As he spoke, bleak images of a dark future loomed in his mind.

"What's the matter? What are you thinking?" Mary demanded.

"Something terrible is about to happen here," he said. "I see buildings burning, people screaming in terror as they die. They scream in darkness. They're calling me, begging me to help."

As quickly as it came, the dark vision receded. When John lowered his eyes, he looked straight into Mary's strained expression. He did not know what she saw in him, but when their eyes met, she gasped in alarm and took an involuntary step back.

She stood a few feet away, her hands to her mouth as some silent conflict raged within her. She acted as if she wanted to run, but needed to stay.

John reached out to her. "Mary, what's wrong? What did I say?"

She backed away, avoiding his touch. Her foot struck the stone walkway and she stumbled, but she never took her eyes off him. She continued to retreat, crossing and uncrossing her arms.

Then, with obvious effort, she took a step forward and lifted a trembling hand to touch his face, but she never did. With her fingers mere inches away, she suddenly pulled back and ran into the house, crying.

John called after her, "Mary? Mary! What's wrong? What did I say?" He started to follow her, but her father's voice stopped him.

"John!"

What does he want? John wondered.

Chapter 15

"John!" Doc Lazlow called again. He walked from the corner of the house carrying hedge clippers from his yard work.

John stopped on the stone walkway, watching Mary slam the front door without looking back. With one last longing look at the closed door, he crossed the yard toward Doc, perplexed and confused. Doc met him mid-way, the sharp shears still clutched in a gloved hand.

"So, you two have been out for a walk, have you?" he said. "What did you talk about? Were you able to remember anything else?"

"We talked about a lot of things. I remembered some things about dark-energy and explained what I could."

"Well, how did it go? Did she understand it?"

"Yeah, I guess so. I mean, there's a lot involved. Most if it is brand new stuff, things she didn't get in school, but she got the gist of it well enough."

"I see." He nodded toward the door. "What's with the tears?"

"I wish I knew. We were just talking when she suddenly got upset and ran inside."

"Well, you obviously said something to set her

off. What was it?"

John shrugged. "She mentioned her husband and what happened. She was disturbed about that, but I thought talking about it would help her deal with it better. Looks like I was wrong."

Doc scrutinized him before he spoke. When he did, it was with a sense of bitterness. "You touched a sore spot with Paul. There are some around here who thought he was a prophet. Others say he was a nutcase who deserved what he got. In any event, it doesn't help matters that you resemble him so much."

"I do?"

Doc squinted against the sweat rolling into his eyes and mopped his brow with the back of a gloved hand. "Not so much in the way you look. It's more your attitude and mannerisms, the way you walk, the things you say and the way you say them. You two were definitely cut out of the same mold, that's for sure."

"What kind of things did he say?"

"Toward the end, mostly doom and gloom stuff. The end of the world, war, and chaos, that sort of thing. He said it was his mission from God to quit his job to and tell people the end of the world is near."

"Well, I did see something like that myself, just now on the trail."

Doc shook his head. "That must be it, then. I advise you to tread softly there. Despite my best efforts with Paul, all he wanted to do was preach things he said came to him in dreams. He didn't have a church or a license, and so he spoke anywhere and everywhere. Street corners, any public gathering, you name it, telling anyone and everyone who would listen.

"Things didn't get bad until he started singling out Governor Logan as the primary cause of all our problems. He even managed to get on TV, though I still don't know how he pulled that off. Anyhow, he claimed Logan was behind all the corruption and drug related murders going on in these parts. He even started a groundswell campaign to impeach him."

Doc shook his head. "Personally, I think that was when he flipped out. I tried getting him to stop his vendetta against Logan and convince him that it was the gangs, not Logan behind it all, but he wouldn't listen. He said Logan would destroy the world and kill us all if someone didn't stand up to him. But in the end, Paul is the one who wound up dead."

"You said he was hung."

Doc nodded, eyes indicating the front of the house. "Right on that tree there."

John turned to see a giant oak shading the front lawn. Fifteen feet up, a thick branch grew from its base at almost a ninety-degree angle, making it perfect for the gruesome job.

"And Logan killed him?"

"He most certainly did not!" His head snapped up. "I don't know what line Mary fed you, but Jack Logan is not the sort who would stoop to such barbaric behavior. The man is our governor. He's my friend, my only real friend.

"He was there that night, yes. But from what I saw, he did everything he could to stop that mob. There were just too many of them, that's all. The mob was out of control. There was nothing he or anyone else could do. He even called in his Special Forces, but it was all over by the time they got here. Paul was dead."

"Well if Logan wasn't responsible, who was?"

"That's hard to say. It was too organized for a simple street gang. I think it was the Mafia. They are deeply embedded here. Paul probably got too close to the truth with them. It may have been one of their outfits that attacked you last week. You might have stumbled on a drug deal or something. You were just in the wrong place at the wrong time that night, that's all.

"But as for Logan, he's clean. You can look it up. He's signed dozens of crime bills. The police conducted raid after military raid, but the Mob has too many people. Every time the police arrested someone, the courts turned them loose. Jack's doing his job. It's not his fault the legal system is screwed up."

He shook his head again. "Paul made a lot of accusations. Toward the end, he got to be an in-your-face kind of guy and he didn't much care who got angry with what he said. He upset a lot of influential people, both good and bad. That's why it's impossible to say who incensed the crowd that night. By then Paul had so many enemies on both sides of the fence it seemed everyone wanted him dead.

"Paul knew this, of course. He even predicted his own death. The day before he died, he came to me saying he didn't have long to live. That's when he told me about the weapons he had stashed under the house and asked if I would take care of them. He had been planning a real war against crime.

"I don't know why he entrusted me. Maybe he saw something in me I didn't, but he asked me to carry the flame, so to speak. He wanted me to stash his weapons, to keep fighting the fight. When I agreed and joined up, there were a good many more in the group. Now there's only half as much. They just got tired of waiting. Waiting and doing nothing to stop the crime.

"Paul told me a man named Harry would come get the weapons when it was time. Harry's the one who's really in charge. I just stockpiled the weapons."

"So you did join the vigilante group," John said.

"Sure I did."

"But why?"

"With Jack's hands tied, I figured the least I could do was to carry on the fight. I just needed to change the group in the right direction, target the people who really need to be exterminated from this planet. Paul's sights may have been off, but he definitely had the right idea. We've got to take the fight to the Mob. We can't afford to sit back and let them destroy our country, our families, and our lives anymore.

"Anyhow, when Paul died, Harry came for the weapons and we moved them out of the house. You know, to hide them from Mary."

"Uh, yeah." John frowned. "We stumbled across your stash during our walk. Actually, it was David who found the cave at the base of Rock Hill. It's where we hid from those men."

"You did, huh?" He mopped his brow, shaking his head. The sun was hot that day. "That's too bad. We're going to have to move them now. I know David wouldn't mean anything, but a child can't keep this sort of thing a secret. He's bound to tell someone."

He paused a moment to pull a towel from his pocket. He took his time wiping more sweat from his face.

"Listen to me," he said. "I've been trying to find a way to broach the subject and I suppose this is as good as any. I didn't quite know how to take it at the time, but Paul said a man would come who was special. He emphasized time and again that only with this man could we succeed. He made Harry and me to promise to wait, to keep the group together until this man arrived. He said he would come out of nowhere, be from nowhere, and show up on my doorstep. It was the last thing he ever said to me. It was the last thing he said to anyone."

"And you think I'm the guy Paul was talking about?"

Doc nodded. "When I saw you that day on my front porch, you fell into my arms and said you came to *save* us. You can imagine my surprise. I didn't know what to think. After all these years, I'd almost given up hope. But when you said what you did, I knew you were the one."

He gripped John's arm with his free hand. "Please, you've got to help us. These people are totally ruthless. They even tried to kill you! And by what you just said about the men on the trail, they're still looking to finish the job.

"Can't you see? You must have seen something, done something that jeopardizes their operation. These people systematically kill anyone in their way and they won't stop until you're dead. You don't have a choice.

It's kill or be killed. That's the way it is around here."

He gestured with the garden shears toward the distant mountain. "You've seen the munitions. We've got it all: rifles, grenades, mortars. We've got everything but the right man to lead us. And I believe that man is you. I'm positive you're the man Paul told me about."

His grip, surprisingly strong for a man his age, tightened on John's elbow, his face pensive and drawn. "We need you, John. Remember, I gave you refuge. I saved your life. Now, you must save ours. It's only a matter of time before they come here. God knows why they haven't so far. So will you help us? The people. Think of the people in town. They're the ones who get it worse. Please, you must help us stop the Mob here. They're out of control!"

John stood speechless, realizing the scope of what Doc was asking him to do. Doc went on to describe the many that were beaten, their arms or legs broken because they would not pay the extortion money. Others died, a sign of what happens if someone interferes.

The more he talked, the more John grew angry. He wondered if Doc was right. Maybe his mission was to lead their fight. With Doc's computer fixed and the power of dark-energy in his control, he could wipe them all out. He was tempted. And had it not been for a persistent small voice in the back of his mind, he might have joined Doc on the spot.

Yet the voice would not let him forget he wasn't there to lead a war and that killing people wouldn't solve a thing. There was a bigger problem at stake, something more profound than the temporary tragedies of life. Unfortunately, it was something Doc didn't want to hear. He had been so focused on his own selfish desires for so long that he could no longer see anything else.

John shook his head with true regret. "I'm sorry, Doc. I am here to help you, but not by killing people. I don't have time to fight a war."

Doc blinked hard. Then he stiffened, his blue eyes glaring. "Don't have time? You don't have time! I brought you into my house. I cared for you. I sheltered you. I saved your life. You said you came to save us, and now you say you don't have time to do that?"

"That's not what I meant," John said. "I *am* here to save you, yes, but in a way far better than any military campaign could ever do."

"Then what, pray tell, do you plan to do?" he said, his arms wrapped in disgust.

"It involves the use of your neural simulator, that computer project you've been working on. The idea came to me while I was talking with Mary. I need that computer to connect my mind to the outside world. And right now, the clock is ticking. I've already lost a week. That means I only have little more than a month to make connection with the outside world. If I don't, then this world, as corrupt as it is, will cease to exist. Then everyone will die, the good and the bad."

"Don't give me any of that other world crap! If you're too scared to fight, then say so. Don't hide behind ridiculous excuses."

"Doc, I'm not making this up. I feel bad for what you people are going through. Believe me, it rips my heart out just thinking about it. But using your neural simulator to connect my mind with the Genesis Machine is the best way I can help you. It's why I came here. Trust me, you've got bigger problems than thugs running around with guns.

"This world is a ticking time bomb. There is a virus in the main computer that generates this world. At its current rate, that virus will destroy all life on this planet in a month if I don't do something to stop it. I've got to connect to the Genesis Machine and find a way to get you people out. I now know the only way to do that was for me to come inside this world and help you fix your machine. Well, that's one of the reasons. Anyway, I know you're stuck. That's why I'm here. That's why I came to you.

"To stop the virus and find a way to get you people out, I need to repair your device. Once we've realigned it with my modifications, it will boost my ethereal signal to where the Genesis Machine can then pick it up. Only then can the next phase begin."

A look of realization dawned upon Doc's face. His eyes widened. He took a step back as if unspoken accusations were festering in his mind. His face transformed from anger into a mask of hatred. His mouth tightened into a white line across a blood raged face, his eyes narrowing to menacing slits.

John was amazed at the drastic change, the sheer amount of fury that now seethed from him was incredible. What had once been a kind old man was now a hard and bitter adversary.

"*Mr. Neumann!*" He sneered the words, taking a belligerent step forward. "It suddenly occurred to me that you are interested in only two things, and those two things happen to belong to me. I admit you had me fooled, but not anymore. I'm onto you, mister. And I'm warning you. Don't even think about getting into my lab. And if you so much as touch my daughter, I swear I'll kill you myself!"

John shook his head. "But why? I know how to make your neural booster work. This project is the key to this world's survival."

"No you don't." He shook his head vehemently. "I don't know how you found out about it, but you just want to get into my lab so you can steal or destroy what I've spent a lifetime inventing. It's going to work. I can make it work. I just need more time."

"But Logan's the one who's messing up your design. You started with something perfect. Now he's got it all fouled up."

"And just how would you know that?" he snapped.

A long, uncomfortable silence followed when John refused to comment. He didn't want to alienate Doc any more than he already had.

"It's obvious Mary is attracted to you," Doc said. "But then I'm sure your boss thought about that before he selected you for this job. You thought you could seduce her and then use her to influence me."

John's head snapped up to look at him. "No. That's not true."

Doc nodded, bobbing his head faster with each confirming second. "Yes it is. Yes, that's it. That's why you've been spending so much time with her. I bet they even beat you up to make it look real, so that Mary would feel sorry for you and take you in. A

Trojan Horse. That's what you are, a Trojan Horse."

He smiled at John's shocked disbelief. "You can stop with that phony surprised act. I'm onto you. Now just stay away from Mary! She's been spoken for by someone more powerful than you'll ever be and he won't like you messing around with what's his. A coward like you wouldn't stand a chance against a real man."

John took another step back from his angry advance. "What's the matter, Doc? Just this morning, you were glad Mary was talking to me. Why the change?"

"I was glad she was showing interest in life again. Since her husband died, Mary's been a recluse, refusing to see much less go out with another man— until you came along, that is. But I won't stand for her getting involved with the likes of you. I can't afford that. Not now. Not ever."

"Come on, Doc." John lowered his tone with a friendly smile. "Sure, there's a physical attraction, and well there should be. Mary is a beautiful woman, but I'm not using her for anything, least of all to manipulate you."

"Say what you want," Doc retorted. "But remember what I said. Stay away. She's spoken for."

"And just what do you mean by that?"

"I mean she's about to be engaged, you idiot! I've arranged for her to marry Jack Logan, the richest and most powerful man in this part of the country. I worked hard for this union and you are not going to wreck my plans."

John didn't know whether it was his hostile attitude or the garden shears pressing into his chest, but that was when he lost control. He pushed Doc back on his heels.

"Jack Logan?" he said with a condescending tone. "Are you saying you promised him her hand in marriage?" He rolled his eyes. "What century are you living in, man? This house is not a castle and you are not a feudal lord. Please, tell me you didn't promise Logan your daughter in exchange for all the money he's given you. Tell me you're not that shallow, that insensitive of your daughter's feelings."

The change in Doc's expression was subtle but significant. What had once been hatred now grew into malevolent contempt. He didn't say a word but his silent stare conveyed volumes.

"Oh, my God!" John shouted. "I can't believe you have the audacity to stand in judgment over me while you treat your own daughter like some possession to barter with. Just who do you think you are?"

Doc opened his mouth but John cut him off. "And Jack Logan? Something tells me 'I don't think so.' Have you even bothered asking Mary how she feels? She hates the guy."

"Our family matters do not concern you, Mr. Neumann. And I will not have a stranger interfering with our lives." He jabbed him with the shears, the sharp point tearing at John's shirt. "How dare you come into my house and tell me what to do! Who are you to tell me right from wrong?"

He thrust the sheers again with aggravated authority. "You keep your asinine opinions to yourself, mister. I know what you're up to and it won't work. If

I were you, I'd walk out of here while you still can. One call to Logan and you're a dead man."

John took a deep breath, forcing himself back to a softer tone. "Look, Doc, you saved my life and I appreciate that deeply. I didn't come here to argue or to fight, least of all with you. Part of my purpose is to help you complete your research. Deep down, isn't that what you really want, to succeed? Mary said you want to prove the soul exists. Ask her, she'll tell you what I can do. We talked about it today. Isn't this project what your life is all about? I can help you.

"Please tell me what I can do to make you believe I'm telling you the truth? What can I say to convince you that my ethereal concept is your, no it is *our* key to success?

"We have to work together on this, Doc. Face it. You need what's inside my head as much as I need you to get it out. Only by working together can either of us accomplish our goal."

He threw up his hands in mock surrender. "However, if you want me to leave, then I'll go. If you don't want to find the answers you've spent most of your life looking for, that's your choice because I assure you the path you're on leads nowhere. What you have is ancient code for a time long past. It's time for a change, but you won't listen.

"*Can't you see that old ideas never breed new concepts?* That's what you're lacking now, the right concept. You don't understand the essence of what you're dealing with. I can give that to you."

Doc jabbed the shears again. John grabbed them and threw them violently to the side. They arched through the air, clattering against the side of the house, but his unwavering eyes never left Doc's challenging glare.

"But make no mistake," he said. "Unless Mary tells me otherwise, I have no intention of abandoning her to a life of misery with Jack Logan."

The late afternoon sun burned hot against his back. The bright glare struck Doc full in the face. Sweat trickled from Doc's forehead and into his squinting eyes. He blinked against the salty sting, but he would not back down.

The tense stalemate endured in baleful silence until, like flipping a switch, Doc's expression brightened and he smiled once more—only this time his eyes were empty.

"No, I don't want you to leave, my boy," he said, his tone soft and friendly. "You mustn't be so sensitive to the babbling nonsense of an old man. It was a bit of a test to see if you were real. That's all.

"Yes, it's true that Logan likes Mary. I was just saying Jack's a powerful man who usually gets what he wants. And he's in love with Mary. If he were to discover you and Mary had a thing going on, well let's just say it wouldn't be pretty for any of us. I've learned it's not wise to make Logan angry, that's all."

"Thank you for your concern, Doctor," John said, eyeing him cautiously. "But no one ever said love came easy."

Doc raised a brow at that remark. John was probably more surprised than he in what he just said, but he could not deny his feelings. He was in love with Mary Lazlow. And no matter whether he left or stayed there was going to be pain and heartbreak in the days ahead because of that.

Doc let the statement go without comment. The raised eyebrow was loud enough. Stooping to pick up his garden equipment, he returned to the original subject. "This energy concept you mentioned, you say Mary understands it."

John's answer came slow and guarded. "Yes, at least the part we covered. We didn't get through it all, just some examples showing value of dark-energy. I took a lot of time proving another energy does exist, and I believe the soul is made of this new kind of non-atomic energy."

"Okay." He nodded. "What do you say we spend some time together ourselves, eh? I would like clarification on some things you said during your trance. That is if you don't mind, of course."

"That would be fine with me." John shrugged. *What was he up to?* "I have nothing to hide. What is it you want to know?"

"I want to hear your version how the soul and spirit interact with the brain. If Mary believes this new energy of yours exists, I'd like to hear how we can apply it."

When John hesitated, he added, "Come on, John. Like you said, we've got to work together on this. If you don't open up, how am I to know whether your theory is worth the time it will take to reprogram my computer?"

Something was wrong. John didn't know what had gotten into him, but he needed to find a way to work with Doc no matter what the cost. And so he agreed to the request, cautioning himself against the possibility of a trap.

He followed him down the slope to the back yard and through the door to his office. Once inside, Doc told him to wait on the couch while he washed his hands in the nearby bathroom.

John waited for over an hour. He passed the time browsing through the stuffed bookshelves. Doc wrote some of them himself. Some were by his father, a prominent psychiatrist in his own right. The others were variations of the same theme: effects and treatments of personality disorders.

One book caught his attention. It described the electro-chemical functions within the brain. It detailed how the brain used chemicals to induce electricity coursing through the neural network—many neural networks constantly realigning themselves in a variety of different patterns. It was Doc's first book, his breakthrough theory, the work that established him as a leading authority on the subject.

John stood leafing through its yellowed pages when Doc finally returned. The towel he used to blot his face only partially hid a devious smile. He offered no apologies for his delay. He strolled into the room acting as if he had all the time in the world. John put the book back on the shelf and flopped on the couch.

Doc tossed the towel over one shoulder and sat down at his desk. The creaky wooden chair complained at the strain of his bulk. He took his time shuffling through a neat pile of papers. John leaned forward.

"Now let me see." Doc donned his gold, half-rimmed reading glasses. "Where did I put that note? Ah! Here it is."

He held up a legal pad, flipping through several sheets before stopping to read. His voice took on the interrogative tone of a trial lawyer. "In your trance, you mentioned the spirit was the root of human consciousness. And the spirit is made of this other form of energy—something you called dark-energy, to be specific."

He looked up over his glasses. "Is that correct?"

"Yes," John answered slowly. *What was he getting at?*

"You also stated the brain acts like a transceiver, implying the energy of the spirit physically interacts with the neural atomic-energy of the brain. Dark-energy provides the power that drives the brain, and thus the body, to living animation."

He hawked an accusing glare over his glasses. "So tell me about the soul-brain connection, and don't give me any technical mumbo-jumbo nonsense. I want to know for certain how an ethereal spirit can exert any force at all on the neural energy structure of the mind."

He took off his glasses and flipped them triumphantly on the desk, a man who just won his case with superior knowledge and cunning. The springs of his chair moaned as he leaned back. He laced his fingers behind his head with a smug let's-see-you-answer-that expression on his face.

John paused, gauging his motivation for such a question. Doc glared at him, ready to denounce anything John said. And that frustrated him. Not in his ability to answer the questions. He felt comfortable in that. Rather, it was Doc's unwillingness to accept the concepts necessary for the answer. It was like trying to explain DNA to someone who refused to learn biology.

Despite feelings to the contrary, John decided to test the possibility Doc might actually be willing to listen to reason. Perhaps by cooperating he might appease the bitterness festering within him.

Over the next several minutes, he reviewed the general idea how dark and atomic-energy co-exist. He described how dark-energy plays a pivotal roll in dictating the locations of those properties via what's called location nodes, a product of interference between dark matter waves. The electrons of the brain *must* migrate to those points. The movement of dark-energy spawns electrical signals in the brain that in turn animate the body to life.

John reviewed by counting off on his fingers. "Let's look at what we have so far. First, the human brain creates a field of atomic-energy unlike anything else in the universe."

He peeled back another finger. "Second, no two brains are alike. This of course implies that no two neural fields are the same. And if the neural structure is unique, we can conclude each spirit is unique as well.

"Third, the dark-energy of the soul needs the neural energy in the brain as much as the energy within the brain needs the ethereal content of the soul. They are a perfect match for each other, one for each human brain. This mutual attraction results in a tightly integrated, symbiotic bond."

Another finger counted, "Because of this bond, movement of the soul's ethereal content induces electrons to move through the brain's neural circuits.

Once resonance is achieved, the particular energized circuit causes electrical impulses to course throughout the body. Thus, the soul ultimately stimulates the brain and animates the body.

"Finally, the soul also receives data through the brain. This is the two-way radio action I referred to earlier. Any disturbance in the neural energy field caused by a stimulus from the body induces a fluctuation in the spirit, thus producing awareness of the event."

John said, "It's important to note that *the brain always responds to a stimulus, but never generates one.* Whether that stimulus is from the body or soul, the brain merely reacts to the event."

John paused, taking a moment to read Doc's stoic mask, but his poker face gave away nothing.

"Okay, let's put it all together," John said. "Let me narrate a hypothetical chain of events to illustrate how the body, brain, and soul work in concert.

"If I were to stick your finger with a pin, chemicals in the skin produce electrical impulses that go racing up nerve fibers in your arm and energize neural circuits controlling that finger. This surge in electrical activity causes a spike in your brain wave pattern. The soul, which is bonded with the brain's neural energy, senses this abrupt field change. This makes you, a spiritual being, aware of the penetration to its host biological body.

"Your first reaction is to move the finger away from the source of harm, but being a living spirit housed in an animal's body, you've got to do it by remote control. Spiritual thoughts are ethereal perturbations. Because the brain and soul are bonded, movement of ether, via location nodes, makes electrons move in the same neural circuits that then travel through the nerve fibers of your arm. This electrical signal originated by the soul then makes your muscles contract, pulling your hand from the pin."

"You forgot the impulse sent to my leg telling it to kick you in the groin." Doc chuckled.

John ignored the remark. "Now, it is common knowledge that your body works on electricity, which is the movement of electrons. You said so in your book where you identified the chemical resources the brain employs to produce electrical current.

"This is to say that every aspect of mental and physical activity is founded on the principle of electricity. But what induces the electrical potential difference that makes the electrons move?

"Most people are unaware that electrical potential in the brain actually fluctuates *prior* to the person's awareness of conscious thought. No one has yet shown why until now, but this has been clinically proven to be true. It's not until electrons start moving in a particular pattern across the brain that you become aware of it."

Doc's eyes lifted in recognition. John recalled reading a section in one of Doc's books relating that very same experiment in which a person was wired with a monitoring unit and asked to move his finger. The experiment proved that electrical potential, the force causing electrons to course throughout the brain, occurred *prior* to the subject's conscious thought to move.

John added, "In my view, brain activity occurs

prior to awareness of thought because movement in the soul's dark-energy stimulates the electrons in the brain to move. This stimulus induces neurons to release essential chemical reactions in a particular pattern via synaptic gaps to resonate that flux of energy. This preceding ethereal movement, which are spiritual fluctuations, produce the shift in the brain's electrical potential. The person doesn't gain awareness of the thought or movement until there is *resonance* within a particular neural circuit. Resonance is the key to it all."

Doc rested his chin on folded hands, studying him. After a few minutes he said, "If the soul is our source of consciousness and being, it would seem our perception could transcend our captivity imposed by the brain.

"Since the soul is ethereal, or dark, in nature, that leads me to believe it is non-dimensional, not bounded by space and time, the part of the spirit that extends beyond the mind. Therefore, if we were free of the brain's captivity we as conscious spirits would be able to experience much more. This makes me think if we weren't caged inside this atomic energy well," he tapped his head, "we could perceive more of reality than we do now."

"From what I've read in your books, I believe you're right, Doctor." John smiled encouragement. "Have you ever considered how extra sensory perception works? Or what about premonitions, dreams that come true? Mothers knowing a son or daughter is hurt the instant it happens, even though they may be separated by thousands of miles—faster than light communication. Almost everyone has had them at some point in their life. Some possess a better ability than others to detect remote or future events, but we all have the ability.

"We can do this because the soul is not trapped within the brain like a genie in a bottle. We are not locked inside our skull any more than a radio signal is trapped within the radio. The soul is non-dimensional."

"So my answer is yes?"

John nodded. "The brain is the soul's point of contact with the atomic side of reality, but that's it. The brain restricts us, to be sure, but it does not define the limit to our existence. The spirit grants human awareness but dark-energy has no form, no spatial definition. Time and distance mean nothing.

"Dark-energy is in constant contact with all of atomic space at any given time, and thus so are we. The reason we don't normally sense these remote events is because our attention is focused on the vast amounts of atomic data streaming into our minds from our eyes, ears, and other bodily senses—but it is possible. It's like trying to hear what someone is saying on the other side of a crowded party. It's possible to tune out the immediate noise, but difficult.

"However, if we could find a way to block out these dominating inputs from out atomic sensors, we should be able to perceive other events—even other realms, like the outside world. And that's why I need your machine.

"If we alter your design to my specifications, we can filter out the stimulus from this world and boost my ethereal signal at the same time. As long as the ethereal signals of your machine match mine exactly, we can establish contact not only with my spirit, but also link my mind to the machine generating this world.

"But I must repeat, the match has to be absolutely exact." He stabbed the air with an urgent finger. "If it isn't, then there will be no resonance. And without resonance, there will be no connection. However, if we do it my way, there is a good chance we'll succeed."

"Your way?" Doc sat upright. "You want me to throw away my life's work to replace it with this nonsense? If this is all you've got, then you're wasting my time. This is nothing. All you've done is read my book and thrown in some science-fiction gibberish.

"In short," he leaned forward, "I don't much care for your trumped up theory. This is nothing. Did you really think I'd fall for a ridiculous story like this?"

He slung the towel off his shoulder and slapped it against the desk. He ignored the papers sent flying. "What kind of idiot do you take me for? I'll have you know that my theories explaining life originating within the brain have been established for years.

"What's more, I have years of documented evidence to back up my ideas. Years! I've written a dozen books on the subject. And what have you got? Nothing. No degrees and no books."

He let the accusing statement hang before adding, "I respected my father. He taught me what he knew when I was but a child. His work shaped the way I approach my own research. His father did the same for him, and his father before that. What makes you think that I'm going to turn my back on my heritage for the sake of some lunatic with a good scam?"

He slammed a thick palm on the desk, littering the already cluttered floor with still more papers.

"I admit, you had me going for a while with all your baffling tales of ethereal this and energy that. But I'm on to you, mister! I know what you're up to and I am not going to let you get away with it!"

"Get away with what?"

"I will not let you steal my mind machine!" Veins bulged on his neck, his face red. "This so-called theory of yours is nothing but a ploy to get inside my lab so you can steal my device. I don't know how you found out about it, but I'll die before I let you touch that machine."

He jumped to his feet, sending his chair crashing hard against the book case behind him. He leaned across the desk to shake his finger at John. "You go back and tell your boss that."

"What boss are you talking about?" John ignored the impotent threat. "You and I both know that as of right now, your neural device is useless. You started out with a great dream, a vision to accomplish the impossible—direct connection with a human soul. But you refused to abandon your old way of thinking. Then you let another lead you in the wrong direction. Because of this, you doomed your project to failure. You're the one at fault here, Doc, not me. You must change your perspective. *You will never invent something new with old concepts.*"

Doc's eyes narrowed. His body tensed. He shook with rage. "Do you know who you're talking to? I'll have you know that I was practicing psychiatry while you were still in diapers.

"I made a good living with my practice. Why, if I had time, I'd tell you a thing or two about family honor and tradition, things you obviously know nothing about. You're nothing but a puppet, a two-bit con artist from the Mob here to destroy an honest man's life. But I won't let you. I may be old, Mr. Neumann, but I can still handle the likes of you!"

John groaned in hopeless frustration. He loathed people who had to have their ego coddled to gain cooperation. Sensing the futility of the situation, he got up and walked out of the study.

"Where are you going?" Doc demanded, but John was already gone.

Doc called again, following him as far as the office door. John stopped at the foot of the stairs and turned to look into the hard, haggard face of an old man. For a moment he almost felt sorry for him, but his patience with his rudeness had worn thin.

With clipped, measured tones he spoke through clenched teeth, "Doctor Lazlow, I now know the circuit arrangements, the firing rates, and the property densities that can effectively simulate the neural activity of a normal brain. I know what materials are needed to create these properties and I know how to wire it all to your computer. Given the right programming, we can tune these circuits to my brain's natural frequencies. Just let me work with you. We will make direct contact with my ethereal spirit. I guarantee it.

"Don't you see?" John relaxed a bit, taking a fervent step toward him. "I can give you the answers you've been looking for your whole life. That's right. Mary told me everything about you. But there's no need to repeat the unfulfilled legacy of your fathers. I can help you succeed where they failed. The only way you can give David the knowledge he'll need when it is his turn to step onto the world stage is for you to prove that the soul is real. Doesn't that mean anything? Don't you care what happens to him?"

There was no reaction, not even a blink.

"Dr. Lazlow, both of us have personal objectives here, but only by combining our efforts can either of us succeed. You want validation the spirit is real by making direct contact with it. I need to connect my spirit with the Genesis Machine. Working together, we both win."

He took another step closer. "But I'm frustrated, man! We're wasting time arguing when there is so much work to do. Please, I implore you, let me help you. Will you do that?"

Doc's blazing blue eyes burned for a long, hard moment. A grandfather clock chimed, its steady bongs beating cadence to the tense silence. He never answered John's question. When he finally spoke, it was with a nasty sneer. "Why does it have to be your spirit we connect to? Why can't we connect to mine like I planned?"

John waited a few seconds before speaking. And when he did, it was with subdued anger. Doc knew the answer. He just wanted to throw one more verbal jab at John.

"Forget about my need of the Genesis Machine for the moment," John said. "Let's talk about you. If the ethereal signals we generate do not match that of your brain exactly, it could overexcite your neural circuits, damaging them beyond repair. It could kill you, Doc. On the other hand, you could wind up in an incapacitated, vegetative state. Are you prepared to take that risk? Are you willing to risk your family?"

Lazlow's eyes glared.

John knew then that whatever they once had was gone. Doc turned on a heel and slammed the door, locking it behind him. The sound of that lock was a deafening condemnation. As long as a barrier stood between them, they didn't have a chance—and Doc held the only key.

John turned to ascend the stairs, his feet jabbing each step. Doc wasn't behaving normally, he consoled himself. Mary was right; Logan had some kind of control over him that he did not yet comprehend. And as long as he remained under that influence, Doc was going to resist everything John said. At the time, he had no way of knowing how deadly that resistance would be.

Chapter 16

Nick Fishetti climbed the seven brick steps of the Lazlow house and knocked on the front door. No one answered. He pounded harder, the sweat from his fist leaving their mark on the aged wood. On his final attempt, the door rattled from the violent impact.

Impatiently, he went to the window and was about to break in when he heard movement inside the house. Locks turned, a deadbolt thrown, and Mary opened the door.

"Yes?" She peered through the narrow opening. "May I help you?"

Fishetti produced a badge and credentials from his hiker's uniform.

"My name is Sergeant Fishetti, Special Force Unit. This is Corporal Miller. We'd like to come inside, if you don't mind."

Mary nervously glanced over her shoulder. She slipped outside and closed the door. Her tone was brave, matter of fact. "As a matter of fact, I do mind, Sergeant. I'm not about to let you two ransack my house."

Then she pointed and laughed. "Those are cute uniforms you're wearing. When did Logan's Storm Troopers start wearing these little hiking shorts? Are the suspenders standard issue?"

Fishetti instantly tensed, but held his temper. His face burned red.

"Move aside, Miss Lazlow," he said through clenched teeth. He reached for the doorknob. "We have orders to search every house in this vicinity."

"Not this house you don't!" Mary stepped in his way.

The sudden rise in tension was startling.

"What did you say?" Fishetti's voice was barely audible.

"Are you aware of the research project Governor Logan is conducting here?"

That made Fishetti stop. Mary knew Fishetti had accompanied Logan on many of his visits to the house. On each occasion, the Governor always instructed him to wait outside for reasons of national security.

"This house comes under state code 57-429-C, declaring this property to be off limits to all unauthorized personnel," Mary declared, her chin lifted high. "It states that no one, repeat, no one shall enter these premises without the expressed and written authorization from the Governor himself. Now, unless I miss my guess, you boys don't have that consent form, do you?"

She looked Fishetti in the eye. "Don't misunderstand me, Sergeant. I'm aware of the manhunt your department is conducting and I understand your need to conduct such a search. However, your authority granting you the right to tear apart people's homes does not supersede my orders to protect the integrity of this research site. Governor

Logan was extremely precise when he gave me my instructions.

"Now, I know you boys are much bigger than I am and would have no problem forcing your way inside. But if you do, rest assured that I will report your actions to Jack the next time he comes to visit me."

When Fishetti did not respond, Mary smiled. "I thought you would see things my way," she said. "Now, if you have something to ask, we can talk right here. What is it you want to know?"

Fishetti turned his back and stared at the stone walkway, his fist shaking as he tried to control his fury. Finally, he turned on Mary, who stood squarely in the middle of the doorway, her arms crossed.

Fishetti spoke through yellowed teeth, his eyes glaring. "Who was with you on the trail today?"

Mary never blinked. "I was with my son, David. We take a walk almost every day. Why?"

"Who else was with you?" He stepped closer, fists still clenched.

"No one, just David and myself."

"You can stop with the games, sister!" Miller said. "We know someone else was with you and it wasn't your old man, either. We saw another set of footprints in the sand, a man's footprints. Now who was it?"

"Footprints?" Mary gasped, her eyes wide. "Someone else was there? Oh, my God! Are you sure?"

"Absolutely. And they were right beside yours."

"They were?" Mary's lips trembled. "Oh, my

goodness! Is it that man you're looking for? I saw the news report. He's some sort of terrorist, isn't he? A murderer? Oh, dear Lord, was it him?"

She shivered, uncrossing and re-crossing her arms while working up a worried frown. "He, he must have been waiting for us in the bushes, watching us every minute, stalking us."

Fishetti and Miller exchanged looks.

Mary faced them. "You know something? I thought someone was following us, but I wasn't sure."

"Why do you think that?" Fishetti said.

"Well, for one I kept hearing things. You know, breaking twigs or rustling leaves like someone was in the woods. David and I got scared and hid in the rocks at Rock Hill. We heard footsteps on the stone. Oh, he was so close. It was terrible. I was so scared!"

She stepped close, grasping Fishetti's muscular arm. "Sergeant! Please, don't leave us here alone. He may still be out there, lurking in the trees waiting for you to leave. If you go, our lives may be in danger!"

Fishetti pulled his arm away with malicious contempt. "I'm afraid we can't do that, Miss Lazlow. Us Storm Troopers, as you referred to my unit, are not responsible for your personal safety. However, if you see anyone suspicious just call 911. The Sheriff's Office will send someone out."

With that, the two men marched down the steps.

Mary called after them, "But they're so far away. It will take at least half an hour for anyone to get here. We could all be dead by then. At least send someone to protect us."

Fishetti turned with a smug sneer. "We don't have the manpower for that right now. But I intend to ask Governor Logan for permission to search this house. It remains the only house in the area that has not been investigated."

With that, he and Miller turned onto the trail heading back to town.

Mary watched them go, deep worry crinkling her forehead. She watched until they were out of sight, then went back in and locked the door.

~~~

"Search the Lazlow house?" Logan said. "Absolutely not! They are working on a special project of mine and no one is allowed inside. You got that? No one."

"But you ordered it, Governor," Lieutenant Carpenter said. "You said to search every house."

"Not that one. Leave it alone. Mary was right in standing firm. That's one of the reasons I admire that girl. She can be, shall I say, rather strong when it comes to that sort of thing.

"Besides, I can't afford for my top secret project to get out. So leave it alone. And no one is allowed to question them, either. Tell the men, including Fishetti, that the Lazlows are to be left alone."

"But they saw footprints."

"It could be anybody's," Logan shrugged. "Fishetti was wrong."

"But he seemed so sure."

"He's just being over zealous. He's been known to be that way, you know. If Mary says no one was there then I believe her. Just leave that house to me. I will be going there in a few days myself to, uh, inspect their progress on my project. I will personally search the premises when I go there."

"Then what should we do? She asked for a few men to stand guard over the house," Carpenter said.

"That won't be necessary. I'm sure the man we're looking for is miles away. Most likely hiding in the city or just outside of it. He would never suspect a small residence in the middle of nowhere to have a computer powerful enough to do what he came to do. What would he have to gain by stalking them? The footprints Fishetti saw was just another hiker. I'm sure of it. They're all over the place up there. Hunting that man by footprints is unreliable in that part of the park."

"Whatever you say, sir," Carpenter consented. "What should we do with the rest of the men? We've completed the search of that area and found nothing."

"Then split them up. Have half of them start with Rock Hill and go south."

"But sir, we've done that twice already."

"Then do it again, Lieutenant! He's bound to be there somewhere. Assign the others to help with the house-to-house search in the city. I'm positive he's headed here—if he's not here already."

"Are you sure, sir?"

Logan instantly turned furious. "Do not question my orders, Lieutenant! Just follow them. That's your job."

"Yes, sir." Carpenter saluted and was about to leave.

"Carpenter."

The lieutenant turned around.

"Have Captain Petra report to my office. I'm not satisfied with the progress of the search. It's been over a week now. We should have found some trace, some hint by now. The man couldn't have vanished into thin air. I want him to redouble his efforts. Put some men in the woods surrounding the city. That's possibly where he's camped out while he scouts the town. Find more men if he has to, but this man has got to be brought to justice."

"Yes, sir. Anything else, sir?"

"Yes. You said you scoured the cliff base and found nothing. No trace whatsoever? No clothes, no blood, nothing?"

"No sir. But with the storm we had that night, any trace would have been washed out to sea. The choppers searched everywhere from the point of impact to five miles in both directions and five miles out in a tight search pattern. There was nothing, sir. Absolutely nothing."

"Keep at it. I want no stone unturned. If he is out there, he may have swum ashore outside of your search grid. I want you to widen it and try again. The tide came in later that night. He may be closer than you think."

"Yes, sir. Anything else, sir?"

"No. Just have Petra here as soon as possible. I have some things I need to review with him, too."

"Sir," Carpenter saluted, and left the office.

Chapter 17

The next few days were uneventful. Mary never said another word about that day on the trail and John didn't ask. With the exception of her father, who maintained his distance, everything seemed normal.

Mary told John of Fishetti's visit. From that point on, John never left the house but that Mary or David didn't check the surrounding forest first. While at home, he kept away from the windows and tried to placate Doc as much as possible.

For the most part, he stayed in his room, trying to keep a low profile from Doc as much as anyone who might be watching the house. But being confined to his room often got to him. That is when he took a chance and studied in another part of the house. It was on one of those occasions that Logan walked through the front door without so much as a knock.

"Mary? Mary, where are you?" Logan called.

John and Mary were in the white piano room adjacent to the foyer going through his notes. John instantly dove for the floor, using the couch for cover while Mary hurriedly collected his hand written pages.

"I'm over here," she answered his call.

John saw the worry in her eyes. She rose, trying to lure Logan away from the music room, but the effort failed.

John saw Logan's feet coming his way and he strained to slide beneath the sofa.

"Where have you been?" Mary asked, casting a nervous glance at John's leg as it disappeared from view. She looked up, pasting a thin smile. "You normally come here a lot more. I haven't seen you for days."

"I've been busy, my sweet," he said. "This business of finding the terrorist has me up to my neck with work. I've taken personal control of the manhunt from Captain Petra. He's an incompetent fool. When your project is over, things will get a lot better around here with me in total control of this world. But I have missed you. That's why I took time out of my busy schedule to drive all the way out here just to see you."

"Well, you shouldn't have," Mary said. Her feet shuffled when Logan sat down on the couch. She hurriedly indicated the papers in her hands. "Maybe later might be good. As you can see, I have a lot of work to do."

"What kind of work?" Logan's voice took on an urgent tone. "I gave orders not to do anything to that computer without my specific direction or approval!"

"I was going to show it to you when I finished. I thought I had a way to tweak the programming, but it's nothing really. A waste of time."

Logan grabbed the stack of papers. "What are you doing?" he demanded. "You're hiding something."

Mary's voice trembled. "Like I said, it's just something I thought might help. After going through it, though, I don't think it will work. That's, uh, that's why I haven't told you about it yet. No use wasting your time with nonsense. I know how busy you are. Trust me. I wouldn't have done anything without your permission. I was just trying to be proactive, that's all. Really."

Logan hesitated. He shuffled through the papers again before handing them back to Mary. "That's not your handwriting."

"Oh sure it is. You've just never seen my chicken scratch when I'm in a hurry. I had ideas flitting through my head and I had to get them down fast as I could. I usually rewrite them before I submit them to you for approval. You know that."

Logan paused, watching her shift from foot to foot. "I admire your initiative," he finally said. "I'm sorry I snapped at you. I've just been under a lot of pressure lately."

He then abruptly changed the subject. "Mind if I look around? I'd like to check on your progress. And it's been so long since we've been alone. Why don't we take a stroll through the house and we'll talk about these changes you're thinking about. I might like them. Plus, I want to see the computer again. I have a few more ideas I'd like you to implement."

With that, the two of them left, leaving John alone beneath the couch. He stayed there for hours, listening to their idle conversation as Logan went from room to room, commenting on the decorations and beauty of the house. But John knew what he was up to. *It's a good thing Doc isn't here*, he thought. There was no telling what that old man might say.

After what seemed an eternity, Logan and Mary came back to the lobby laughing about something.

John could see their feet.

"Okay, then," he said. "I'll leave you alone to continue your work. And don't worry. I've ordered my men to stay away from here. That will give you the privacy you need to continue your work unimpeded. I can't stress enough how fast I need your neural device to be up and running. I need it operational within a month."

"A month?" Mary repeated. "That's not much time. Why do you need it so soon?"

"Don't worry about that," he said. "You just make the changes I specified."

"Ok. I'll tell Father when he comes back."

"Yes, where is the old man?"

"Oh, he's on one of his walks. He should be back in a while."

"Oh, well, that gives us a little more time, doesn't it? We are all alone. How about that kiss I've been waiting for? You've put it off long enough. It's about time you and I got more acquainted."

Mary pulled away. "Not now Jack, not now. I'm . . . I'm just not ready yet. You know with Paul and all. I just need a little more time. Please, you must understand that."

"It's been long enough," Logan said, coming closer. "It's time to stop being the grieving widow."

"I know, but I'm having a tough time of it." She wiggled away. "Just give me a little more time. I'll come around. I promise. Just a little more time."

Logan said nothing. He was an impatient man, but best not to pressure her at this point. After a brief moment, he agreed and left the house.

Mary instantly ran to the music room. "John? John, are you okay?"

Neumann crawled from under the couch, stretching his cramped muscles. "Yes, I'm fine. That was a close call. How often does he do that, just come into the house like that?"

"Not as much as he used to, thank Goodness." Mary handed him his notes. "Still, there's no telling when he'll pop up. I'm afraid that's going to be a problem."

"I wish we had a way to give us more warning. If I had been in my room today, he would have found me for sure."

"Yes," she said. "He even checked the closets. I'm sure he was looking for you. Though Lord knows why he would look for you here."

"Probably your argument with Fishetti. Plus, that pet project of yours is critical to his plans to take over this world."

"What do you mean? He said he needed it operational in a month. I thought it was just an experiment to prove the soul exists. But then he said something about world control. What's going on? I know why you need it, but why does he need it in a month?"

"He needs to beat me to the punch. That's not just a neural simulator you're working on," John said. "Once you've proved you can make the connection with a human soul, he plans to use the device to control people's mind. If it becomes operational under his design, he can control everyone here like a robot, make them do anything he wants. With a machine like that in his power, there's no telling what he can do.

Ruling the world would be child's play, and he can do it all from here."

"Oh, my God! I never dreamed of that."

"That's another reason why I have to stop your father and alter his programming to what I've sketched out in these notes. We've got to change his current design to work with my spirit, not Logan's.

"By the way, what do you think about your father? Is he still willing to hide me? We were just lucky today he wasn't here. But what if Logan was to question him?"

Mary shook her head. "I don't know. I'm worried about that, too. He sees you as a threat, but says he hasn't made up his mind. When you turned him down to join his vigilante group, he just got hurt. I think that's most of it. But something about you intrigues him. At least you've got that going for you.

"I think he may still be holding out hope he can change your mind. So if he ever brings it up again, maybe you should play along. Make him think you're interested in the group. You know, just to keep him appeased. If you do, he's bound to agree to hide you a while longer. It may give me enough time to work on him from the other side and convince him to let you in on his project."

~~~

Throughout the coming days, Logan came by several more times and each time John had to duck into a closet or behind a convenient piece of furniture, trusting Mary to lure him away. So far, he had been lucky. Still, it was only a matter of time before one of Logan's surprise visits caught him in the open. Then it would all be over. All his planning, all his preparations, his hiding out, would be for naught.

John tried Mary's advice to play along with Doc's idea of joining his vigilante group without actually committing to it. It was a tight line, but it was enough to keep Doc at bay. Yet as the days passed and John made no outright effort to participate, Doc's attitude grew ever more distrusting and combative—though he never turned him in.

To her credit, Mary fought hard to keep her father from doing so, but this came at a steep price. Eventually, tensions rose to the point that Doc forbid her from speaking to John. From that point, if Mary and John wanted to talk, they had to sneak out of the house and rendezvous in the forest.

Despite the stress, it was those times together John cherished most. They would sit on the side of the cliff, feet dangling, holding hands as they experienced the sunrise together. The ocean scenes were breathtaking. Each morning, the sky was decorated with fabulous colors that seemed to have been invented just that morning. He loved to hear her laugh and feel the warmth of her body next to his.

Doc began avoiding John. Mary said it was getting harder to convince her father to let him stay. It wasn't long before Doc sequestered Mary with him in his lab, forcing her to work long hours on his machine in an effort to meet Logan's timeline—or was it to keep her away from John? With David in the last days of school, John was left totally alone.

It was during those long and lonely times that he reflected on the revelations of his dream. He spent time deriving the technical programming details of its message in the hope that Doc would one day come to his senses. The time to connect with Genesis was drawing closer each passing day. If Mary could ever convince Doc to let him into the lab, John wanted to be prepared.

He desperately needed to get his hands on that computer, but he played the waiting game he was forced to play. To do otherwise would have taxed Doc's eroding tolerance to the breaking point. And so John waited, trying to feed him suggestions through Mary. But from what she whispered when they were alone, Doc adamantly refused any idea that varied from his determined path. The project was still going nowhere and the Genesis clock was ticking. Every passing day brought the world closer to destruction if he could not modify that machine.

Late one evening, John figured out the firing circuit programming that could effectively control the new computer design. He was excited, to say the least. For days on end he had been searching for the right approach and he was certain he finally found it. To be sure, however, he wanted Mary's opinion. He valued her mind. He hurried down the hallway to her room, reviewing his notes as he went.

He was about to knock on her door when he stopped and leaned close. Angry voices came from inside.

". . . I tell you, I don't trust this guy," Doc shouted. "We should throw him out of here. Turn him over to Logan. We should do it now, while we have the chance. If Logan finds out we've been hiding him, there's no telling what he will do."

"How could you possibly think of throwing him out? John still doesn't know who he is. His body may be healing, but he only has bits of memory. If you throw him out, where could he go? With everyone searching for him, he'll be dead before he can reach the city. He needs us, Father. And whether you admit it or not, we need him, too."

Mary's voice softened as she changed tactics. "Why don't you trust him, Father? What has he done wrong?"

The subtle ploy had its effect. The edge came off Doc's harsh attack. He breathed a heavy sigh. "Days ago, I asked him to, well, join my fighting group. But he turned me down cold. The coward walked away like he couldn't care less! And then a few days ago he starts acting like he's interested again, but he never commits.

"I tell you, Mary, nothing about him adds up. He says he's here to help us and yet he refuses to. As for my project, he knows too much for a man with amnesia. Neural simulation is a top secret project and yet it's all he's talked about since he came here. And he won't be satisfied until he gets his hands on it.

"Personally, I think this whole thing has been one big setup. I wouldn't be surprised if his injuries were self-inflicted to gain our sympathy. And his energy ideas are nothing but a ploy to work his way into our trust. If you ask me, he's working for the mafia. Yes, that's right. You heard me. I don't know how they found out about it, but they would do just about anything to have my computer."

"Oh, and how would you know that, the mafia, I mean?"

"Logan told me. That's why he moved us so far out of town. Jack says the isolation makes it easier to protect us, and you know he's doing everything he can to do that. You should be thankful, Mary. If it wasn't for Jack Logan, we would have nothing. The Mob could have killed us all and taken control of our computer a long time ago if it wasn't for him. And you know what that could mean. The power they could wield, the destruction, it's unthinkable."

"Oh, Father! Do you honestly think the Mob is concerned about the existence of the soul?"

"It's not just the soul. It's what they could do with it. That's what Logan told me. And now consider Neumann. I'm becoming more and more convinced they're trying to steal my ideas by his trickery. That's why he's here. I said it before and I'll say it again; beaten up, he played on our sympathy, assuring we would bring him inside our house.

"I've watched him. When he's alone, he pretends to be working on the house fixing things here and there. Oh, it sounds nice, but he's actually casing the place, looking for my lab. And when he finds it, you can bet he'll kill us and be gone before anyone suspects a thing. He's already found my stash of guns. Lord help us! For all we know, we could be dead by morning!"

"Oh, Father!" Mary sounded exasperated. "Really?"

"Don't try to convince me otherwise." Doc said. "His smile is a nice disguise, but he's with the Mob. If what you tell me is true about what our machine can actually do, probe and even control people's thoughts, the exploitation possibilities are limitless! I can't afford for that to happen. Not with him, anyway.

"You think his friends are ruthless now. Humph! Ruthless doesn't come close to describing what they'd be like. If the Mob gets my computer, they could scan your innermost secrets, make you do what they want you to do—even make you kill for them. Then you'll know what ruthless can be!"

"How can you even begin to think John is working for Logan?" Mary sounded incredulous. "Logan is trying to kill him!"

"Who said anything about Logan?" Doc snapped.

"Who do you think controls the crime here? Jack has been masterminding what you call the Mob for years. He's the one who started altering your computer. John just wants to bring it back to its original design, the one you abandoned the minute you let Logan into your life."

"Stop changing the subject! Jack Logan is doing everything in his power to wipe out organized crime and you can't convince me otherwise. Check the record. He spends millions of dollars each year. He even gets personally involved with his own Special Force Unit. He makes dozens of arrests each week. With all he's doing to stop the Mob, how can you say he controls it? That doesn't make sense. Why would he fight against himself?"

"Oh, when are you going to wake up to reality?" Mary's sarcasm was clearly evident. "Those arrests are just to placate the Press and make Jack look good. They're petty criminals who work for him.

"And speaking of Logan's Special Force Unit,

why does he have over fifty people? Does a state governor need that much protection? Has it ever occurred to you their true function is to enforce his criminal wishes?

"You've seen his house. Tell me how he could afford a three million dollar home on a governor's salary? He gets a cut off every drug deal, that's how. If you want protection around here, you have to buy him off. Surely, you've seen that by now."

"I don't know." Doc faltered. "I don't want to go through all of that with you again . . . but if John is not one of them . . . well, how could he have known about Alice? I've never mentioned her to anyone since we've been here. He must have inside information."

Mary was not the type to quit easily. "That's my point! Who's going to have a personnel file describing how Mom used to bake cookies, pinch your stomach, and blow you kisses? Certainly not the Mob. Jack wouldn't, either. They only way John could have known about Mom is if he is what he says he is, and he came from where he said he did."

Doc fell silent and Mary continued with tenacity. "I checked public records. There's no trace of a John Neumann. If this place is a virtual world like he says, and he's from the outside, then that could explain how knows about Mom. It explains how he knows about our project, about this new form of energy. It explains everything. Think about it. It makes sense."

She paused. John pictured her steeling herself for what she was about to say. "I believe John is the one Paul prophesied would come to save us. And he can save us. That's why he's here. He just needs to do it in a way we did not expect and you're too stubborn to accept that."

Doc exploded in furious rage. "No! That's a lie! And I won't hear you mention it again! Do you hear me, Mary?" There was a second of silence before he yelled, "Did he tell you that?"

"No, but it's true. I can sense it in the way he talks, the way he knows so much about how the world and soul are made and how they all link together. Everything he says makes sense. If you would only listen to him, you would know what I mean."

"That's not it," Doc stated. "You've fallen in love with him. That's why you believe him. You believe him because you want to believe him. But me, I'm not blinded by his charms. He's a lying devil and in the end he will get us killed! We should have left him alone, Mary. We never should have gotten involved."

A tense stillness hung in the room before the conversation resumed. This time, his tone was weaker, more subdued, like a defeated old man.

"Mary, you know our financial problems." He groaned. John heard the faint creak of bedsprings. "Our only way out of debt is for you to marry Logan. He's rich, he's powerful, and he's going places. Jack's done a lot for us, and he's promised to do so much more if you marry him.

"I can get my neural simulator to work, I know it. I just need more money, that's all. And Logan promised to give us all we need. Plus, I'd be assured of a high-level position when he becomes President—and he will become President. I'll be on his medical advisory staff. He promised me that. But what can

John do for us? What can he give us? Nothing!

"I admit I can't prove John's in with the Mob," he continued. "That and your persistence on the subject are the only two reasons I let him stay, why I haven't turned him in. But he's up to something and I don't like it. That's why I say proof or no proof, the time has come we throw him out. You know how critical our project is. It's better safe than sorry and I don't feel safe with him around."

"Father, listen to what you're saying," Mary pleaded. "Listen to what I'm saying. If John isn't what he says, would he know these energy theories he's trying to teach us? If he wasn't genuine, would he know what an ethereal field was – not to speak how to set one up?

"Don't you see? If he was trying to steal it, the man would be pumping us for information. Instead, he's trying to give us our answers! Would the Mob do that?"

Her only answer was silence.

"I don't think so, either," she replied for him. "If he wanted to kill us, he would have done so by now. He's had plenty of opportunities. If he were a spy, he'd be demanding information, not patiently waiting for you to talk to him again. If he were any of the things you claim, he would be trying to force his way in."

"Well, what about him turning me down?"

"You mean that stupid vigilante group of yours? If you'd asked me, I would have turned you down too. Does that make me bad? John turned you down because he doesn't want to kill anybody. He said next time he comes things will be different. But for now, he has something better, a more important way to help us.

"This world is infected. This world is dying. By connecting his mind to the outside world, he can find the way to get us out of here. But to make contact, he needs your computer. And you're endangering millions of people's lives by rejecting him."

"Find a way out?" It was Doc's turn to be sarcastic. "Virus ridden world? That sort of thing is nonsense. There is no outer world. If there were, don't you think we would have found it by now? So just get over it. I'm not endangering anyone or anything. You're just sticking up for him because you're a love sick whore."

Mary took a startled breath. The verbal slap must have hurt her. There was a slight pause, and then she said with heavy bitterness, "Okay, fair is fair. You've bared your soul. Now it's my turn.

"The way I see it, the reason you want to get rid of John has nothing to do with his refusing to join your petty band of rebels. You hate him because he knows more about your project than you do. You're afraid if you let John in your lab, he will prove your theories are outdated and moving in the wrong direction—and you'd be right.

"Face it. Ever since you let Logan take charge, we've been getting nowhere. This project has been dead for years. We're no closer to proving the reality of the soul than we were five years ago. The only reason we're still on this dead horse is because of Logan and because you're too stubborn to admit the two of you are wrong.

"When are you going to realize that *if what you*

continually tried before doesn't work, you've got to try something new? John's theories can breathe new life into your dream and make it come alive. Yes, his ideas are radical. Sure, you've never heard anything like them before. But maybe, just maybe, radical ideas are what we need to succeed.

"We can still do this, Father, but only if you drop your stupid ego and pride. Stop blocking him out. If you kick him out, you're never going to succeed. You're going to fail like you have a thousand times before."

She must have hurt the old man because he countered as if he didn't hear a word she said. When he spoke, the words came slow, thick with jealousy. "Well, I still think he's playing us for fools. But if he thinks he can get the better of me, then he's sadly mistaken. I'm the only one around here who hasn't been fooled by his lies. Someday you'll understand what I'm talking about. Someday you'll thank me for protecting you."

There was another long pause followed by the soft creak of bed springs. "Mary, maintaining the social status of our family is more important than John Neumann. We have a heritage to consider here and John is a stranger from nowhere. We hardly know him. We can't afford to sacrifice what little we have for the likes of him. He has too many secrets, too many unknowns for me to risk everything. The stakes are too high.

"You know the money is gone. Since my retirement from the University, I've lost everything. All my investments—gone. If it weren't for Logan's money, I wouldn't have a computer, a house, or even be eating three meals a day. Do you hear what I'm saying? I am broke.

"I owe Logan my life, Mary. The University Board didn't believe in me. The only one who's ever believed in me if Jack. With Logan, our future is secure. Without him . . .

"I'm too old to find another job. Mary, Jack Logan is our best chance to regain our identity, to return to what we once were. When you and I are gone, David will continue our legacy. But if he inherits nothing . . ."

There was a pregnant pause before he uttered, "You were promised to Logan. Marry him. It is the best way."

John quietly retreated to his room and closed the door. This was bad. He never suspected Doc's hatred ran so deep. With his frame of mind, he would never accept changes to his design. And if he didn't do that, they were all doomed.

He sat on the edge of the bed, confused by his twisted logic—but emotional responses are not subject to the logic of rational thought. When emotions dictate one's decisions, their distortions preclude accurate analysis of facts. And his mind was definitely wrapped in too much emotion to hope for reason.

That must be how Logan is controlling him, he thought. Somehow, Logan had wormed his way into Doc's mind and got his thoughts so muddled with pride and passion that the truth was now impossible to see. John had to find a way through that mental barrier, if only for a moment. If he could do that, he knew Doc would see the light. He had to.

John laid on the bed, hands folded behind his neck, and stared blindly at the ceiling. Darkness breathed through the open window, the ocean air thick and humid. His mind raced, desperate for a solution as he drifted off to sleep.

That night, he had a dream. The images were strange and yet strikingly real. At first, he didn't understand what it meant. In hindsight, he wished he had.

In the dream, he saw a huge beast floating above the Earth, conquering all it surveyed. The creature was ghastly. It was half human, and yet to his eyes it was not a man. Its face was grotesquely deformed and resembled a rabid wolf with small, maniacal eyes of malevolence. It had four claws like that of a bear. In its fangs was the rotting, decayed flesh of the human carcasses it consumed.

The beast went wherever it wished, breathing pain and destruction on whoever stood against it. With strange powers it annihilated all opposition, destroying everything in its path. And what it did not destroy, it gathered to itself. The people gave themselves to the beast willingly, openly, and with great desire.

The beast was hideous, but no one would see that. They ignored its bloody fangs and vied with one another to do it homage. They worshiped the beauty of its power and performed all manner of degrading services in hope of receiving its favor. Though some tried, no one could kill it. And after a while, no one wanted to. The beast had become their chosen king.

A star fell from Heaven. Rumors began of one who could destroy the beast, a baby child born with power to return people to their stolen soul. And yet the people were not pleased, content with their chosen lord.

The king was enraged at the news and started a host of wars, killing all in search of this child, the babe that threatened his sovereign reign. The beast coerced the unsuspecting people to fight, which they did with vigor, betraying and killing each other with religious fervor. Only a few survived who understood the truth. Though forced into hiding, they maintained their stand against the king.

And so despite the efforts of the beast, the one who had been foretold came under the cover of darkness. The beast charged forth with a mighty force to crush the newborn threat, but a woman with wings of an eagle swooped from the sky and snatched the infant from its clutches. She flew deep into the wilderness and there hid the babe until such time that his power was strong enough to fight the beast, and to prevail.

The creature was furious. It feared the boy's power and razed the land, desperate to kill this chosen one. The beast opened its mouth and issued forth a flood of terror against those who might nurture the infant. It was a flood the woman drank.

And the beast came toward this house with death in his eyes. As it approached, the creature transformed into the image of a man, draped in expensive robes. His image was perfect, beautiful. And when he smiled, gleaming teeth flashed in dazzling array. But his eyes! His eyes were black as death, echoing the wailing of a lifeless soul.

The man-king came forward, seeking to solve

the mystery shrouding the chosen child. But alas, Doc held no answers. He fell before the king, crying out to the beautiful one. "I do not know the child whom you seek, my lord. However, I have one request I implore of you. A man has come into my house. This man is a thief. He schemes to steal all that is yours. With charm he enchants my family against me. He has entranced my daughter and treats David as his own."

The beast snarled at the old man's approach, jealous for the woman. "What else have you not told me?"

Lazlow's white beard scraped lower to the ground. "My lord, you truly know all. The man claims no past but preaches a new form of energy. I fear it is a ruse to gain my inner lab and there perform his deeds of destruction. With clever words he changes my theories that took generations to build. He seeks to alter my holy computer. And when he does, he will surely kill me."

"This energy," the dark one demanded, "does it speak of the soul?"

"Why yes, my lord." Lazlow's head rose. "How did you know that?"

"Bring him to me at once!" The beast roared. Lazlow immediately lowered his face. "If you do not, he will tear down your house and build another. He will steal your heritage to himself. The mother of your heir will stand by his side. She will leave, taking her son with her, and nothing you have will remain."

He pointed a gleaming scepter to lift Lazlow's head. "Do not let Mary know our plan. This man's spell is strong and word of this will only strengthen her resolve against us. Then I could not have her. And if she is not mine, you will not live in the mansion I promised."

The beast tapped the scepter against his hand. Seven times, he struck his open palm, grasping it again on the eighth. "This is what you shall say: the man is wanted for murder. At the noon hour, my men will come into your house. Be sure this man is there."

A beast-like snarl curled his thin lips as he finished with a warning. "Keep clear if you do not want to get hurt. And do not interfere."

"As you command, my lord," Lazlow said with quivering voice. "The man is in the upper room at the noon hour. For this, you have my eternal gratitude."

John awoke with a start, sitting upright in the bed. His shirt was soaked with sweat. He frantically looked left and right, expecting to see Logan's men surrounding him, actually surprised he was alone. The dream seemed so real.

After a few minutes, he shrugged the nightmare to the back of his mind, hoping it was just subliminal fear. He was not a superstitious person, but he did make it a point to be more cautious of Doctor Lazlow from that moment on.

The next afternoon, he chose to do his studying in the ocean-side cave. He tried telling himself he wanted some fresh air, but who was he kidding? The dream scared him. He didn't know what it meant, but he was taking no chances.

When he returned home, he did so cautiously, watching the house from the protection of the surrounding forest for almost half an hour. He saw no one. Finally, chastising himself for being naive, he rose and went inside.

They came the next day.

The Awakening

Chapter 18

John was in his room putting the finishing touches on the circuit logic for the simulator's firing controls when he heard a knock on the front door. Mary burst into his room in a wild panic.

"It's Logan! This time he brought his troops with him."

He snatched up all his notes and followed her out of the room. As he fumbled to keep the mess of papers from falling, she grabbed his arm and pulled him toward the front door.

Instinctively, John held back, wondering why she would take him *toward* Logan and his men. She felt his resistance and pulled harder. The flash in her eyes screamed urgency was vital if he was going to survive that day. He had to trust her, and so he submitted to her persistence and fell in step. They were descending the upper stairs when the beast beat the front door again. The booming echoes died slowly in the vast foyer.

They slipped around the foyer floor corner and then down the basement stairway. Mary's eyes never stopped moving. She paused on the broad landing to feel the grooved wooden wall with the finger tips with her right hand. Her left still embraced John's. Finding a concealed switch, she pressed it and a section of the wall moved inward to reveal a small, dark room beyond.

"Come in here. You'll be safe. They won't find you," she whispered. She unscrewed the overhead light, pulled him close, and latched the panel shut.

The cramped chamber was lit by faint sunlight filtering through a wall mounted vent. But even in the tense desperation of that moment, he couldn't help but notice her intoxicating perfume and the freshness of her auburn hair.

"Why is he knocking?" he murmured in her ear. "Doesn't he normally just barge in?"

"Door's locked." She placed an ear to the wall.

John fell silent.

Another thundering knock sounded throughout the house. Doctor Lazlow must have been close behind them because no sooner had they closed the panel than his footsteps clicked across the hard, white tile of the foyer above. His steps were quick and shuffling.

Fortunately, David was still at school.

Doc called out in a hoarse whisper, "Mary? Mary! Where are you?"

A final impatient rap threatened to shake the door from its hinges. Seconds later, John heard it unlock and open.

"Good afternoon, General," Doctor Lazlow's voice trembled. "What a surprise! Yes, a surprise. Come on in. Come on in. It's a pleasure to see you again."

Logan's chilling voice pierced the darkened walls of John's hiding place. Mary gripped his left arm and nestled close against his side. The voice was deep and rich and spoken in the precise manner of one who chafes at being cordial to those less important than him.

"Good afternoon, Doctor. May we come inside?"

Before Doc could reply, the sound of many heavy boots ran through the open door. They pounded up the steps and then quickly faded down the upstairs hallway.

"Yes! Yes, come in! Come in . . . What's wrong?"

Mary and John looked at each other, knowing what was coming next.

The distant sound of splintering wood signaled the destruction of John's bedroom door. This was followed by the crash and tumble of broken furniture. After a momentary pause in the violence, they heard quick steps overhead.

A strong voice near the upstairs handrail reported to the foyer below, "No sign of him in the room, sir! He's not here."

"*What?*" It was Logan.

John envisioned Doc cowering in fear.

"Search every room, Fishetti!" Logan commanded. "I want that man found at once."

"Sir!"

Logan's voice called out. "Lieutenant Carpenter, set up a perimeter around this house. We know he's here. Do not let him escape!"

Another series of running footsteps. Only then did Logan turn his attention to the old man. He spoke loud, as if wanting anyone in the house to hear. "We are looking for a terrorist. He was shot while trying to escape a few weeks ago. He is injured, perhaps critically. He could not have traveled far in his condition.

"My men have checked all other houses in the area. Yours is the only place we have yet to inspect."

His disgust at having to ask Doc for anything was resoundingly obvious. John was baffled by the show of cordiality. Perhaps Logan knew Mary was listening and needed a cover for the military intrusion. His voice strained the perfunctory request. "I understand the sensitivity of the research you are conducting here, Doctor, but may we have permission to search your property?"

It was all polished and polite but for the sound of his metal cane striking on what sounded like a ring. The metallic tap made his "request" infinitely more imposing.

"By all means, please do." Doc sounded worried. "What has this man done?"

"He killed an innocent man. Murdered him in cold blood."

Mary released her embrace on John's arm. She backed away, staring at him through the waning light with wide, tearful eyes. But her face didn't hold fear. It was pain. She shook her head slowly, as if fighting against bitter memories of that horrible night when men took her husband away. And now it was happening again.

"A murderer?" Doc echoed his daughter's unspoken anguish. "Who did he kill?"

"Man by the name of Odom McCain. A farmer."

"Oh, my goodness! I know him. He was a peaceful man. He was a guest in this very house not long ago. He was my friend." Doc sounded sincerely mournful. "How was he killed?"

"Beaten to death. The man we're looking for is a terrorist, a sociopath of the worst sort. We know he's been traveling the country using various identities. He lures his victims into a false sense of security, gaining their trust and entrance into their homes – and then murders them. We know he is around here, probably hiding. I fear you and your family are in imminent danger.

"One of my men happened upon the scene of crime," Logan continued. "But he was too late to save Mr. McCain. Sergeant Fishetti called for backup and we gave chase. It was most unfortunate that freak storm blew up when it did or we would have captured him that night. He got away and we've been looking for him ever since."

Their voices faded toward the back of the house, replaced by the sounds of organized destruction as the small army tore through the house. Mary and John looked up to trace the sounds of scraping boots, tumbling furniture, and breaking glass that marked their torrid progress.

Some men came down the lower stairway.

Fortunately, Mary had the foresight to turn off the stairway light. One of the soldiers stumbled and fell against the door panel to their hiding place. Mary covered her mouth to stifle a scream. They both expected the men to come bursting into the room with guns blazing. But the impact did not engage the opening mechanism and the door held fast. The man cursed the darkness and continued on his way to search the basement area below.

Mary and John took a collective sigh, completely unaware they had stopped breathing. He looked at her and tried to smile, but the strain was too thick. She only managed a half-hearted response.

Hours ticked by and the world outside gradually grew quiet once more. During this entire time, Mary stayed in the corner, staring at John through the gathering darkness.

Toward the end, she approached him. Without a word, she peered into his eyes as if looking for something lost. John stood motionless, hands by his sides, saying nothing. She placed a soft palm against his cheek, a nervous smile twitching the corners of her lips at something she found.

Torment streamed down her cheeks. She never said a word, but she didn't have to. Her eyes cried out, "I love you."

With that, she silently held him, saying nothing, which said everything.

They jumped when the front door slammed shut. Their attention once more turned to the unseen world outside. This time, however, there was just one set of footsteps. They crossed the foyer, paused, and then shuffled slightly. Suddenly, the pace quickened, rapidly descending the stairway. Then they stopped outside their door!

The light came on.

Mary and John tensed, their hands clasped in tight embrace. They faced their fate together with anxious anticipation. John tried to move Mary aside, out of harm's way, but she would not budge. She only held his arm tighter, as if determined that no matter what happened she was not going to leave his side.

Her hands trembled, but she would not let go. It seemed obvious that no matter what happened she was not going to let things end like they did with Paul—even if she had to die trying. John smiled, thankful for that kind of love. She smiled back, those deep brown eyes pouring into his.

The door panel exploded in a shower of splinters. The glare blinded them to a man's silhouette rushing through the opening. And in his hands was a shotgun!

He pumped a shell into the chamber and quickly crossed to where John stood. His face emerged from the shadows. It was Doctor Lazlow, his face a mask of hatred, his eyes ablaze with murderous intent.

"Get away from my daughter!" he shouted, and raised the shotgun to John's face. In the stillness, his finger tightened on the trigger.

Chapter 19

"No!" Mary shrieked. She grabbed the gun barrel with both hands and shoved it toward the floor. Doc tried jerking it away, but kept his eyes locked on John.

"Let go!" he shouted. "Get out of the way."

"Father, please stop! You can't do this."

"Mary, this man murdered Odom and now he's come to kill us. There's no point in protecting him anymore." He jerked his head toward the corner of the room. "You get over there. I'll deal with you later."

"How do you know he killed Mr. McCain?" She gasped. His push made her lose her footing, but Mary maintained her grip on the gun and stood to face him once more.

"You heard what Logan said."

"Yes, I heard him." Her voice cold and bitter. "He said the same thing about Paul."

Doc stiffened as if he had been slapped. He blinked a few times. For the first time since crashing into the room he took his eyes off John and gave her a long, hard look.

"Who?"

"Oh, don't tell me you've managed to block out my husband along with everything else." She stood tall, no longer trying to hide her emotions.

Doc didn't respond. He cast a quick glance at John but quickly returned his attention to Mary.

"Logan's the one who accused Paul of killing that girl," she said. "Why else do you think he was there? He's the one who incited that mob to do what they did. Can't you see? He's a master at playing both sides of the fence. While whipping the people to a frenzy, he made certain no one suspected his direct involvement.

"Logan always gets someone else to do his dirty work. That's why he paid off those men that night. That way, when the job is done, he always claims plausible deniability—and he's doing the same with you. Yes he was there, but only to make sure you and I saw his feeble attempt to stop the people who hung Paul on that tree.

"Even you must admit he didn't try very hard. When he spoke, he made sure we couldn't hear. He just stood on the fringes, doing nothing that mattered. Don't you think if he really wanted to help, he would have had the Police or even his Special Force Unit there at the beginning, to dispel the crowd? Oh, he called them, but not before it was all over."

Tears began pouring down her cheeks, glistening in the harsh light streaming through the broken door, but their mist only served to reflect the fire blazing in her eyes. "After all that's happened, after everything he's done to us, how can you keep on blindly believing everything he tells you?

"Just open your eyes! Logan's been stringing you along from the beginning. He gives you money and classified your research as a top-secret project.

Why? Because he knew your ego would feed on that sort of thing, make you feel important.

"The only reason our neural simulator is top-secret is because when we're done, no one else will know it exists. This computer is his key to world domination. Why else do you think he wants such a thing? For the betterment of mankind? Ha! He's planning to use our computer to control people's minds. But if anyone knew such a device exists, his plan would be compromised.

"Don't you see? He has to keep it secret. That's why he put us out here so far from town and made our house off limits to everyone. When we're done, our isolation makes it easier for him to take everything for himself—and we will be dead."

The old man stepped back, staring at her with a comprehending glare.

"Oh, look who's surprised!" Mary's sarcasm hit hard. "Here's another news flash for you: Logan doesn't like you. He doesn't respect you. He never has and he never will. He was never going to appoint you to his cabinet." Her voice grew more bitter as she went. "He just told you what you wanted to hear, and your ego fed on the crumbs he tossed your way."

She let go of the dangling gun barrel, standing ramrod straight to confront him. The gun stayed where it was.

She threw her head back. "You've always considered yourself special, a little bit better than everyone else. That's why you never understood how the University could terminate you so unexpectedly. Well, let me be the first to clue you in." Her disdain thickened. "Guess who influenced the Trustees to let you go."

Doc didn't respond, but his eyes knew the answer.

"Yes, that's right. It was your buddy, Jack Logan. I went to the University President on your behalf right after it happened and while I was waiting in the administration office, I saw a transcript of that meeting on the secretary's desk. I asked if she would let me read it. She did.

"Logan told the Board your idea of the soul is deranged nonsense brought on by psychosis. He said your experiments were filling your students with religious superstitions of spirits and ghosts. He even gave them a counterfeit report from a doctor that certified your condition was incurable.

"He convinced them you were a liability, and an expensive one at that. He said it was only a matter of time before someone sued the school because of your statements or actions and that they were better off severing ties with you immediately. But even then, the Trustees were reluctant to let you go. After all, you were the Dean.

"But Logan desperately needed your research on the soul for himself. You were essential to his plan. He alone knew the value of having a machine that could invade the thoughts of people. And so that's when he played his final card. He bribed them with a new mainframe computer system. He said he would donate it if they would allow you to retire honorably under an oath of secrecy. Logan claimed you were his dear friend and just wanted what was best for you. His speech was a real tear jerker."

She gestured with both arms wide. "He said he would build this place for you, a house where you could live the remainder of your life in peaceful seclusion where you couldn't hurt anyone. But I ask you, are we secluded here or peacefully imprisoned?

"Since Logan took over your research, we've been confined here so he can keep this project secret. And when our job is done, he will likely kill us. Yes, that's right. You've been worrying about John, but Jack's the one you should be worried about."

Doc's eyes flashed, his head slowly nodding. His face drained of blood, his eyes staring blindly into space.

"Surely, you must wonder why none of your friends who saw that computer ever came back," Mary said. "And that includes Odom."

Doc's eyes widened, his mouth slightly agape.

"Who was the first one you showed it to?" Mary continued. "Arthur Jordan, I believe. Was it a coincidence that he died the next day? And when did Odom McCain die? A few weeks ago, wasn't it? Isn't that when you took him in the lab to show off? Logan says John killed him, but Logan is the one killed Odom. I bet he had that murderer Fishetti do it."

Doc blinked hard, shaking his head vigorously from side to side. His teeth gritted, his hands clenched the gun stock in white-knuckled bewilderment.

"You know it's true." Mary stepped closer. "He gave you the things you wanted. You thought he was your buddy, your pal, your connection back to the high society you miss so much.

"But didn't you notice Logan started acting like

that only after Paul died?" She looked at his dumbfounded face. "No, of course not. You were so infatuated with your new toys and money that you never realized Logan was putting on an act. Logan is the ultimate con artist, not John.

"With his first objective of controlling your computer firmly in his grip, he put the second part of his plan in action. He thought befriending you would make me love him. He gave you new cars, TVs— anything you wanted. And then he talked you into forcing me to marry him, which you tried in grand fashion. A day didn't go by that you didn't harp on me, telling me what I should and shouldn't do, laying countless guilt trips on me for refusing." She stepped forward. "Do you have any idea how you made me feel?"

"Why, why didn't you tell me?" his weak whisper barely audible.

"Tell you?" Mary groaned. "God only knows how many times I tried. But you refused to hear anything bad about your precious benefactor. Every time I told you the truth, you shut me out. You turned everything around until I felt like trash."

With that, her frustration became more than she could stand. After years of mental anguish, isolation, and emotional torment, everything crashed together in one raging torrent. Sobbing heavily, she fell against his chest, beating him with both fists.

"How can you be so blind you stupid, stupid old man?"

It surprised John that Doc didn't try to defend himself. Hollow eyes stared unseeing at her tearful attack. Mary quit hitting him and leaned against his

234

chest, still crying. He raised a hesitant, halting hand to stroke her hair.

"I . . . I don't know what to say, Mary." His voice was detached, strained. "I thought you and David deserved the best. That's my role as your father. Since my termination, Logan was my only source of income. I had no choice but to accept his money. This is my job. So why not get you to marry him? I thought it was a simple matter. If you married him, we were set for life. Everyone's happy, but I guess it's not as simple as I thought."

Mary turned away. Doc tried to hold on, but Mary would have none of it. She jerked from his grasp and went to the back of the room, facing the wall. His shoulders slumped, his face went slack, eyes filled with hollow dejection.

It was clear Mary was leaving him. And not just physically, but emotionally—and emotional rejection was the worst separation possible. Love can span vast distances and time, but hate is a barrier that can not be breached even across a tiny room. Spurned by his only child, he was alone in the world.

John said, "Doc?"

Doc stared at his daughter's back, sighing heavily. When he didn't respond, John called again. "Doctor Lazlow?"

His eyes could not muster the once malicious glare. He didn't say anything. He simply stared at him with a what-do-you-want look on his face.

"I know what Logan told you about me," John said. "But before you make up your mind, let me state my case. All I ask is that you hear me out. Please, if not for your own sake, then do it for Mary and David. They are the ones in the most danger here. However, if we act now, I can still save your lives."

Doc never said a word. If John was ever going to reach him, it had to be now, while his mental anguish blocked his fabricated defense. With Mary's tirade, all of Doc's carefully manufactured feelings were muted. He was vulnerable now, and John seized his chance.

"When I came here, you helped me because you thought I was the one who could put a stop to all this, that I can save you. And I am, just not in the way you want me to."

"If you're not willing to put a gun in your hand," his voice was soft, distant, "then you're no use to anyone. You just want to ruin my life."

"I'm not trying to ruin anything," John said. "Yes, I need to change your program, but only the parts that are wrong. The main core is fine. That part came from true inspiration, your original dream. It's the rest we need to weed out. You let your dream decay, and it shows in your design, your plans. I'm willing to bet that redirection started when you gave Logan control."

The petulant hostility returned to his glare but John stepped in front of him, no longer searching for carefully chosen words to protect his fragile feelings. The time for coddling egos was over.

John said, "I know how he's getting his information. He has some sort of connection with the outside world. That's how Logan knows why I'm here. Ask yourself this: Of all the scientists in this world, why did he pick you? The reason is he knew I also chose you."

"But why?" The shake of his head was slow.

"Logan knows there are three things that can stop me. One is if he can adapt your device to work for him. That would allow his mind to connect to the Genesis Machine and give him ultimate control. From what Mary tells me, and this is fortunate for us, he either doesn't understand the logic or doesn't have the whole plan.

"The second is if he kills me. The last is if he gains control over you. Right now, he has two out of three. He's got you in his hip pocket. He came very close to number two. In light of that, we should be glad your computer doesn't work. If it did, Logan would be unstoppable right now. And Mary's right. Your family would be dead."

Doc's head snapped up at that last remark. His hostile expression waned, his face slowly melting into a passive brood. John pressed his opportunity.

"Deep down, you know Mary's right," he said. "I'm not your problem. I'm not the one who destroyed your life, and I'm not the one trying to steal your computer or your daughter. The one you should be fighting is the same man you let rule your house. When you embraced Logan, you were defeated without ever knowing a battle waged for your soul."

John studied the old man a moment, waiting for a reaction. His quivering gaze took him in and then wavered back to Mary's cold shoulder. John could see he was making progress, but was it enough?

As Mary sniffed her frustrations, Doc's brow furrowed with a despondent, lost expression. Soon, he turned back to John and his emotional ride took another turn. His look of despondency now changed to distressed confusion.

He brushed back a shock of thick, white hair with an angry hand. "Oh, I don't know what to think anymore! Both you and Logan say you've got all the answers. You both claim to be right and accuse the other of being evil. How can I know who's telling the truth?"

He looked up as John stepped into the light streaming from the shattered door. The gun was a forgotten threat, dangling at the floor. "I need more facts," Doc said. "I need to know which one of you is right."

"I can give you proof," John said. Even Mary turned around at that. "When we have rebuilt your machine and established an ethereal link with the real world, then you will know I am telling the truth."

Doc flashed an annoyed scowl. "No, I meant now! Everything I have is on the line here. My life, my reputation, even my family. I need concrete evidence before I can make that kind of commitment."

John shook his head. "That's never going to happen. Admit it, no matter what is said or done, there can never be enough said or done to prove anything beyond all shadow of doubt—anything.

"The proof you seek is at your journey's end. The answers line the path. If you want to make direct contact with a human soul, you must trust your original dream. That's all I'm asking. Let me take you back to where you once were, before Logan corrupted you."

As he talked, John gradually moved away from

Mary such that she was now clear of danger. Doc followed him with troubled eyes as he spoke but did nothing. Streaks of light from the doorway cast half his face in deep shadow. When he finished, Doc simply stood there, looking at him with a blank expression.

John raised both hands.

"That's it, Doc," he said. "You've heard all I have to say. The decision is up to you. If you still believe I'm a murdering thief, then go ahead and shoot me now. Because you shut me out, I only have two weeks left. I can still do it, but if you don't let me make that connection on time, we and this world will be dead anyway. If you won't let me help you, then you might as well kill me now and get it over with. It's up to you. You make the choice whether or not millions die."

Doc looked around. His eyes opened as if realizing he had a clear shot. He scowled, but the grimace wasn't the satisfied smile of a hunter cornering his prey. Rather, it was the strained and painful look of a man struggling against his conscience, a man who no longer believed in his murderous task. Slowly he heaved the shotgun, catching the heavy stock in the palm of his left hand.

Mary heard the noise and turned, gasping in horror. She started forward, but John stopped her with an outstretched hand. The tiny room fell deathly quiet. No one moved. At that moment, Doc held John's life in his hands. He could kill him and resume his life with Logan, or he could accept him and risk Logan's wrath. It was a difficult decision, but one he alone had to make.

The seconds ticked by, but he did not fire. The dark muzzle wavered unsteadily. His eyes remained on John, wide and unblinking, his hands shaking. Beads of sweat sprinkled his brow.

Just when Doc's finger moved to the trigger, David's head peeked around the broken doorjamb, gawking at the destruction with awestruck wonder. He set his school books down outside the door and stepped over the threshold. Eventually, his eyes grew accustomed to the relative darkness and noticed the three of them standing there.

"Hey, Mom! Last day of school. I'm free! I'm free!" He giggled, holding his arms high. Then his laughter stopped.

Mary was by the back wall, a look of confused horror on her face. Doc stood in front of John, his back to David. The shotgun pressed firmly against John's chest, his finger tight against the trigger. David's eyes squinted, his head tilting curiously.

"Grandpa?" he called. "What are you doing?"

"Nothing, David." The old man labored to answer. "We're just playing a game."

David stepped through the door's scattered remains, his wide, curious eyes soaking up the strange mysteries of a room he had never seen. He returned his attention to Doctor Lazlow. "Don't do it, Grandpa. We need him. You need him. Please, put the gun down."

Doc still glared at John. His finger quivered against the trigger, gripping and releasing it.

"Grandpa, put the gun down! Mr. Neumann can help you. I know he can. You have work to do, and so does he."

John held his breath, expecting an earsplitting

roar and the pain of hot lead ripping through his chest. But somehow, in that moment, the words of that little boy penetrated his mental fog—and Doc heard him.

The old man blinked hard a few times, trying to clear his vision. And when they finally opened, whatever had possessed him was, by that simple phrase, gone.

"You have work to do."

Doc staggered unsteadily. With trembling hands he reached up to rub bloodshot eyes. That's when he noticed the shotgun still clutched in his right hand. He stared at it a lingering moment as if wondering why it was there. He followed the gleaming barrel and glanced up at John. And when he did, a look of sincere bewilderment twisted his tired and haggard face. Slowly, he lowered the muzzle to the ground.

David was instantly beside him. Taking his hand, he said, "Thank you."

Doc looked down at his grandson. Before him was a curious young boy hungry for knowledge, a boy constantly studying everything around him with an insatiable need to learn. To David, everything was new and still a mystery, his mind unfettered with the predilections of a corrupted world. He saw only what there was to see, not the preconceived notions yet to be drilled into him by society. The child's mind was fresh, open, trusting—and with that he could see what others could not.

Doc looked again at the gun. Swelling tears blurred his vision. To kill a man! He shook his head at what he had become. It was a far cry from where he started.

During one of their walks, Mary told John a lot about Doc, how as a young man he, too, had thought of the soul as being the source of life. The idea came unbidden, as if from nowhere, but he knew that had to be the answer. The soul somehow generated the electrical potential that ultimately drove the body to animation. It began as a notion that quickly became an obsession. But after years of toil, he was no closer to proving it than when he started.

Out of money, out of a job, he considered abandoning his dream. That's when Logan entered his life and offered him money and a lab to continue his research. That, he now realized, was the turning point—and his biggest mistake. The money. That subtle change in motivation drastically shifted his focus and altered his course in life. What was once a sparkling effort to seek new understanding became a dreary prison-like existence in his own home, chained to the computer laboratory under the authority of a tyrant master. He was now lost, his dream of proving his theory farther away.

Doc reached an age-spotted hand and tousled the boy's hair, smiling in fond affection. He set the butt of his gun on the ground and, looking directly at John, answered his grandson's question. "Yes, son. We have a lot of work to do."

The crazed glare was gone. For the first time in weeks, he spoke to John in a normal tone. "John, you were right, and I apologize. Your ideas on dark-energy are exactly what I need to prove my theory.

"If you're still willing." He took a deep breath. "I need your help to prove the soul is real. I'll do whatever you say. You can have complete access to my lab. All I ask is that you tell me about the changes you make and allow me to witness the connection process. With a monitor in place, I can see and document what you experience when you make ethereal contact. It's the only way I can prove once and for all that I'm right."

"Fine by me." John sighed with relief. "Time is running out. The sooner we get at it, the better."

Like a vanishing mist, the air of malevolence was gone. Mary rushed to her father, grabbed his arms and spun him toward the hallway light. She peered into his face with expectant hope. What she saw brought more tears to her stained cheeks, only these were tears of joy. Her father had returned.

The old man's own tears glistened through his white beard. He stroked her soft cheek and said, "I'm sorry, Mary. I had no idea what I was putting you through. Can you ever forgive me?"

She flung both arms around his neck and cried, "Oh, Father!"

They both sobbed as they held each other. Sorrow and joy mingled with what was lost, but now was found. For the first time in years Mary had a father again, and Doc had regained his daughter. That alone was worth all they stood to lose when Logan learned of Doc's defection.

Mary looked at John. "Thank you," she said. "Without you, he never would have come back."

John shook his head. "Not me. I just drove him to the breaking point. David's the one who got through to him."

The boy's freckled face beamed with a pleasant

smile. "What's everyone talking about?" he said.

Doc patted his shoulder. "It's over, son. Now it's time to get to work."

David nodded. "Good. You get to work 'cause I'm hungry!"

Everyone laughed and took the cue to break up. Mary took David's hand and sniffed the last of her tears. "Well, come on then, David. Let's celebrate the end of school. We'll start by getting you something to eat."

As they walked out of the room, David picked up a shard of wood. His make-believe sword clicked noisily along the wooden wall planks. John turned to follow but Doc held him back with a clandestine hand.

He waited until they were alone before turning to him. "I've got to be honest with you, John," he said. "I'm still not sure about everything going on here. But I do know I was wrong about you. That's why I figure, uh, well you should know what I've done."

He shifted uneasily. "John, you can't stay here. No, it's not about me this time. It's Logan. He told everyone you're a terrorist assassin here to kill him. He's called in the National Guard, the City Police, and is using his own Special Force Unit to hunt you down. Every citizen and law officer in the state has orders to shoot you on sight."

"But I'm not here to kill anyone!" John said.

"Well, that's not the point now is it? Logan's the one calling the shots. The fact is he's more fanatical than I've ever seen him. Whoever you are or whatever it is you can't remember has him extremely worried. With each passing day, he becomes more desperate. One thing is sure: He won't stop until you are dead."

He raised a curious brow. "Now, why would a man like Logan be so afraid of someone like you?"

"When I connect to Genesis," John said. "Not only will I put Logan away for a long time, I'll completely destroy his power base forever."

Doc hesitated at the unexpected response, but let it go. He had something more imminent to talk about. He dropped his eyes, toeing the floor. "Well, he knows you're here. It's, uh, well, I told him." He lowered his head. "I'm sorry."

John stepped forward and placed a hand on his shoulder. "Don't worry about it, Doc. I knew you would tell him sooner or later, but it's okay. Once your computer is repaired, everything will be all right. I know it. I have a feeling Logan needs to find me—just not now."

"I don't know what came over me," he blurted as if he didn't hear him. "All I could see was you stealing everything I loved!"

John shook his head. "What are you talking about?"

"It's been years since I've been able to talk with my daughter the way you do." His voice broke with sorrow. "She respects you. She trusts you. And what's more, she loves you. David feels the same way. Ever since you got here, he can't wait to get home from school so you two can play. And then, when you wanted to reprogram my computer. . ."

"Maybe you don't spend enough time with them," John said. "They both love you. Sometimes, words aren't enough. You have to show them how you feel."

Doc stiffened. "Oh, you don't have to pacify me! You're not the problem. I know that now. All you did was give me the slap in the face I needed to wake up. My problem is with Logan. I had every reason to believe him. After all, he gave me everything I asked for.

"But now," he hit the wall so hard dust fell from the ceiling, "now I see him for what he is and it makes me sick. I let him corrupt my program. Like a mindless puppet, I made so many changes, I hardly recognize my own invention anymore. And through it all he was so smooth and slick I never even suspected."

He slammed the wall again, then again. "Why? Why couldn't I have seen it before?"

John turned Doc to face him. "Listen to me. You've got to forget the past. What's done is gone. Let it go. The important thing is what you do with your future. Believe me, you may be old, but your life plays a crucial part in saving this world. You're not dead yet."

His head came up, but he could not bring himself to look John in the eye.

"Doc," John said. "Do you still want to prove your theory about the soul? Wouldn't it be nice to show everyone that, after all these years, you've been right all along?"

With that, Doc looked at him, his sour expression transforming into grim determination. John looked into his eyes and saw the fire that had once burned so bright.

"I thought so," he said. "Old dreams never die, do they? Doc, your time of waiting is over. I promise you will realize your dream, but we have a lot of hard work to do before then."

Doc blinked and shook his head. "I don't understand. You, you forgive me for telling Logan, for everything I've done and said?"

"There's no need to forgive when there is no blame. What's done is done. But like I said, I have a plan. And, it turns out, I need him to know. It's a little early, but trust me, everything will be all right."

The corner of Doc's lip twitched. And then the smile broadened as if a tremendous weight had been removed from his shoulders. "Thank you," is all he said.

He stepped away for a moment, running pudgy fingers through sweat matted white hair while he struggled with a difficult choice. It was his point of no return, a monumental decision that would impact his family and his life. If he walked away from Logan now, his life would be in danger. Despite the enormous consequences, it didn't take him long to make up his mind.

He turned to John and said, "We've got a lot of work to do, John. We should start now. We don't have much time left." He extended his arm toward the broken door, allowing him to exit first.

"You're right about that, Doctor Lazlow," John replied and preceded him out the door.

Chapter 20

"I don't like it, Fishetti," Logan said. He was in the passenger seat of a white four-wheel drive Jeep. He turned toward the muscular war veteran as they drove down the two-lane road heading to the city. "Neumann should have been at that house. We looked everywhere." He glanced at the burly sergeant. "You're sure you looked everywhere?"

Fishetti nodded. "Absolutely, sir. Every room and closet. I even checked for tracks outside and the forest—nothing." He looked at Logan. "It's possible this Neumann saw us coming and escaped, but then there would have been tracks. I don't know, sir, if you ask me the guy's not there. If he were, we would have found something."

Logan sat silent a brief moment, looking out the window. "You may be right. If I didn't know better, I'd say the old man made up the whole thing. But that doesn't make sense. It's not like him."

Fishetti shrugged, his eyes fixed on the road. "Maybe he just wanted attention. He's like that, you know."

Logan shook his head, his gaze still out the side window. "That old fart wants attention. It's all he wants, but not the kind that's going to come down on him if I find out he lied to me. It's something else. I've got a feeling . . ."

Logan tapped his head against the window. He stopped and closed his eyes, placing two fingers against each side of his forehead.

Fishetti asked, "Sir? Are you alright? Got a headache?"

"Shut up!" Logan snapped. "I need absolute quiet."

For a brief second, Fishetti stared at the contorted face confronting him. It wasn't natural.

Logan resumed his studious pose. His eyes were closed, squinting with effort. "Where is he?" he said. He lurched upright and covered both ears. "Where is he? I can't . . . ah, I've lost him!"

"Uh, excuse me, sir?" Fishetti cut his eyes at his boss. "What is going on? Who were you talking to?"

Logan looked out the side window and never said a word. Fishetti nodded at the silence and returned his attention to the road ahead.

They drove for almost half an hour before Logan finally spoke. "Sergeant, I have an assignment for you."

Fishetti smiled.

"After you drop me off, I want you to gear up and stake out Lazlow's place. If Neumann's not there, he's definitely on his way. The Lazlows are working on a top secret project that deals with a computer of mine. It must be protected at all costs. Neumann wants that computer. That's the bait. You're going to be the trap.

"I want you to set up camp in the forest out back where you can get a good shot at Lazlow's office and the back entrance. Set up surveillance equipment around the perimeter. Nobody goes in or out without your knowing about it, you got that?"

Fishetti's smile broadened, his eyes still on the road. "Yes, sir."

"I'll direct the search teams farther south to get them out of your way. I couldn't quite make out that last transmission . . . oh, never mind. Anyway, by moving the teams out of this area, Neumann might relax and show himself. Besides, it will give you the opportunity you've been waiting for. You can take him out and no one will be the wiser about that first shot thing you got in your head."

He looked at Fishetti. "You're going to do this on your own. No one else. And be prepared. It may take some time."

"That's okay, sir. I prefer to work alone. And I've got all the time in the world when it comes to killing him."

~~~

When Doc and John entered the study, Doc turned left and pulled on the blue book on the middle shelf. A muffled, metallic click and the bookcase swung inward on silent hinges. The little shop was unchanged. An assortment of test equipment filled the workbench on their left. Flashing lights and computer panels adorned the other walls. And in the center of the room, still on its mobile cart, was the alpha-generator device.

Doc walked to a computer panel in the back right corner of the room. He pulled an electronically encoded card from his pocket and inserted it into one of the panel's three parallel slots. A tone sounded. A servo-motor hummed to life and the entire panel recessed and swung inward.

John stood in astonishment at the grand façade. The entire outer lab, the computer panels, was nothing but a decoy, an elaborate secret passage to the real lab beyond. But as he followed Doc inside, he looked back and realized the real purpose for this antechamber. It was a trap.

A miniature television camera above the outer door saw everything. The bookcase panel operated on hydraulic pistons. With the push of a remote button, anyone caught snooping could be quickly isolated long enough for Logan and his henchmen to arrive.

Stepping through the inner portal, John entered a large, lavish laboratory brightly lit by dozens of fluorescent ceiling lights. Doc donned a long, white cotton lab jacket. He pointed John to another hanging on a coat rack to his right. He put it on. It was cold in there.

A workbench spanned the two left walls. Above these were shelves stocked with multimeters, oscilloscopes, tools, and various electronic spare parts. The other side of the lab contained power supply controls. And in the back, metal storage cabinets filled the wall.

But the object in the center of the room commanded all attention. A monolithic computer towered over them, cylindrical, made of black metal, and spanned at least ten feet at its base. Multiple color monitors filled the single workstation in grand array. This was why it was so cold. He had to keep the temperature down to prevent the sensitive electronics inside the cylindrical giant from overheating.

"This is amazing, Doc," John said, inspecting the massive structure. "It's all I expected and then some."

"Thank you. It took a lot of years to make it."

"But this must have cost millions! How could you afford such a colossal machine?"

"I told you, Logan paid for everything. I don't know how he came up with the money and I never asked. And right now, I really don't want to know."

"You're probably right." John nodded. "It doesn't matter."

"Doesn't matter? Who knows how many people he robbed, killed, or strung out on drugs because of," he gestured at the computer in disgust, "because of this? Mary's been right about Logan all along. That means this thing was built with blood money and it makes me sick to be part of it!"

"Doc, you can't keep beating yourself up. Yes, people suffered for this, but the fact of the matter is that we need this machine. Think of it as Fate's way of financing your destiny."

Doc looked at him. "You have a twisted way of seeing things, young man."

John shook his head. "No, not that twisted. Okay, so people died to finance your dream, but don't forget we're fighting a war here. And there are always casualties in war. In a way, Logan was necessary. Otherwise, this computer would never have been built, and then we couldn't do what we need to do."

Doc dropped his head, his shoulders sagging.

"Come on, Doc," John said. "Snap out of it. Sure it's sad, but their suffering gave us the means to set them free. We're going to take what Logan built and use it against him. With the changes we're going to make, we can bring Logan's entire organization down and help those he hurt in the process.

"The people may not know it, but their future depends on us. We can't let them down. Look up. You can't quit. Not now, not when we're so close, not when so many have already paid the price."

Doc gave a half-hearted shrug and despondent nod, but John could tell he was still beating himself up with guilt. He had to get him focused and so he walked to the computer, beckoning him to follow.

"So tell me, Doc. How does this thing work?"

Doc shuffled beside him and looked up at the computer that in one way or another had monopolized his entire life. He took a long, deep breath and let it out slowly.

"Most computers fall into one of two categories," he said. "Analog or digital. This one is a hybrid design, combining the continuous input and output characteristics of an analog computer with the extreme accuracy afforded by digital circuitry. It has a multiple parallel circuit architecture that allows trillions of instructions to be simultaneously executed. It can process over a trillion quintillion calculations per second."

John whistled softly. "Why do you need such massive power?" He knew the answer, but getting Doc to focus on the present was the only way to escape his past.

Doc gave John a strange look. He moved to the workbench and pulled back a cloth. He stepped aside to reveal two spherical glass bowls. They looked like ordinary two-gallon aquariums, the kind kids put goldfish in. One was empty, the other filled with thousands of hair-thin wire filaments suspended in clear plastic. The tiny wires collected at the base to form a thick, braided cable that lead back to the mainframe computer.

He stroked the assembled bowl affectionately. "This was supposed to be an artificial brain. A few years ago, Logan demanded we incorporate it into our computer design. I didn't think it would work and told him so, but he was very emphatic—if you know what I mean."

"Why? What can this thing do your program can't?"

"He said something about using this to create an analog energy spectrum, something the computer's digital circuits could never do. Theoretically, by placing these filaments in a precise pattern, this bowl was to simulate the analog energy spectrum of a human brain."

Doc looked at John. "Logan didn't give me details, only orders to figure out a way to make it work. I had the distinct impression someone else gave him the idea." He almost managed a smile and said, "I have to admit, the idea did seem out of this world. Maybe that's where he got it."

"I'm sure it was," John said. "Logan seems to have a unique connection with the outside world. I've got to find out how, but go on. Tell me more."

"He came back many times trying to describe what to do, but he didn't know what he was talking about. He'd tell me to do one thing and then next time he'd tell me to do something almost completely opposite. He didn't make sense.

"I told him I didn't have enough data to go on and that it would be foolish to proceed. But when the money man talks . . . well, you get the idea."

He placed both hands around the bowl, caressing the smooth glass. "Years ago, someone took the time to map the neuron connections within a portion of a real brain. We used that as our pattern. It took thousands of hours to place these filaments into that meticulous pattern."

Using tweezers, he picked up one of the filaments off the workbench and placed it in the palm of his hand, holding it up for display. What looked to be a very thin human hair was a wire. Closer inspection revealed other filaments branching off from the first, each of varying length, like limbs of a tiny tree.

"We designed these things to resemble the neurons they imitate."

He pointed to the thick cord of wires leading back to the computer. "The plan was to use my computer program to input electrical energy into this bowl. The computer's digital analyzers were to monitor the loads within the network and control the energy transients within the filaments."

He turned the bowl around to reveal a smaller cable exiting a hole in the top of the glass. This cable connected the bowl to a mechanical arm still half buried beneath the cloth. He pushed the cloth back and picked up the arm.

"I thought if we could create an analog

resonance in the artificial brain, the induced current would be enough to power the arm's servomotor. But it never worked. We never could achieve resonance in any of the transient fields."

He tossed the lifeless limb on the workbench, shaking his head. "What was I thinking?"

"But what about resonance with the soul?" John asked. "Wasn't that what you originally wanted to prove, the existence of the human soul?"

"That's what I've been talking about!" He beat the workbench with a heavy hand. "This is all wrong. I wasted years on this stupid brain approach. And now, Logan's got my computer program so twisted it doesn't do much at all. The whole thing is useless."

He hit the worktable again and again. "Why did I listen to him? How could I have let Logan waste my life like this?"

"Come on, Doc." John shook his shoulder. "Stop beating yourself up. You did not waste your life. As a matter of fact, this artificial brain idea is close to what I want. It just needs a little tweaking, that's all."

He looked up. "It does?"

"Yes. And this proves what I suspected. Logan didn't come up with this idea out of the blue. Someone from the outside world is definitely communicating to him." He shook his head. "I shudder to think what else he knows, and what might have happened had he succeeded."

"What do you mean?"

"If your machine worked, Logan would have mental access to everything. And I'm not just talking about the Genesis database, but people's thoughts, even the main control system for this virtual world."

"Control system? You mean he could have had control of this entire world?"

John nodded. "With the power of the Genesis Machine at his command, there's nothing he would not know, nothing he couldn't do."

Doc stepped back, his face pale. "Oh, my God!"

"Well, he certainly would have seemed like a god to everyone on this planet," John said. "With his mind connected to Genesis, he could make anything happen with just a thought. But like you said earlier, it's fortunate that he doesn't understand any of this."

"How do you know he doesn't understand?"

"Because if he understood the concepts involved, you wouldn't be using the artificial brain like this. The reason you're not getting resonance is because he's mixing old techniques with new concepts. Like old wineskins and new wine, you know the saying."

"I know the saying, but I don't have a clue what you're talking about."

"I'm talking about your design," he said. "It's not only wrong, it serves a completely different purpose. But from what Mary told me and what you just said about your main program, I think I can make it work."

"So my computer isn't worthless?"

John shook his head. "Far from it. The overall design is fine. We'll talk about the program changes we need to make later. With a little tender love and care, you'll see what I mean. The only problem we have is that there are only fourteen days left before the Genesis Machine starts listening for my signal. If I'm not ready then, well, you know what will happen. That means we've got a lot of work to do in two weeks. Just plan on a lot of late nights with no sleep."

They talked a few more hours until Mary's voice floated down from the top of the stairs. "Hey, you guys! Are you going to eat dinner or what?"

John looked at the clock. "Wow! Look at the time. No wonder I'm hungry. Come on, Doc, I'll explain the rest over dinner and plan out next move."

Chapter 21

When they entered the kitchen, all the window blinds were closed. Mary answered John's unasked question. "You never know who may be watching outside."

"Where's David?" Doc asked. "Wasn't he starving?"

"Oh, you guys were down there so long he ate and left already. Ryan and his mom came over to make sure we were all right. They saw the trucks and police vans headed our way and thought maybe something might have happened.

"Anyway, Ryan asked if David could stay at their house for a few weeks." Her tone was curt, business like. "I figured we are going to be working pretty late hours if you're going to make your deadline. And with David out of school, it wouldn't be fair leave him by himself.

"Debbie, that's Ryan's mom, said she didn't mind. Ryan was bored. The kids seemed excited. Before they left, they were already planning a trip to the beach. David's in seventh heaven. So that's good."

She removed a glass cooking dish from the oven, filling the room with an enticing aroma.

"Ummm." John smiled over the dish she placed

on the table. "Smells good. What is it?"

"It's not much, just a chicken casserole." She blushed, pulling off the oven mitts. "What took you guys so long?"

"Doc was showing me around the lab and we got to talking about the computer and the glass brain," he said, heaping huge mounds of steaming chicken and noodles onto his plate.

"Oh, that's wonderful!" she said. But then she looked at her father and her smile quickly faded. "Father, what's wrong?"

Since entering the kitchen, Doc never said a word, choosing to sit at the far end of the circular alcove alone, his hands folded in front of him. At her beckoning, he looked up and addressed his troubled thoughts.

"Mary, when did you know all that about Logan?"

She sat back and sighed. "From the beginning. To someone with an objective viewpoint, Logan is not a hard man to figure out."

Doc stabbed his food. "Then why couldn't I have seen him for what he is? Why didn't I believe you? How could I . . ."

She laid her hand on his, stopping his agitated thrusts. "It doesn't matter, Father. That's behind us. You've got to let it go."

"How can I let it go?" he said. "Don't you see? I'm responsible for ruining countless lives! How am I supposed to live with that?"

"You had a lot more invested in this than Mary did," John said. "Logan knew that. He knew your weaknesses and how to control you. You wanted respect; he made you feel important. You wanted to be rich and popular; he gave you money and attention. He's a master at manipulating people. When the University kicked you out, you felt lost and abandoned. He gave you a place and a purpose. With all that on you, how could you possibly have seen him as anything but a savior?

"Face it, you were taken in by the best con artist there is. Emotions block rational thought, and nobody knows that better than he. Your emotions were purposefully contrived such that it was impossible for you to see the truth. But don't be too hard on yourself. You weren't the first to fall into his trap. And unfortunately you won't be the last."

Doc looked at him a thoughtful moment, his fork hovering over the plate. "Manipulated. Out of emotional control, eh?" He nodded with a slight smile. "You may be right. Yes, that may be it."

He took a bite of food, his words muffled by his bulging cheek. "John, I think you missed your calling. You would have made a great psychologist. You have a knack for making people feel good."

"Maybe next time around." John smiled.

With that, the conversation died. They ate in silence for some time before Doc spoke. "John, you know Logan is obsessed with killing you. He knows you're here. For all we know, he's probably setting up surveillance on this house right now. They could come back any minute. Why don't you leave while there's still time?"

John shook his head. "Right now, leaving is the last thing on my mind." He put up a hand to stop further protests. "Yes, I know they'll come back. Keep all the doors locked so they can't barge in. Logan won't come back. Not him personally. Don't ask me how I know, I just do. But just to be safe, I'll stay in the lab. Buried in the ground like it is, no way any surveillance equipment they might set up could find me there."

"Surveillance equipment? How do you know he'll do that?"

"Wouldn't you if you thought someone was going to use your own computer?"

"Then why not just leave before they get here? Surely, you can tell us what to do. I promise Mary and I will do whatever you say."

John shook his head. "Because I'm the one who has to merge my mind with the Genesis Machine. Regaining my entire memory is the first step in knowing how to get you people out of this world, and I can't do that without your computer. That means I've got to stay."

"But merging your mind with my machine is dangerous," Doc said, leaning both elbows on the table. "There are so many unknowns. There's no telling what kind of power surge will go through your mind. Your brain could be cooked to mush. You said so yourself."

He stopped Mary's unspoken protest. "Don't get me wrong. I'm just concerned about John tackling something that's too much for any mortal man to handle. Even if this spiritual connection is possible, I'm not sure it's morally right. The implications of coming in contact with the power of the Genesis Machine is unsettling, to say the least. Like you said, whoever connects to that machine well be like a god. Your very thoughts will control the world."

"I built this world." John extended his arms. "I wrote the program, I designed this place, and I put you people in here. That makes it my responsibility to get you out of here – whether or not I survive the effort. My point is I've got to try. There is a way back. I know there is. I just have to find it.

"Connecting my mind with Genesis is the best and only way to stop Logan and the virus threatening to destroy this planet. Let's not forget about that. So you see? I have to do this. There's no other choice."

There was a brief moment of silence before Mary asked, "So, if Logan is to be stopped, it's got to be us and it's got to be now. Is that what you're saying?"

"Yes."

"Then let's get to it!" Her mind made up, she stood to leave. "We don't have much time."

"But how?" It was her father sounding defeated again. "We never got the artificial brain to work. You know that. How can we be sure John's additions to my program will do what he says?"

"Oh, Father, please!" Mary turned on him.

"I'm sorry. I don't mean to be negative, but I'm still not sure about his ethereal-energy concept, or dark-energy, or whatever you want to call it. How can you be so certain there's another energy realm beyond this one? Another world outside of this one? It sounds preposterous. For all I know, this may be a big waste of time."

Mary took another step toward him. "I've had

enough of this. Every time John tries to help you slam on the brakes."

"Hold on, Mary." John said. "You must remember your father doesn't know what you know. I described my vision to you. You've read my additions to the program. You know what this thing can do. Doc doesn't.

"To someone who does not know how, any task is insurmountable—and this is about as difficult as they come.

"We need your father's help and shouting isn't going to convince him. I don't blame him for having reservations. That's normal. Remember, he's been in seclusion. He's also taking an awful chance bucking Logan. He stands to lose everything, including his life and family. I think that earns him an explanation."

John looked back at Doc who shifted in his chair. "So tell me, Doc. What do you need to know?"

He hesitated. "Well, I suppose it would help if I knew how to make this dark-energy you keep referring to. And after we make it, how do we control it? Your design changes hinge on the existence of this new form of energy and I still don't know how to make it. Just answer me that. I think I can deduce the rest."

"Fair enough," John said. "But first let me remind you that we can't make energy, even if it's ethereal. That's the most basic rule of Nature and it applies on both sides of the energy spectrum.

"However, although we can't make ether, we can form ethereal darkons the same way we make atomic photons. I'm sure this is what you're driving at. And then you want to know how to control the ethereal field once we've created it."

Doc nodded.

John pushed his plate away, trying to think of some simple terms to describe the general process by which ethereal particles are made. Mary, who had heard this lecture before, began clearing the table.

John looked around for something to use as an illustration. He settled on the color of his sweater.

"Okay, try this," he said. "It's kind of like separating the color gray into its components. We both know gray is a combination of black and white. These two colors represent the atomic and ethereal forms of energy together."

He held out both hands, palms held together. "If we start with the two colors mixed uniformly, we have the color gray. This is to represent the Absolute Energy Medium. But if we remove the black and place it in my right hand." He moved his right hand away. "Then all that's left is the color white. Do you see it now? If you isolate one, you necessarily isolate the other whether you intended to or not.

"The same holds true when we form a pocket of atomic-energy out of the Absolute Medium. Isolating atomic-energy leaves a pocket of dark-energy behind.

"So actually, it's not hard to make darkons. We do it every day. We don't notice them because our eyes and lab instruments only detect the atomic bubbles in our energy pool."

"Are you saying that everything generating electromagnetic radiation is also producing ethereal darkons?" He sat upright in his chair.

"It's at least affecting them, but don't get too excited. Although it's easy to make them doesn't help us with the second part of your question and that is how to control them. How can we manipulate something we can't see? Just being able to make them doesn't do us much good."

"Why not?"

"Because just as a random production of atomic photons will be seen as static on your TV, a random production of ethereal particles will be seen as 'static' by my spirit, and that won't help us here. To attract my spirit to the ethereal plasma I plan to create, your glass artificial brain must produce an energy field that is the exact match of my soul, only stronger. That's the hard part. If we can do it, however, we'll force an out-of-body experience where my spirit will connect with the matrix."

"So how can we do that? Is it possible?"

"If it wasn't, I wouldn't be here." John nodded. "While locked out of your lab, I spent a lot of time writing a program to mimic the electric potential oscillations within the brain. This will make your glass brain generate a suitable ethereal signal. At that point, it's all about making the field strong enough to attract my spirit like a magnet."

Doc shook his head. "But I'm still not clear on how we can manipulate something we can't see. You said yourself we can't detect ethereal photons, darkons, because our atomic sensors are limited. How can we control something we can't see to any degree of accuracy?"

"By observing and controlling the effects on what we can see."

"And what is that?"

"Brain waves."

"Brain waves? I thought you said that was old stuff. What good will that do?"

"I'm not interested in the brain waves themselves," John said. "It's what they leave behind that is essential. You see, brain waves are atomic photons, just like the light shining from a bulb—only at much lower frequencies, of course."

Both Doc and Mary exchanged knowing looks.

"Are you getting the picture now?" John asked. "Brain waves are photons produced by neurons, the same energy separation process we just talked about. If your artificial brain can produce an electromagnetic wave pattern like mine, then the ethereal content left within that bowl will match that of my soul. All we have to do is make that ethereal field stronger than what's up here," he tapped his head, "and my conscious spirit should move to this artificial environment."

Mary said, "It's kind of like bringing a large magnet near two smaller magnets that are stuck together. If we hold one of those small magnets in place, the larger one will eventually draw one of the small magnets away. Once the force is strong enough, the small one will break free and attach itself to the larger one."

"She's right," John said. "At that point, once my spirit is free, it will be captured into your computer. With the code we'll add to your main program, your computer will then amplify the ethereal signal of my spirit, elevating me to the Ethereal Boundary—the point where the real and virtual worlds come in contact.

"All your machine needs to do is magnify my spirit. On the fortieth day since my arrival here, the Genesis Machine will begin searching for my signal. Once it locks in on me, my computer in the real world will take over and do the rest."

"Fortieth day?" Doc shook his head. "Why is that so important? Could you do something to extend the deadline? We could sure use the time."

John shook his head. "That's my appointed time, a pre-set moment I made before coming in here for the merging process to initiate and at this point I can't change that. It's a one day window of opportunity. Too early, and I project myself into who knows where. Too late, and the Genesis Machine shuts down—and I've told you what happens then. Secondly, Mary's right. Logan's people are probably watching this place already. We don't have much time."

"Before they come back," Doc said. "And if you run, then this world shuts down."

John nodded. "That's why my time is so important—most of which is gone, I might add. We've only got two weeks left. That means we have to work hard and fast."

Doc studied him a long moment, his fingertips brushing pursed lips in a prayerful pose.

Mary asked, "So what do you think, Father?"

His eyes shifted to her. "It's starting to come together. But if that's all there is to the mystery of dark-energy, I think I can handle it."

"Good!" Mary's manner was all business. "I'll start reading through John's code while you two wash the dishes."

She spun toward John, her auburn hair whipping across her dark brown eyes. It was an alluring and seductive look of which she seemed completely unaware.

"Where's your notebook, the one with the code?"

"It's still in that hideaway room we were in," he said, starting to rise. "I grabbed everything when Logan and his men came and in all the excitement I forgot that I set all my notes in the corner. I'll get them for you."

"Don't bother. I'll get them on the way down." She was already halfway to the door. "We've talked about it before. I don't think I'll have any problems following what you wrote, but give me an hour to go through it. When you finish here, come make sure I'm on the right track." Her last few words faintly floated up the stairway, her footsteps already gone.

John glanced at Doc. "Has she always been like this?"

Doc grinned, gathering the remaining plates off the table. "You haven't seen the half of it. Come on. Let's get this stuff put away. She's going to want you down there exactly fifty-nine minutes and thirty seconds from now and we have a lot to talk about before then."

As they washed the dishes, the old man became a veritable machine gun of questions, each query probing deeper into the energy concepts. No sooner had John responded to one topic than Doc jumped to something else.

His questions may have appeared to be the

disconnected rambling of a senile, old man unable to keep a single track of thought. But it didn't take John long to realize that Doc's apparent random attack was, in fact, his way of confirming various astute observations that struck at the very heart of the concept. He was amazed at how Doc's mind assimilated vast amounts of diverse information at once. He couldn't get his answers fast enough. The old master had not lost his touch after all.

Doc turned on the dishwasher and they headed for the lab. The sailfish lamp was on its brightest setting. Mary sat with both legs tucked beneath her and one hand propping her chin, studying the notebook. As usual, her attention was so focused on what she was doing that she didn't seem to notice them come in.

Doc headed for the lab to begin re-mapping the computer's Input/Output addresses, how the computer would communicate with the artificial brain. Mary would need that information to insert the new code. John sat down on the couch to rest. It had been a long and trying day and he was tired.

He looked at his watch and smiled. Fifty-eight minutes. Two minutes to spare. He laid his head back on the couch, closing his eyes in welcome relaxation.

Chapter 22

"John?" Mary shook his shoulder. "John, are you awake?"

John lurched upright and immediately wished he hadn't. His head throbbed with the ache that often follows a short and interrupted sleep.

"Oh, man!" he groaned, trying to rub the drowsiness from bloodshot eyes. "What time is it?"

"It's time we got started!" she said, her tone harsh and abrupt.

He looked up, but she was already heading for the inner lab.

"I finished reviewing your notes." She didn't bother turning around. "You've made changes to your program since the last time we talked. I'd like you to explain them to me."

"Sure," he groaned. Massaging both of his temples, he shuffled behind her.

She stopped at the door and turned on him, waiting until he was close beside her.

John asked, "What do you want to know?"

"The truth would be nice!"

"The truth about what? Why are you so mad?"

"Nothing!" she said with a withering glare.

Without another word, she stomped into the lab, leaving him to stare after her in bewilderment.

Warily, John entered the cold room. Doctor Lazlow knelt beside the giant computer, peering through an open portal with a small flashlight. Mary sat down at the console, her arms crossed, waiting impatiently. As John approached, she stabbed a finger at an open page of his notebook.

"What is this section about?" she demanded. "The logic is convoluted. You're making calls to embedded subroutines of embedded subroutines. You've got data traffic going so many different ways I'm not sure what you're trying to do anymore."

"Oh, that's nothing. Just my way of programming."

She shook her head. "I doubt it. You're a better programmer than this. From what I can gather, you want the computer to send and receive trillions of data bits at the same instant. Not only that, you've altered the data streams. The interactions are incredibly intense. The load is enormous. It's going to push the upper limits of our operational envelope, but I think we can handle it."

"Fine, so what's the problem?"

"The problem is this series of convoluted subroutines you added. They're in a language I've never seen before. Why would someone write a subroutine in a different language from the main program?"

Her fingernail ripped the page, her voice strained with anger. "I want to know what's going on here, John! You don't write code like this. You're hiding something. What is it?"

He rubbed his eyes again, giving his groggy mind time focus. She opened her mouth to say something else, but he held up an irritated hand, stalling her impatient demands. Her mouth went tersely shut as he walked to their artificial brain, the smooth bowl on the workbench behind him. He picked it up and pulled hard on the thick cable exiting the plastic filler at its base.

"What are you doing?" She jumped off the stool, reaching for the bowl.

"I'm trying to show you what the program is supposed to do," he snapped, turning to keep her hands off the bowl. "Isn't that what you asked? Don't worry about this thing. We can't use it anyway."

The clear plastic groaned with a high-pitched creak before finally breaking free, sending splintered plastic fragments clattering across the tile floor. Doc's head jerked up at the sound, his eyes wide with horror when he saw the frayed cable in John's hand. Bits of plastic still clung to the ends of the thin filaments.

John stripped away the clinging debris to reveal a blossom of tiny wires. He fanned them evenly in all directions, like a metallic dandelion. He held it up and said, "This is what I wanted to show you."

He tossed the wrecked bowl onto the workbench and pointed to the frayed ends in his hand. "The initial sequence of my program will excite these lead wires, which for our purposes will serve as the base ganglion in a new brain we'll have to build.

"We have to cut each of these leads so they extend various lengths into the brain, thus traversing a specific pattern of neurons. Then we'll fill the bowl with a new dielectric material I've described in my notebook. This dielectric is better than plastic. It has the ability to isolate each filament while at the same time facilitating current flow throughout the entire structure, just like the fluid in a real brain."

"So what happens then?" Doc groaned as he got up off his knees. He stopped rewiring the computer terminals to approach them. "How do you plan on creating resonance?"

"In a way not unlike your initial approach." John turned to face him. "But there are significant differences. First, each input lead will need its own channel. That's why we need those I/O addresses you're mapping now. Each of these wires in this dandelion will need its own specialized computer input and output address.

"However, unlike your approach, these lead wires won't connect to any specific neuron filament inside the brain. Instead, they will extend random lengths into the bowl, passing hundreds or even thousands of separate neuron filaments before they end, inducing current to flow in each one they cross. The excitation process continues in a cascading effect until the entire structure is virtually alive with a specific atomic-energy wave pattern—my brain wave pattern.

"During this entire process, the computer will monitor the input signals from my brain and check them against the induced electrical fields developing inside the artificial brain. If there is no resonance, the computer will make minute gain adjustments on each lead wire until it attains resonance on that channel.

"The intense data you picked up on in my

programming is the computer adjusting the gains simultaneously on all leads until the entire structure begins to resonate. At that point, the bowl will be radiating an energy signal that should mimic my own brain wave patterns. Theoretically, the ethereal content left inside the bowl will match that of my own soul."

Doc removed the unlit pipe from his mouth. "But how do you put your neuron filaments in place? With your method, or perhaps it is especially with your method of achieving resonance, it would seem neural placement is critical.

"Remember, it's not just any neural field we have to create here. It is your brain we have to duplicate, and laying all these neuron filaments in a pattern that matches your mind seems impossible. When Mary and I made the last one, the neural map we followed came from a cadaver. How do you propose we mimic your brain structure without cutting open your head?"

"Well, I'm not sure," he muttered. "I'm still working on that." He noticed Mary's eyes shift before she turned away.

"What do you mean, you don't know?" Doc yelled.

Mary looked at the ground.

Was she relieved? What was she thinking?

"Do you mean to say that you destroyed the most vital piece of equipment and you don't know how to make another one?" Doc said.

He ripped the pipe out of his mouth and spun away to pace the floor in aggravated circles, running one hand through his thick white mane. After a few moments, he marched straight at John, a pudgy finger stabbing the air.

"It took us years to make that one. The neuron layout is the most essential, fundamental element to artificial brain design! It is key—no, it is absolutely essential that it be accurate. How can you have such an elaborate plan as this and not remember the most vital element?"

"I don't know!"

Doc shot him an angry glare before turning to resume his pacing.

John didn't mean to respond so sharply, but the same question had been nagging him for days and was an irritant concern to him. The arrangement of these strips of wire had to be exact, but he could not as yet remember the plan for constructing something so complex. Of all the data that streamed into his mind that night in his trance, he could not recall the bit about how to make the artificial brain.

He mumbled an apology. "I'm sorry to snap at you like that, Doc. A lot of data was dumped into my brain that night with your alpha machine. It's taken weeks just to decipher as much as I have. Give me a little more time. I'm sure it will come to me."

Doc stopped pacing. "More time? More time! We have two weeks to make something that took us years to build. How can you demand more time?" He turned away fussing about how John had ruined everything.

Think! John told himself. *The answer must be right in front of me. Why can't I see it?*

Throughout Doc's tirade, Mary sat, her eyes shifting left and right. Suddenly, she snatched a pad of paper and began scribbling calculations. Over the next few minutes, John switched his attention from Doc's reprimanding oration to watch Mary punch more calculations and then reference the notebook again. She flipped through several pages, scanning them with a finger until she would nod, write something, make a few notations, and then repeat the process.

Doc was in the middle of yet another long diatribe when she cut him off in mid-sentence as if she didn't realize he was speaking—which, John knew, was probably accurate.

"How about running your program in reverse?" she said. "We could connect your mind to our computer and use it to magnify the intensity of your brain waves. By my calculations, we have enough power to polarize the filaments in the new brain into proper alignment."

Doc stared at her, his mouth still open. Mary stopped too, her eyes wide with the sudden realization she interrupted him. She looked apologetically at her father, but something about her idea intrigued John. Doc seemed impressed as well.

"Go on," he said. "What else?" He sat down with an expectant air.

She took a deep breath and continued. "First we fill the bowl with a mixture of these filament neurons and your dielectric gel. No particular order, we dump everything in together. The gel must be liquefied so we'll have to heat it. We can calculate the mixing temperature and viscosity later, but it must be thin enough to allow the filaments to move, yet thick enough to keep them from sinking to the bottom.

"We can use Father's alpha-helmet to pick up your brain's energy signature and feed it into the computer. We'll have to alter the helmet such that each transducer has its own sensing lead. These leads will be assigned its own I/O channel, one address per lead wire, just like you specified.

"We'll then use your program in reverse to collect your neural signal, pump up the intensity, and then channel it to a similar helmet we'll place around the bowl. If I'm right, this will create an energy field exactly like yours around the artificial brain, only millions of times stronger.

"At the proper intensity, the neuron filaments will come into sympathetic alignment with the induced lines of flux—just like iron filings lining up with a magnet field. All we have to do then is keep the artificial neurons in position until the dielectric gel hardens.

"It won't be a replica of your neural structure, but then it doesn't have to be. That's where we went wrong before, thinking we had to model the brain's exact internal configuration.

"These filaments will move into a shape caused by your neural field. Once it hardens and we run the process forward normally to energize this new brain, it should produce the exact same field that created it— namely your neural field. And isn't that what's important here, recreating your neural field?"

Even before she finished, John knew she was right. Doc rapidly jotted notes on a piece of paper, quickly nodding. John jumped off his seat to hug her.

"That's it!" he shouted. "Mary, this is great. I can't tell you how many days I've struggled with this.

And here you come up with a solution in just a few minutes. You're brilliant. What made you think of it?"

"I don't know." She averted her eyes and turned away, shunning his embrace.

Her sad tone and rejection surprised him. He thought she would have been glad at her dramatic breakthrough.

She said, "When you were talking about how the resonances are supposed to set up, it just came to me. At first, I wasn't sure it would work. After all the trouble Father and I had setting up the first one, this seemed too easy. But I checked your notes in this section here." She indicated the open page. "That's when I knew my idea would work."

"Well, I never thought about using it in reverse like that, but you're right. I'm so proud of you." He hugged her and said, "Thank you."

She stiffened and cast a nervous eye toward her father, but he didn't seem to mind. In fact, except for an all but imperceptible smile, he appeared to ignore them completely. He returned to his task of remapping the computer's I/O addresses as if nothing happened.

Mary relaxed a little but there was still no smile in her eyes. It didn't make sense. John couldn't understand how she could be so despondent after finding such a fantastic solution.

She squirmed from his embrace and walked away. John rubbed his forehead. During the last few weeks, he had grown to love Mary more than he thought possible. He was certain she felt the same way. Because of her father, they had been forced to hide their love. Yet now that Doc knew, even condoned their feelings, she acted like she didn't want anything to do with him.

Shunned and embarrassed, John glanced about absently for something to fill the awkward silence. Slowly, his cluttered thoughts came back to her solution.

"Do you, uh," he stammered. "Do you have another alpha-helmet around, for the bowl, I mean. Or are we going to have to make one of those, too?"

"Oh, there's another," she said. She went to a cabinet at the rear of the lab and pulled open the double doors, revealing an identical helmet to the one used on him earlier. She returned to the workbench and dropped it.

"Here," she said, her tone all business. "I'll start loading the code. You start rewiring the helmets. When you're done, connect them to the computer's transmitting cable."

With that, she was gone. Without a backward glance, she picked up the notebook and sat down at her workstation to begin the long and tedious process of inputting the program's massive line code. John watched her a full minute, ruefully rubbing the back of his neck as his emotional roller coaster slowly ground to a depressing and agonizing halt.

It hurt that she could turn him off like that. Didn't he mean anything to her anymore? She saw him watching her and turned her back on him, focusing on her job like nothing else in the world mattered.

With a long, slow sigh, John lifted the alpha-helmet to examine it more thoroughly, but he was looking with unseeing eyes. His preoccupied mind searched in vain for clues about Mary. It took some time, but he finally managed to focus on the helmet, exerting extreme effort to suppress his feelings and concentrate on the task at hand.

~~~

From that day on they worked late into the night, every night, racing to beat the deadline. Even with a brutal round the clock schedule, there was no time to spare.

As for Mary's plan, it worked beautifully. After just a few days of work, he donned Doc's modified alpha helmet and she initiated the magnification portion of the program. She slowly increased the intensity controls until Doc signaled the tiny wire filaments were beginning to squirm and vibrate in the jell-like dielectric goo. As if by magic, unseen hands moved the thin pieces of wire into what looked like a tangled spider web. And there they stayed.

When Doc saw this, he got more excited than John had ever seen before. After years of fruitless research, this was real progress. There was a sense of expectation in the air. He was like a kid again.

But they spent little time celebrating. There was still a lot of work to do and only a few days to do it. After a few congratulatory hugs, they set the new brain aside, allowing the dielectric gel to harden. And then began the dreary, drawn out process of re-connecting the bowl's thousands of lead wires to the main computer.

The work was boringly slow. Thousands of tiny wires and each one had to be tagged. That same wire had to channel through the same I/O port on the back of the computer and connected to the proper transducer in the helmet John would wear. If anything went wrong—a wire attached to the wrong port, a short in one circuit, or the wrong parity in just one of the leads—and resonance could never be established.

But that wasn't the worst fear. Even if all the wiring was perfect, one small coding error could cause too much current to surge through his brain, killing him instantly.

To her credit, Mary never left the keyboard, spending every waking moment clicking in the long lines of code required to drive the process. With the completion of each page, she diligently checked and rechecked her work, pouring over each character to ensure its absolute accuracy.

It was terribly taxing and mind numbing work, but she never quit and she never complained. And whatever troubled her, she kept to herself.

Chapter 23

Nick Fishetti shifted, stretching his aching muscles. Concealed in the bushes surrounding Lazlow's back yard, he had spent hours in a prone position. Although to Fishetti, this was nothing. During the war, he sometimes spent days in one spot waiting to get his shot. It was just part of a sniper's job.

He lowered the binoculars and dug into his utility bag to retrieve a nutrition bar. He ripped open the aluminum foil package with his teeth and wolfed down half the bar in one hungry bite. Twelve days. Almost two weeks lying in the dew dampened grass. Twelve days of ant bites, mosquitoes, and wasp stings. That's how long since he had a decent meal.

Around him lay an array of complex, state-of-the-art surveillance equipment, all of it aimed at the rear of Lazlow's house. Tiny lights blinked silent activity as the black boxes maintained constant vigilance. But in all that time, none of the high-tech gizmos detected a thing.

Fishetti's eyes scanned the LED monitors. A thermograph of the interior revealed no life forms whatsoever. Laser sound sensors centered on each window detected only stony silence. Fishetti shook his head. If he didn't know better, he would have sworn the place was empty.

The problem was that he did know better. On sporadic occasions, his equipment indicated movement. Fishetti tracked the thermal images throughout the house. But once they reached Doc's study, they just disappeared.

Nick stared at the back of the lonely house, wondering where they could be.

His thoughts were interrupted by the faint but urgent warning tone of a motion sensor. Instantly, the nutrition bar forgotten, he silenced the alarm and grabbed his binoculars. He quickly searched the house, scrutinizing each window.

The thermograph's multi-colored display revealed a pseudo-colored body heat image. Someone had appeared from the study and was climbing the stairs. Fishetti smiled. He grabbed his rifle, popped the lens protector off each end of the high-powered scope, and settled once again into a prone firing position.

Slowly, the long, dark barrel protruded from the heavy bush, its silenced muzzle aimed at the upper row of bedroom windows. His finger closed against the trigger, knowing when his opportunity came, he might have only a second to act. It wasn't long before his prey came into view.

It was Mary.

Fishetti lowered his rifle and gazed at the second floor window, switching on the safety to his weapon. He swore softly and turned to retrieve his nutrition bar.

He washed the remains down with a slug of water and then stopped. An evil smile smeared his pockmarked face as he screwed the top back on his canteen. He then slowly slithered back into position and raised his rifle to the window once more, snapping off the safety with a soft, metallic click.

Mary Lazlow sat in her room.

He pressed the rifle against his shoulder and sighted through the scope, taking his time to adjust the elevation settings. There was no hurry. Mary was sitting in front of the window brushing her hair, taking a moment to enjoy the cool night breeze wafting through the open window.

In seconds, experienced fingers made all the necessary adjustments. He shot the bolt, injecting a shell into the chamber, and spun the bill of his cap backward to provide an unobstructed view. He then braced his left arm beneath the barrel stock and shuffled into a more comfortable position. He was ready.

With cold-blooded patience, he lined the cross-hairs on Mary's head. He watched her roll her neck and shoulders. He could have fired, but Fishetti wanted the sure shot, preferably behind her left ear.

Mary stopped rolling her head and closed her eyes to take deep, relaxing breaths.

"Okay, Sweet Thing," he said. "Nothing personal, but I've got a gut feeling popping you will bring the others out. So, say good night, princess."

Fishetti's finger wrapped the trigger with a gentle squeeze.

"What do you think you're doing?" A solitary figure emerged from the shadows and kicked the rifle just as Fishetti fired. There was a soft, metallic *poof* from the silenced muzzle, followed quickly by the small puff of shattered brick beside Mary's window.

Fishetti jumped to his feet and spun around, his eyes blazing lethal fury. And when he did, he looked straight into the face of Sergeant Olson.

"We're not supposed to shoot these people!" Olson stressed, his voice a whispered scream. "You start knocking off the Lazlows and you'll get us all in trouble!"

Fishetti glared for a brief second before looking back at the upper window. Mary was no longer there. His opportunity was gone. He turned back to Olson, cursing a flagrant stream of oaths.

"Oh, cut out the tough guy routine, Fishetti. I did you a favor. Logan likes that girl. You better get control of yourself before—"

Fishetti's arm struck like a coiled snake. Steel fingers closed around Olson's windpipe, crushing the larynx and blocking the blood flow in both carotid arteries. His eyes were wide and fixed, filled with glazed insanity that glowed in the silver backwash of the full moon.

Olson's eyes bulged. Frantically, he grabbed at the vice around his throat, but he could not break the grasp that was slowly squeezing the life from him. Fishetti was too strong.

Olson swung a heavy fist at Fishetti's head and lifted a knee into his chest. But Nick brushed the futile efforts aside, his wild eyes watching the man die with a cold and indifferent stare.

"Sergeant Fishetti!" Private Parker ran up beside him. Parker was a young recruit assigned to work with Olson. "Fishetti, let up, man. You're killing him!"

Olson's tongue protruded from his blood gorged face. Parker grabbed Fishetti's arm and pulled hard, but Nick didn't seem to notice. His eyes remained fixed on Olson, his unrelenting grip cutting deeper into the man's neck.

Parker persisted. He tried hitting Fishetti's arms, but to know avail. After a few more seconds, Olson's eyes fluttered and rolled to the top of his head. His hands stopped their frantic efforts and dropped sluggishly to his side. Only then did Fishetti release him.

Gasping and coughing in uncontrolled fits, Sergeant Olson collapsed at Fishetti's feet. He laid face down in the matted grass, clutching his reddened throat and sucking huge gulps of air.

"Are you nuts?" Parker said.

Nick turned as if noticing the young recruit for the first time. "What do you want?" he said, his voice an evil slur.

"We're your relief. Lieutenant Carpenter said you should take a break. You've been here too long as it is. Go home, man, get some sleep."

"Uh-uh." Fishetti shook his head. "I ain't going nowhere. I'm staying right here."

"Go home, dude," Parker said. "You're driving yourself over the edge. You've lost control."

"I said I'm staying here!" Fishetti stepped toward Parker with clenched fists. "If you think your man enough to make me leave, then let's see you try."

"Sarge, stay cool, man," Parker backed away. "When are you going to realize Neumann's not in there? If he was, don't you think we'd have found him by now? Even Governor Logan doesn't think he's here. He's got everyone down south near the border."

Fishetti's answer to the young man's stuttering tale was a baleful glare. Blood veins bulged in his grimy neck.

Parker took another step back. Hurrying as fast he could, he hooked both hands beneath Olson's arm and helped the barely conscious man to his feet. Together they shuffled into the darkness, immediately lost in the thick foliage.

Fishetti watched them go and then snatched the last bit of his nutrition bar from the dirt. Shoving the grass-covered remains into his mouth, he folded the empty wrapper and placed it in his vest pocket.

With reverent respect, he picked up his rifle and returned to his prone firing position, using the scope to scan each window. There was no sign of Mary. He checked the thermograph screen, but it showed no activity either. She was gone, somehow vanishing once again.

He peered at the house through the bright moonlight. "What is going on? There must be something in the old man's study." He nodded. "Yes, that's it. That's where you are. All of you."

He picked up the binoculars and studied the downstairs windows, but all the curtains were closed. He lowered the glasses.

"I know where you're hiding, John," he said. "I know where you are, but you can't stay down forever. Sooner or later, you're gonna show yourself. And when you do, I'll be waiting."

He stroked his weapon softly, caressing the

barrel's soft blue gleam with loving affection. "All I need is one more shot. I don't care how long I have to wait. And I don't care what Logan said. You're not getting away from me again."

He shook his head, those wild eyes showing bright in the pale moonlight. "Ain't no way you're gonna live."

Chapter 24

It was early morning. Doc, Mary, and John had worked non-stop in the laboratory. They practically lived there, taking turns catching short naps on a metal framed cot.

With just two days left, John woke from a shallow slumber. Vaguely, dreamily, he heard the soft tapping of a computer keyboard. He lay there a moment, gathering his foggy thoughts before staggering to pour a cup of burned, pungent smelling coffee.

He looked across the lab. Mary had worked all night and looked particularly drained from the effort. Three computer manuals covered the desk around her. She looked up as he approached, her red-rimmed eyes piercing him with fiery glare.

He mustered a cheery hello and sat on a nearby stool. "What's the matter, beautiful? You look upset."

"How long did you think you could hide it from me, John?" Her tone was hard and bitter.

The point blank question caught him off guard, his mind numb from lack of sleep. He blinked confusion, shaking his head. "Hide what?"

She jabbed the screen in front of her, a monitor filled with lines of program code. "This! Did you really think I couldn't break your code? These subroutines are creating an energy plasma I never heard of before.

"I knew you were up to something when I first saw your notes. I gave you a chance to be straight up honest and tell me what's going on. When you didn't, I took it on myself to find out. I've got a stake in this too, you know. I love you. I have a right to know what's going on."

John hung his head and sighed, wishing she wasn't so observant, so smart. He should have known she would have figured it out.

"Why did you lie to me, John?"

"I never lied to you."

"You said we were just going to establish a virtual connection with the Genesis Machine." He couldn't tell if she was angry or hurt, maybe both. "I thought you were just forcing an out-of-body experience. But from what I've uncovered, this program will tear your spirit from your body and merge it with the ethereal matrix."

She stepped toward him, screaming. "You never said anything about completely separating your spirit and giving it to the Genesis Machine. You'll be killed for sure. Tearing your spirit from your body will kill you. Is that what you want? Do you want to die?"

"No, I don't want to die. And it's just going to take the spirit, not the soul from my body. That's what the stabilizing field is for. You know that."

Doc came in slurping coffee. "What's a stabilizing field?"

Mary snapped him a quick look. "John's program is going to create an energy plasma to surround his brain. I want to know why."

"Mary," John said, "Nothing has changed. I told you everything. I'm not going to rip out my soul, only my spirit. This will be the out-of-body experience I spoke of. It's just that your father's machine must first free my spirit from its bounds within my brain before it can link with the Genesis computer."

"Then tell me about this other ethereal plasma. What's it for?"

He walked to the artificial brain and laid his hands on it, admiring its gentle smoothness. Its dielectric gel was a beautiful hue of deep blue and gray. The thick braid of cable was almost completely attached now. Only a few lead wires remained to be soldered.

"When this thing is energized, it's going to extract the spirit from my soul. The ethereal field generated by the helmet is to ensure my soul remains in contact with my brain, just like we talked about before."

"But didn't you say the spirit is the source of life in the body?" she cried. "If you completely remove your spirit, your body will die!"

He deliberately kept his voice calm and soothing in stark contrast to her frantic behavior. "No, I said the *soul* is the basis of bodily life. There are significant differences in intensity and amount and frequency content between the soul and spirit. The soul is the primary energy source, the ethereal catalyst in all animals. That's why it is so important to keep my body and soul together.

"And that's one reason why I need this energy plasma. Consider it like a protective shield, a stabilizing field designed to do just that.

"But I won't lie to you. If things go wrong and the stabilizing field doesn't work, well, that would be bad."

"What do you mean by 'bad?'"

"Let's just say the connection between body and soul must be maintained at all costs. If that atomic-ethereal bond is broken for the slightest moment, then my body will most certainly die. It would be like taking the batteries from a toy doll. Remove the soul's power source and everything stops, with little or no hope of restoring its connection with the brain."

Doc said, "Is that because the brain's neural field shuts down if the soul's stimulus is removed?"

John nodded. "Once brain activity stops, there's no chance of return. It may take a few seconds or minutes for all neural activity to cease. But once it has, the bond with the soul is broken and can never be restored. The body then dies."

"Then what about the spirit?" Mary said. "How is it different from the soul?"

"The spirit has a higher, more complex ethereal structure. Thus it provides a higher order of intelligence, even self awareness. Merging the spirit-type ether with the base energy of the soul establishes the unique human life form."

"You know something?" Doc sipped his coffee while keeping an eye on Mary. "I never considered there was a difference between soul and spirit. I thought they were different words for the same thing."

Another loud slurp seemed an ostentatious effort to distract Mary's distraught mind. He was overacting, but John was grateful for the effort. Though poorly done, his actions had their desired effect. Mary's worried frown momentarily dropped when she turned and motioned him for silence.

"So, what's the difference between them?" Doc said. "Physically, I mean."

John winked an appreciative smile. He was trying to arrest her emotions, and the best way to do that was get her to think, and so John quickly answered his question.

"Let's go back to the radio analogy. By coincidence, the radio signal provides a good mental picture for the relationship between spirit and soul."

He found a pen and drew a wavy line across a sheet of paper.

"The AM radio signal is actually two sets of waves combined into one, just like soul and spirit. The first signal is called the carrier wave, which in our example represents the soul. On paper, it looks like a sine wave—a simple up and down wave like you might see on water. It looks like this:"

"Why is it called a carrier wave?" Doc's expression was overtly studious.

"The sole purpose of this wave is to carry another wave to your receiver. It's stronger, the main part of the signal. This second wave, though weaker than the first, is actually what contains all the information—you know, voice and music. Everything noteworthy is in this second wave.

"If you'll notice," he pointed to the smooth contours of the drawing, "the carrier wave has a uniform shape. This means that although it possesses the rudiments of sound, there is no intelligence in that sound. A station broadcasting only this carrier signal would sound like a steady, monotonous *beep* coming from your radio.

"The reason we hear music is because, back at the station, they merge the second wave with this first wave. If you've ever seen a voice print, you have an idea what this second wave looks like. When they are combined, it looks something like this:"

"My point is that your radio, like the brain, is actually receiving two separate energy signals that have been combined into one, much like the brain receives the soul and spirit. The carrier wave by itself has the essence of sound, but like the soul it doesn't have articulation. It has the power to drive your radio, but little else.

"Any animal that has a brain means it resonates a soul. This is to say animals have life, but no more intelligence than what their relatively simple soul and brain combination can provide. As a whole, animals use the soul-type ethereal content of the Absolute

Medium. Animals and humans communally 'breathe' this life source. This is the common ethereal link of all Nature.

"This common sharing of dark-energy produces the cohesiveness we see among and between all species in Nature—including humans. Each species' behavioral pattern is the result of how their neural structure is formed. The personality or variation of each species, and individuals within a species, is due to the uniqueness of their specific wiring of their brain structure.

"Like a snowflake or fingerprint, no two brains are wired exactly alike. Thus, every goose acts like a goose. Every dog acts like a dog, but each one varies with how it resonates the soul-type energy, giving each dog its own nuance.

"The human brain, on the other hand, can resonate and interpret this second signal, the spirit-type ether. The ethereal content (or dark-energy content) of the spirit is much more complex than the soul. Thus, only a very complex brain can resonate with it."

"The cerebrum," Doc said. "You're talking about the outer brain."

"Yes," John nodded. "All animals possess the base and some even the middle brain in various forms and complexity. This region connects to the spinal cord or nervous system. In tiny insects, the base brain may only be a primitive grouping of nerve cells. Larger animals have the middle brain that is bigger and more organized than the base. They have a two-part brain. This region controls the more complex body functions like breathing, muscle movement, and heartbeat—and maybe some sort of rudimentary thought.

"Of the billions of species populating this planet, only a scant few have the third brain—the outer cerebrum. And of these, the *human* cerebrum is the most advanced biological system ever created. The cerebrum resonates the complex spiritual frequencies thus, at least for humans, producing conscious awareness within the brain.

"So you see, the soul may drive the body to life, but the spirit gives that life self-awareness. That's why only my spirit can be removed without harm. However, the soul must remain in contact at all times with the neural energy field of my brain. Thus, the need of the stabilizing field, that ethereal plasma. You yourself even paraphrased it like pulling one magnet from another with a larger one. So you see? I didn't lie. You knew what was going on from the beginning."

"But what happens if the helmet doesn't work?" Mary persisted. "The extraction process could take everything, soul and spirit. What happens then?"

John took a deep breath, stalling for time. He didn't want to alarm her, and he knew the truth would do just that. But her eyes blocked him from any evasive maneuvers. She pierced him with a relentless stare, demanding a confession of what she already knew.

"There's something out there," she said, her eyes opening with sudden revelation. "Something sinister, evil. That's it, isn't it? That's the purpose of the energy shield. It's not just for keeping your soul intact. It does something else."

John's shoulders slumped and he looked away,

wishing he didn't have to go through this. After a moment, he looked at her. "I was telling the truth about the stabilizing field. It is to keep the soul connected to the body, lest my body die. But you're right. It is a protective shield as well. There is something out there. And whatever they are, they're definitely not human."

He paused to take a deep breath. "Human beings possess all three forms of energy. The atomic-energy of the body and ethereal energies of the spirit and soul. We are the only beings beside God Himself to possess this energy image. Perhaps it's more than coincidence that we also possess a triune brain.

"Animals have the atomic body and dark-energy of the soul, and correspondently only two parts of the brain. Since the spiritual energy is so weak by comparison, that in itself is a balanced combination of atomic and ethereal, but it's not human.

"However, there are beings which are neither human nor animal. These other beings possess the atomic and the spirit. These creatures exist in the darkness, the unseen ethereal plane that surrounds this realm, something I call the Netherworld. Because they have spirit, they have intelligence, but they are definitely not human.

"What these creatures lack is the soul, which is the strongest and main contributor to the ethereal life matrix. The ethereal content of the spirit is small in comparison, and so their lack of soul creates a tormenting, insatiable wanting, a pain-filled void they desperately want to fill.

"Ever hear of an angelic possession? No, only demon. This is why.

"As I said, humans possess all three forms of energy and in that we are unique creations. But separate the atomic-energy from the soul-spirit configuration, not only would my body die but also give my exposed soul-spirit to these creatures. The agony would be indescribable! Setting my skin on fire would pale in comparison. Unless something can be done to maintain the soul-spirit bond with atomic-energy when the body dies, this is the reality of spiritual death. Not just possession, but death."

"So the alpha helmet is supposed to keep your soul here, connected to your body. I get that part. But what happens if this energy shield doesn't work?"

John sighed, knowing she would not accept anything but the truth. "If the containment shield doesn't work, then my soul would be captured as well my spirit and be exposed to those beings. Without the advantage of a complete energy shell for protection, namely atomic-soul-spirit combined together, I would most assuredly be attacked by that wanting horde. Without the complete triune human structure, I'd be defenseless against their ravenous assaults; a naked man thrown to hungry wolves. I would, in effect, be truly dead."

"But I thought you said energy couldn't be destroyed!" she said. "Energy can't die. Didn't you say that? And isn't the soul-spirit made of energy?"

"Yes, that's true. Energy cannot be destroyed, only altered in form. But I didn't mean my soul or spirit would cease to exist. What I meant was the combination of three energies that make up what is me, John Neumann, would no longer be together.

"This separation of body from the soul-spirit can best be described as absolute death because without atomic-energy bonded with the dark-energy of the soul and spirit I would become less than human."

"And then what?"

"Technically, because consciousness resides in the soul-spirit, I would still be alive, but it is a life you cannot imagine. To me, Hell is not fire and pitchforks. Hell is having a third of your being ripped apart. You're alive, but without atomic-energy you can never be whole again. Hell is forever enduring that torturing, insatiable need, a burning thirst that can never be quenched.

"Hell is having the soul constantly and savagely attacked by those demonic creatures, each one fighting the other to tear at you, gnawing into your soul, feeding off you for eternity.

"You're right. Energy doesn't die, and thus neither does the spirit. I'd be alive but forever in torment, screaming as they fight to consume my soul. There is no worse fate within the human realm of existence."

She looked at him a brief moment and then walked quickly from the room. When she was gone, John looked at Doc, who watched the empty door with a sympathetic frown. "Well, that didn't go very well, did it?" He sighed.

"Maybe you shouldn't have told her about the spiritual death part," he said. "It's tough enough what she's gone through already. It's obvious she's very fond of you. If you wind up dying from all this, well, I'm not sure what she's liable to do."

John shrugged. "I couldn't lie to her, Doc. She

deserves to know the truth."

"Well, you may be right." He glared a fatherly frown as he rose to his feet. "But you may also be wrong." He lingered on that final word before turning to follow Mary out of the lab, calling her name.

John sat alone after that, facing the black computer, the electronic whir of its cooling fans his only voice of solace. It hurt him to upset Mary like that. He tried consoling himself that he put it off as long as he could. Still, he didn't tell her the worst part. That was yet to come.

Chapter 25

The final two days went by uneventfully. If anything, Mary's apprehensions made her work harder then before. She hardly slept. And what little she ate was done at the console as she tirelessly checked and rechecked everything. She said if she couldn't stop him, she was determined to ensure John came back alive. However, each keystroke echoed frustration and concern, but she never said another word about those things haunting her.

At last, the final day came when the Genesis Machine would initiate its contact sequence. After working the entire previous night, they each ran through their checklists one last time. Everything was set. Doc's machine was ready.

"We need to test this thing before we use it," Doc said. "Let's power it on and see what happens."

"Okay," John said, "but first let's disconnect the artificial brain. I don't want to go spinning off into the darkness if this thing goes wrong."

When finished disconnecting, he called, "Mary, would you please initiate the start sequence? Doc, I want you to monitor the input and output levels. I'll monitor the alpha helmet to make sure the stabilizing field is working."

They each took their stations. Mary tapped the

keystrokes to start the process. Immediately, the massive computer hummed, surging with energy. Smoke rose from the back and Doc raced to check it out. John shouted, "Shut it down! Shut it down! Turn it off. Turn it off!"

Mary and Doc looked to see John throwing a towel on the flaming alpha helmet.

"What happened?" Doc asked. "What went wrong?"

"A power spike," Mary said. She looked at John. "If you had been connected to that helmet, you would be dead right now."

"Some of the lead wires burned out," Doc announced, examining the connection at the back of the computer. "They're fried. Some of the transducer wires are also burned."

"Well, we'll just have to make some more. We have to. We only have today and then the Genesis Machine will shut down. It has to be today."

Mary turned to John. "Please, John. Don't do this, not right now at least. You say this is the last day but maybe your memory is wrong. We might have more time. Even if we could manufacture some more leads, which we can't, we will have to go through every one of them, and there's no time for that. Re-checking the leads will take at least a week."

"What about the leads from the original alpha helmet?" John asked Doc. "We could use those. I can splice the I/O leads at the back of the computer"

"Didn't you hear me?" Mary said. She came to him, her eyes pleading. "We don't have the time."

"Yes," Doc said, "we could use those and still

meet the deadline. I'll get right on it." He immediately picked up the spare alpha helmet and started disassembling it.

"What is wrong with you two?" she shouted. "Isn't anyone listening to me? This thing is going to kill John. I can't allow that to happen."

John took her aside and held her hands. "Mary, you *know* I've got to do this."

"But are you sure it has to be today? You know I'll support you, but we just need more time to check it out. That's all I ask. Just give us time to make sure it's safe."

John shook his head. "We've run out of time. I know the Genesis Machine is already listening. I can feel it in my soul. It's got to be today. Whether this setup is ready or not, I've got to try. This is my only chance."

"Fine!" She turned on a heel and stomped back to the controls while Doc and John busied themselves re-wiring the back terminal of the computer.

"Do we have all the leads we need for the helmet you're going to be using?" Doc asked.

"Yes. You take the lead wires from the old one and I'll connect them to the transducer wires. That's not a problem. The big problem is making sure we have all these leads matched right. I'm not sure what caused the spike. We're all tired, which should be obvious from this mistake. We'll just have to do the best we can."

Mary looked up from her console but didn't say a word. She didn't have to.

"It's okay," John said. "We have till midnight. That should give us plenty of time to run more tests."

He went to Mary. "Listen. I know your programming is perfect. We've both been through it a dozen times. We just had the energy density settings set too high. It's a simple mistake."

"Yes, and those simple mistakes will get you killed."

John smiled, wrapping an arm around her shoulders. "Why don't you take a break and get something to eat? Doc and I won't be long in replacing these leads and matching the address codes again. By the time you get back, we should be ready to start testing them again, but at a lower power rating this time. We don't have any more lead wires and we can't afford to burn any more."

Mary gave him a hard look then left. John went to the computer and laid down on the floor, hooking up and connecting the replacement wiring leads while Doc called out the address numbers from the I/O chart one more time. After a few moments, he slumped against the workbench. Frankly, John was amazed he lasted as long as he did.

Doc's pudgy fingers brushed back an unruly shock of white hair while he watched John finish securing the mass of wires with plastic tie wraps. He leaned both elbows on the counter and cleared his throat. On his third attempt, John glanced at him and smiled.

"What's on your mind, Doc?"

He immediately straightened, bushy eye brows reaching high. "Hmm? What's that? Oh, nothing, well, nothing much."

And then he added, "Well, now that you

mention it, I did want to tell you good luck. I didn't want to say anything in front of Mary, but she is right, you know. No one has ever forced an out-of-body experience before. You're taking a big chance with no certainty if you'll make it back. You've got guts."

"Thank you." He rose to his feet, dusting his hands against his pants leg. "Now, tell me what's really bothering you."

Doc reached across the bench and grabbed John's arm. "John, is this really something worth risking your life for? Even if we have time to test everything properly, who knows what it might do to you? Why, even the smallest power variance could destroy your brain. You said so yourself. Even if you don't die, your mind could be damaged beyond repair. Are you sure this is worth the risk?"

"Yes."

Doc blinked. He waited a moment, seeming to expect more. He stood by his chair, idly shuffling his feet, looking at John. He started to say something else, but shook his head and walked out of the room.

John spent another hour stripping out the bad and wiring in the new leads. When finished, he stepped back to admire the machine and smiled. They had done the impossible. Even with all the tests needing to be done, he was certain they could beat the deadline and he couldn't help but feel a sense of pride. He made no effort to stifle an exhausted yawn and tried to focus bleary eyes on the clock.

Why haven't Mary and Doc haven't come back? He didn't want to cut things too close. There was still the testing to be done and more work if necessary. He decided to go get them.

John trudged up the stairs. He rubbed the stiff stubble on his chin and tried to remember the last time he had slept more than two hours at a time.

The first stairway seemed unusually high. He lifted his leg but it felt like lead. He grabbed the handrail and had to pull to assist his climb. He had been running on coffee and adrenaline and hadn't realized how tired he was till it was now almost over. By sheer determination he finally pulled himself to the top, the final few steps coming laboriously slow.

John stretched a loud yawn and shuffled into the kitchen doing neck rolls. That was when he heard a man's voice, but it was not Doctor Lazlow! He saw a man's leg extended from behind the alcove wall. By then, John was already in the kitchen door, so shocked he never saw the pool of grease until his foot slipped in it.

His leg flipped high and he lurched across the floor in an uncoordinated sprawl. With arms flailing, he tried to catch his balance, but fatigue slowed his reactions and he fell flat on his face. John lay there a moment, stunned and groggy. And when he opened his eyes, he was looking at a pair of high topped black boots. He knew who it was without looking up.

Jack Logan!

John lay face down on the floor, hands clenched in muted frustration. Again and again he beat his head and fist on the floor. All this time spent hiding. All the work they had done. And now that they were so close, it was all wasted effort by one stupid mistake.

Mary called from across the room, but John barely heard her.

"Peter!" she said again.

Still dazed, John looked at her, wondering who she was talking to. She set down a skillet of sizzling bacon that was strangely absent of grease and rushed to him. With both hands around his arm, she helped him to a sitting position on the floor.

Softly, she stroked his disheveled hair and cooed in a singsong voice as if addressing a small child. "Are you all right, baby? That was a big bad fall you had!"

John didn't know how to respond. Had she gone crazy? He stared at her in dumbfounded shock.

"Here you go," she sang, pulling him to his feet. "Why don't you sit at the table and Aunt Mary will get you some cereal. You like cereal, don't you?"

With her back to Logan, her head nodded ever so slightly. That's when John realized her plan. Logan would never suspect someone mentally impaired.

Staggering to an empty chair, John acted like a retarded fool. He leaned forward and slumped to one side, a blank expression gazing about the room. Drool dripped from his open mouth, forming a wet stain on his shirt. He was, he hoped, a pathetic sight.

"Who is this . . . this imbecile?" Logan recoiled.

"This is my cousin, Peter," Mary's tone cut harsh. "And you be nice! If you hurt his feelings, he's liable to throw a fit."

John turned his head to stifle a smile. He was certain Mary was the only person on the planet who could get away with speaking to Logan like that.

She set the bowl of cereal in front of him and patted him affectionately on the head. "Peter is suffering from the ill effects of lead poisoning when he was a child. Too many paint chips, I'm afraid. Because of that, his mind never grew to match his body."

She wagged her head, looking at John with sad eyes. "The doctors say he has the intelligence of a five-year-old. But I doubt he has even that much sense."

John suddenly lurched in a convulsive fit, but that wasn't an act. Mary had pinched his ear and he flinched in pain.

Logan complained, "Well, does he have to drool like that? The idiot's getting slobber all over the place."

"You watch your tone, Jack!" Mary snapped. "Peter doesn't know what he's doing! Just don't pay him no mind."

Logan snatched a napkin and wiped a fleck of spit off the table. He then dropped the soiled paper to the floor and scooted his chair farther away, just as John hoped he would.

Mary placed the cereal bowl in front of John and Logan started to rise. That's when he noticed the thick scar still visible across John's forehead. After a month of healing, the hundreds of cuts and bruises that once covered his face were distant memories. But the bright pink of newborn flesh of that particularly deep gash was unmistakable.

Logan sat back down and squinted at John with instant suspicion. John lowered his head, scooping cereal into his gaping mouth. This, however, only made Logan lean forward to peer at John's down turned face. The closer he came, the more John lowered his head, slopping milk and spilling cereal everywhere.

Logan turned on Mary, menace thick in his gravel voice. "How did he get that scar?"

He started toward John but a spoonful of cereal splashed in his direction. That did the trick. Not wanting his neatly creased uniform soiled, Logan backed away. But he wouldn't let the question go.

He pressed Mary for the answer. "Well?"

Mary never missed a beat. "He was in a car wreck, poor thing. It was terrible. What with all that broken glass flying around, it's a miracle he's still alive."

She paused a moment, but with John's head buried in the bowl, he couldn't see why.

"His father was driving," she said. "Killed instantly, I'm afraid. His mother, my Aunt Edna, is still in the hospital. She asked if we could take care of Peter until she gets back on her feet again. It's the least we could do, him being family and all."

Logan shot her a dubious look and then addressed Doc. "I didn't know you had a sister."

The old man was not as quick on the uptake as John. "Sister? Uh, what, I mean, yes! I mean, well, uh, she isn't really my sister. Actually, she was my wife's, uh, sister. We didn't see much of her, though. Not a good relationship, I'm afraid."

Doc shook his head. "We, uh, didn't keep much contact through the years. Sort of gotten out of touch, you might say. I guess that's why I never told you about her. Kind of forgotten them. But he's family, all right."

Doc clapped John on the shoulder, knocking the spoon out of his hand. It clattered across the table, making a bigger mess.

Logan stayed where he was across the room, his arms crossed, inspecting John from a distance. He stroked his chin and though John never looked up, he sensed Logan's malevolent stare.

Finally, Logan turned on a heel with a guttural "Humph!" and signaled Mary to follow him outside.

When the door clicked shut, Doc and John rushed the window to spy from the safety of the concealing curtains. Doc eased the drapes aside. John peered over his shoulder to see Mary standing with her arms crossed in front of her, a cool contrast to Logan's agitated gestures.

He made several attempts to touch her, but every advance was met with a stiff hand holding him at bay. After a few minutes of repeated frustration, he looked at his watch and said what John assumed to be an excuse to leave. With a forced smile, Mary endured a kiss on the cheek and then hurried inside the house. She closed the door and leaned against it in emotional exhaustion.

"A five-year-old brain damaged idiot?" He smiled, still watching Logan through the curtains. "Couldn't you have made up something better than that?"

"Who says I made up anything?" She said with a coy grin.

Logan opened the door of his Jeep and then stopped, staring off into the distance. Rock Hill was but a few miles away, its lofty plateau clearly visible above the tree tops. Suddenly, he snapped around to stare at the house, his eyes narrowing.

"What's he doing now?" Doc said. Unable to

watch any longer, he had turned to pace the kitchen floor.

"I'm not sure." As John spoke, Logan leaned into the car and produced a cellular phone. He turned his back and started talking emphatically, gesturing wildly as he barked a series of orders. For most of the conversation, his face was averted. Only once did he glance at the house. And when he did, it was quick, so fast it could have easily been missed. But John saw it, and he knew what that look meant.

"He's onto us!" he said, turning from the window in a rush.

Doc stopped his pacing. John dodged around him and hurried toward the lab. Mary snapped one final look through the window and hurried to catch up.

"How do you know?" she said. "I thought we did a good job of fooling him."

"Well, it wasn't good enough. Right now he's either checking out your mother's family tree or the number of recent car accidents involving one oversized mental retard. Either way, knows he's been had. It's just blind luck he didn't bring his normal detail of goons today."

"He said he wanted some quality time with me alone," she said. "That's why he drove himself this time. You've seen him out here many times by himself. That isn't unusual, especially considering our project."

"Great!" John said. "Sounds very romantic. But in a few minutes, we're going to have an entire platoon of Nazis swarming all over this place!"

They were halfway downstairs. Mary caught John's elbow, Doc right behind her. John turned to see apprehension in both their faces, but this wasn't the time to be gentle.

He said, "Right now, Logan is frustrated and angry. At this point he'd gladly kill any stranger this close to your computer. My guess is that's the real reason he's here. He wants to try the connection process himself, today. He knows about the connection time limit."

He turned to go and Mary called after him. "But you don't know that. If he suspected you, wouldn't he have killed you himself?"

By now, John was in the game room, running toward the office. "You know Logan better than me. He's a coward at heart, not the kind of guy who does his own killing. For all he knows, I have a gun. But trust me. When his men arrive, they'll storm this house with orders to kill."

Mary and John entered the lab. Doc, with his massive bulk, lumbered far behind.

"Mary, your family is no longer safe. It doesn't matter that Logan likes you. He will kill anyone who knows his plan or stands in his way, including you."

Mary's hand shot to her mouth and he realized his harsh tone only made things worse.

"What can we do?" she said.

"It's a good thing David is still at Ryan's. That gives you an alibi. Tell Logan I abducted you at gunpoint and I'm holding David hostage. Tell him I forced you to put on that act in the kitchen because I would have killed David otherwise. If you play it right, he might believe you. If you don't get out now, it's your only chance of coming through this alive."

He was in the process of arranging the cot and the new alpha helmet when he looked up to see her face. Although time was of the essence, he stopped and reached out to her. She immediately rushed into his arms.

"I'm sorry, Mary," he said. "I'm sorry to have brought this on you. But you can't stay here. Please, go get David. Go while there's still time, before Logan's men get here. Get to the cave. When your father and I are finished here, we'll meet you there. The connection itself is almost instantaneous. It just has to be done. I won't be long."

He caressed her cheek with gentle fingers. He paused a moment longer, memorizing her deep, mournful eyes. Doc finally lumbered into the lab, wheezing from the effort.

"Come on, Doc," John said, his loving eyes still on Mary. "We've got to hurry!"

"But the computer. We didn't test those final few leads."

"It doesn't matter. We're out of options. We've got to take the chance they will hold."

John finished strapping on the alpha helmet and commanded him to initiate the startup sequence. When he turned around, he bumped into Mary. "What are you doing here?" he said. "I thought I told you to leave. Now go. Get out while you still can."

"Don't worry about me," she said. "Logan needs us. Without Father and me, he can't do a thing with this machine and he knows it. It's you I'm worried about. I don't want you to die. I couldn't take losing the man I love. Not again."

John turned to lie down but she grabbed his

arm, forcing him to look at her. "Please, John. It's you he's after. We'll be alright. If you go out the back door, you can still get away."

He shook his head. "Mary—"

"John, think about it. If Jack kills you, you'll be no good to anybody. You've got to save yourself. As long as you're alive we have a chance. Besides, Father's right. We haven't tested this thing thoroughly. The last test failed. There's no of knowing what it will do this time."

John shook his head, pushing her gently away. "Don't you see? If I don't make this connection now, there won't be a tomorrow. Everything you see here will be gone, including you. I'm doing this for the people, Mary, but I'm also doing it for you. I need you. I love you. And don't worry, I will come back. I will come back to you. I promise. I will never leave you alone."

She smiled but her shoulders sagged. "But you don't know that for sure. Your memory still isn't complete. Surely, there must be another way."

"You're right. My memory isn't complete. That's why I need to do this. Mary, Logan is not stupid. He'll know I've been here once he sees the modifications we've done to the machine. If I run, he'll just use it to make the connection himself. And with Genesis in his control, there's no limit to what he could do. I've told you that."

He shook his head. "I'm sorry, but I can't run away from this. I've got to make this connection and I've got to do it now, before he does. I must become who I am. I simply must know what I am to do."

With that, he kissed her. Her passionate hands held his face as she returned his love, unwilling to let him go. Reluctantly, he pulled away with a forced wink and smile.

"Trust me," he said. "Everything will be all right."

He laid on the cot and called out, "Are you ready, Doc?"

"All channels have completed their test sequences. As far as I can tell, all systems are go," he said. From his console, he looked at John. "I'm ready when you are, John."

John looked at Mary one last time. Her sad eyes silently begged him to stop. He hesitated only a moment, lingering on her beauty. "Let's hit it!" he said.

Mary turned away when her father punched the keystrokes to start the program.

Not knowing what the effects would be, John gripped the cot's aluminum poles. But nothing happened. He waited a few minutes. Still nothing.

"Doc?" He shouted. "Did you start it?"

"Yes."

Tension filled the room. John rolled up on one elbow to see Doc squinting at one of the computer monitors. Without his glasses, he had trouble reading the tiny, constantly moving graphs that indicated the electrical current associated with each lead wire.

"Everything seems to be functioning normally," he said. "At least it's not blowing up. The leads seem to be holding. But there's no indication of resonance on any channel."

John expected Logan to charge through the door

any minute. He ripped off the helmet and rushed to the computer, taking the keyboard from him. "We don't have time to wait," he said. "Let's try increasing the charge densities. Maybe that will speed things up."

The room went deathly silent but for the echoing sounds of John's agitated clicks on the keyboard. Mary and Doc exchanged worried looks. Within a minute, he gave the controls back to Doc and donned the helmet again.

Mary walked away. She sat on a stool near the wall and gazed at him. John returned to the cot and smiled at her. She sniffed back her tears and tried a supportive smile, failing miserably.

He forced himself to look away and yelled, "Okay, Doc. Hit it again."

Almost instantly, a surge of current vibrated the artificial brain setting on the workbench. His vision became distorted. The room grew dim followed by severe muscle spasms.

"We've got resonance, I think," Doc called out. "It's building. Ten percent on all channels and climbing! Twelve! Fifteen!"

Suddenly, everything within ten feet of John's body exploded away in all directions. Books, tables, chairs—everything not bolted down went flying. The ethereal shockwave knocked Mary out of her chair. She skidded across the floor shrieking with fright.

"Amazing!" Doc breathed, pulling himself upright. He took his eyes off the controls to admire the flying debris radiating away from John. "I've heard of telekinetic power, but I never dreamed it could be demonstrated so forcefully."

Mary shouted a warning, pointing at the computer. "Father! The monitors!"

Doc's mouth dropped open. "Oh, my God! It's building too fast. There's too much current!"

John reached for the connection straps on the helmet but only got it partially off. By then it was too late.

Knocked to the ground by the ethereal blast, Doc was off the keyboard but a few seconds, but it was enough for the energy inside the partially removed helmet to shoot beyond the danger point. It was a power spike, capable of cooking John's brain like a microwave oven, the one thing they feared most.

John's body convulsed violently, jerking about with increasing speed and violence. Doc's hands went through his thick hair. "Good, Lord! What have I done?"

"Stop the program!" Mary screamed, running at him. "Do something! You're killing him!"

Searing pain knifed through John's mind. The agony swelled like an oncoming wave before bursting through his body without mercy. His brain was on fire, his soul burning. His body contorted with such violent seizures that his grip bent the cot's aluminum support bars.

Fortunately, built-in protective circuits tripped the device. Doc shut down the rest of the system while Mary ran to where John lay face down on the floor. Rolling him over, she gasped at the blood pouring from his nose and mouth. She knelt beside him and listened to his chest.

He wasn't breathing.

"No!" she screamed. "Don't die! Please, don't

leave me here alone. Not again. Not again!"

She fell across his body, weeping.

"Mary, move!" Doc commanded.

But she refused to let go, hugging his head to her breast, she rocked him back and forth, sobbing uncontrollably.

Doc pried John's body from her arms, but she still would not release her hold. She remained on her knees, grasping his hand as Doc laid him out and tilted his head upwards. He pinched his nose and breathed hard into John's mouth three times before rising to pound his heart.

It only took one blow. John coughed and gagged, gasping for air, spitting up blood and phlegm. As he regained consciousness, he noticed his head cradled in Mary's lap. He looked into her tear-filled eyes and she smiled sad relief. She gently wiped the blood from his face with a gauze pad she retrieved from a first aid kit.

John wasn't as bad as he looked. When he lurched off the cot, he landed on his nose. That was the source of all the blood. But other than a pounding headache and being terribly weak, he seemed to be okay.

"Turn it off, John," Mary said, softly stroking John's hair. "We failed. It's over."

"No," John strained to speak.

"John, this thing is killing you. If you try it again, you'll die!"

"It doesn't matter," he said, his voice drained to a groaned whisper. "I'm dead already."

She looked at him, her mouth agape, her eyes

wide. John held her hand, squeezing gently. "Don't worry. I'm fine. Just give me a minute to re-group."

He closed his eyes to rest and said, "Would you mind going upstairs to check on Logan? I want to know what he's up to. While you're at it, bring me something to drink."

She hesitated and then looked at the wall clock. She looked down at him with a worried frown. "Okay," she said. "But you've got to rest, John. You can't take any more of this. You may already have damaged your brain beyond repair."

He nodded silent understanding. She turned the bent cot upright again and helped him lie down. She sat with him a few moments, caressing his head as he lay there with eyes closed.

Reluctantly, she left the lab. He heard hurried footsteps heading for the door. He opened one eye to be sure she was gone. Satisfied, he rolled over to find Doc, his words slurred with pain. "It was a mistake to build the resonance so fast."

John struggled to sit up, but didn't have the strength. He tried again, only to slump back in exhaustion. On his third effort, Doc stepped over and propped him up. John motioned for the alpha helmet.

"Help me put that on." He gasped from the exertion. "Reset the charge densities to their initial values. Let the currents build naturally. The leads are holding. Just give the computer time to accurately monitor all the signals being inputted. Hopefully, there won't be any more power spikes."

Doc nodded. He didn't argue or agree, but no sooner had he strapped on John's helmet than he was already resetting the program to its initial values.

Within seconds, he was done.

"All set," he said. His face showed the strain, his shaking hand poised over the start button.

With a shuddering breath, John sighed, resigning himself to whatever fate held for him. "Okay, I'm ready. Start it up."

As with the first attempt, nothing seemed to happen. There were no sounds, no feeling, no movement of the channel resonance indicators on Doc's display. He lay on the cot in anxious frustration. *How long before Logan's men arrived?*

John's head throbbed with each pounding heartbeat, a side effect from the electronic punishment already inflicted on his mind. Another minute dragged by and still nothing happened. He looked at the clock, watching time slip away. He drummed the cot with nervous fingers.

"Doc?" he said. "Getting anything yet?"

"Not much. Just a little . . . I . . . wait a minute. What's that?"

Mary came back carrying a tray of coffee and cups. She backed through the door to push it open. That's when John's mind began to hum once more. The air around him sizzled and popped with tiny sparks of light. Her back still turned, Mary said that Logan was still on his cell phone. Turning around to push the door closed, she stopped dead in her tracks.

Her eyes immediately locked on the heightened computer activity, studying them a moment before glancing back at John. She knew what was coming next.

The coffee cups rattled on her tray, her eyes

wide. She opened her mouth to shout a warning, but was cut off when Doc yelled that the first resonant wave had been established. One by one, growing at an exponential rate, every channel locked on a stable resonant pattern.

The old man yelped and hollered, dancing around his chair like a kid. He had seen his dream come true. Mary set the tray on a nearby bench and hurried to Doc's console, checking the monitors with a mixture of excitement and worry. This time there were no power spikes, no energy surges.

John felt no pain, only a slight tingling in the middle of his brain. A faint, blue light began emanating around his body, the air crackling with energy. He tried focusing on the eerie glow, wondering where it was coming from, but he couldn't. There was no point of origin that he could see.

"Ethereal nodes," Mary breathed. "It's working, just like you said."

And then everything went completely black. John looked about frantically but couldn't see a thing. He started to panic. He was about to call for help when he suddenly found himself standing in the middle of the room. He looked down with odd confusion to see his own body still lying on the cot, his head enveloped in that odd looking helmet. He saw his body breathing, his chest rising and falling in steady rhythm. For all appearances, he seemed sound asleep.

At first, John wondered what was happening. But realization came quick. He looked around the room. They had done it. His spirit was free!

Doc scrutinized the dozen screens in front of him. His emotions back under control, he resumed his duty of monitoring the displays. His finger remained poised above the termination button, ready to press it at the slightest provocation.

Mary left the console and sat next to where John's body lay. She lifted his limp hand and held it tenderly. She stroked his cheek, soft fingers lingering a tender moment on his lips. On impulse, she leaned over and kissed him.

John was surprised, especially when he saw his body's lips flinch in pleasant response.

"Mary, I'm over here," he said, but she couldn't hear him. John stood right beside her and yet she could not see him. He tried to touch her but couldn't. There was nothing to touch her with. He looked where his hand should be and saw nothing, nothing at all.

Doc gave a sharp yelp. "The monitor. I forgot to turn it on." He whirled around, punched the switch, and peered closely, anxious to see what John was experiencing. Mary left John's bedside to stand beside her father. As the screen's image flashed to life, it showed two people standing in front of a computer panel.

"Why, it's us!" Mary shouted. She spun around to scan the room. "Where is he? What's happening?"

"His consciousness must be in transition," Doc said. "His spirit has been extracted from his body, but he must not have been captured by the artificial brain's ethereal field yet." He nodded at the workbench. Mary looked to see the glass brain glowing, pulsing with blue energy.

"But how are we seeing this?"

"We're monitoring his brain's neural circuits

via the helmet. As long as that energy connection is maintained, then whatever his spirit perceives, we see."

He pointed to the screen, his eyes wide. "Look! He's moving!"

And he was. An irresistible force drew John across the room, pulling him toward the artificial brain. The blue light was no longer pulsing but glowing bright. The tiny wire filaments hummed and throbbed as they beckoned him ever closer. There was no resisting its attraction. As the energy glow flowed around him, unseen hands pulled him inside. And then everything went black.

"What happened?" Mary shrieked when the monitor went blank.

"Don't worry." Doc's voice remained calm. "The artificial brain has no external sensors. Once John is bound by its atomic field, he'll have no sensory input. But this should only be a temporary . . ."

His voice faded away as that magical force dragged John deeper into the machine, pulling him down a long, dark corridor. He didn't know how long he traveled. Outside the atomic domain, time has no meaning. A white light appeared, small at first and then gradually growing bigger and brighter.

Drifting closer, he noticed the light was actually a translucent wall, a flaming shield of glowing radiance. It was the energy barrier between the two worlds, the end of his journey. Its brightness was dazzling, much brighter than the sun, and yet it did not hurt to look at it. It gave off no heat, no sound, simply an amazing white light.

Beyond this portal was the secret to his life and

purpose; the answers to how stop the virus that had corrupted the virtual world's ethereal matrix and repair the spirits of those living there—and how to get them home again. But there was something else. Why did he have to come inside the virtual world to do all this? What was next? What did he have to do? With the limitations imposed on his memory by the virtual world, he did not know for sure. To find his answers, to unlock his mind, he had to rise above the ethereal plane. Only then would he discover the means of getting the people out.

And there were other mysteries, like how to stop Logan. He was linked with the virus but in a way John could not yet explain. Stopping Logan was key to stopping the virus, essential to his as yet unknown overall plan. He had to remember that plan. He had to remember what to do.

So many questions. So many unknowns. Only one thing was certain. His answers lay behind that wall of flame. To find the truth and reveal the mysteries of this world, he had to go beyond it. And so he faced the fiery wall, and moved into the light.

Continued in
The Genesis Project, Part Two
"New Beginnings"

Made in the USA
Lexington, KY
15 August 2018